tomboy, and her heroes…well, they're all 200% grade-A male. YUM! Her love scenes left me breathless . . . and I'm surprised I have any nails left after the suspense in this last book."
— *Queue My Review*

"Vivid battles, deceit that digs deep into the coven, and a love that can't be denied."
— *Night Owl Romance*

"Besides a fabulous finish to a great urban fantasy that sub-genre fans will relish as one of the best series over the past few years, the romance is the one readers have been waiting to see how it plays out since almost the beginning. Master magician Cheyenne McCray brings it all together in a superb ending to her stupendous saga."
—Harriet Klausner

SHADOW MAGIC
"Erotic paranormal romance liberally laced with adventure and thrills."
— *Romantic Times BOOKreviews* (Top Pick, 4 ½ stars)

"A sensual tale full of danger and magic, *Shadow Magic* should not be missed."
— *Romance Reviews Today*

"Cheyenne McCray has created a fabulous new world. You won't be able to get enough!"
—Lori Handeland, *USA Today* bestselling author

WICKED MAGIC
"Blistering sex and riveting battles are plentiful as this series continues building toward its climax."
— *Romantic Times BOOKreviews* (4 stars)

"Has an even blend of action and romance. . . . An exciting paranormal tale; don't miss it!"

"Cheyenne McCray shows the best work between good and evil in *Wicked Magic*. The characters are molded perfectly . . . sure to delight and captivate with each turn of the page."

SEDUCED BY MAGIC

"Blistering passion and erotic sensuality are major McCray hallmarks, in addition to a deft and exciting storyline. This magical series continues to develop its increasing cast of characters and complex plotline; the result is erotic paranormal romance liberally laced with adventure and thrills."

"The slices of humor, the glimpses of the characters' world through fantastic descriptions, not to mention fascinating characters, landed this book on . . . [the] keeper shelf."

"Witches, drool-worthy warriors, and hot passion that will have readers reaching for a cool drink. Cheyenne McCray has created a fantastic and magical world where both the hero and heroine are strong and are willing to fight the darkness that threatens their worlds."

FORBIDDEN MAGIC

"Wildly erotic and dangerously sensual, this explosive paranormal thriller sizzles. McCray erupts on the scene with one of the sexiest stories of the year. Her darkly dramatic world is one readers won't mind visiting again… McCray knows how to make a reader sweat—either from spine-tingling suspense or soul-singeing sex… McCray cleverly combines present-day reality with mythological fantasy to create a world where beings of lore exist—and visit the earthly realm."

— *Romantic Times BOOKreviews* (Top Pick, 4 1/2 stars)

"McCray will thrill and entrance you!"

—Sabrina Jeffries, *New York Times* bestselling author

"A yummy hot fudge sundae of a book!"

—MaryJanice Davidson, *New York Times* bestselling author

"*Charmed* meets Kim Harrison's witch series, but with a heavy dose of erotica on top!"

—Lynsay Sands, *New York Times* bestselling author

"McCray's paranormal masterpiece is not for the faint-hearted. The battle between good and evil is brought to the reader in vivid and riveting detail to the point where the reader is drawn into the pages of this bewitching and seductive fantasy that delivers plenty of action-packed sequences and arousing love scenes."

—*Rendezvous*

"*Forbidden Magic* is a spellbinding, sexy, superbly written dark fantasy. I couldn't put it down, and you won't want to either...[a] fabulous plot... [Cheyenne McCray has an] incredible skill at keeping readers engaged in every moment of the action. Longtime fans and newbies alike will be enchanted and swept away by this enduring tale of courage, love, passion, and magic."

—*A Romance Review*

"If one were going to make a comparison to Cheyenne McCray with another writer of the supernatural/sensuality genre, it would have to be Laurell K. Hamilton... *Forbidden Magic* definitely puts McCray in the same league as Hamilton. The book is a very sexy work... *Forbidden Magic* is dark and filled with danger at almost every turn. Magic and mystery abound in San Francisco, with a major battle between the forces of good and evil, and the outcome is always in doubt when it comes to demons."

—*Shelf Life*

"Cheyenne McCray has written a sexy adventure spiced with adventurous sex."

—Charlaine Harris,
New York Times bestselling author

"Erotic with a great big capital E. Cheyenne McCray is my new favorite author!"

—Bertrice Small, *New York Times* bestselling author

NO
WEREWOLVES
ALLOWED

Cheyenne McCray

St. Martin's Paperbacks

This is a work of fiction. All of the characters, organizations, and events portrayed in this novel are either products of the author's imagination or are used fictitiously.

NO WEREWOLVES ALLOWED

For information address St. Martin's Press, 175 Fifth Avenue, New York, NY 10010.

EAN: 978-0-312-94642-5

Printed in the United States of America

St. Martin's Paperbacks edition / June 2010

St. Martin's Paperbacks are published by St. Martin's Press, 175 Fifth Avenue, New York, NY 10010.

10   9   8   7   6   5   4   3   2   1

To Tara Donn, one of the bestest friends a girl could have. It's time for another appletini-and-lychee martini marathon!

ACKNOWLEDGMENTS

Thank you, Daniel, for being my cheering section and sounding board.

Many thanks to Frank, for information that sparked just the right idea.

A huge thank you to Vincent Abbatiello for your support of Brenda Novak's fifth annual online Auction for Diabetes Research.

Congrats, Nancy, on new beginnings.

WELCOME TO NEW YORK CITY'S UNDERWORLD

Present Day

Dark Elves / Drow: coming right up.

Demons: eh, got rid of the loose ones a while back.

Doppler: a paranorm who can shift into one specific animal as well as their human form. You should see muscle-bound Fred turn into a golden retriever. Way cool.

Fae: sigh. We could be here all day if you want to go through every single species. Your choice.

Gargoyles: live inside statues. You so do not want to get in their way if something wakes them up.

Light Elves: how art I better than thou?

Magi: delicate, frail beings who forsee the future and vision the past. If an evil force were to possess a Magi, the Magi's abilities, used for evil, would be beyond catastrophic.

Metamorph: paranorms who can mirror any human. And not in a good way. But when it comes down to facing a Tracker's blade, they're all big wusses.

Shadow Shifter: a paranorm with the ability to shift from human into shadow. If your shadow looks like the Incredible Hulk and you're the size of Pee-Wee Herman, *hide*. Behind a door with at least a dozen bolt locks and tape any cracks with duct tape. Most importantly, make sure you have the space under the door blocked. With something made of steel.

Shifter: can transform into any animal of their choosing as well as take human form. Apparently they have one weakness, but they're not telling. Well, I'm not sharing my version of kryptonite with anyone, either.

Vamp: bloodsucking, waxy-faced . . . They have the ability to mask themselves in an illusion of beauty or handsomeness. Stay away if you want to keep your blood. And your life.

Werewolves: can take normal wolf form almost any time. However, during the full moon they become dangerous creatures that resemble neither man nor wolf. Creatures that are not self-aware and would rip a non-Were to shreds . . . *so* not good.

Let's save Necromancers and Zombies for when we have a little extra time to spend. Like never.

Fair warning: having your soul stolen by a Succubus or Incubus might not be exactly the direction you want your life to go. The sex isn't *that* good.

Or so I've heard.

I know indeed what evil I intend to do,
but stronger than all my afterthoughts is my fury,
fury that brings upon mortals the greatest evils.

—Euripides (484 BC–406 BC)

NO
WEREWOLVES
ALLOWED

PROLOGUE

Abominations.

From his hiding place behind a stand of large-trunked oaks surrounded by thick bushes, Johnson narrowed his eyes. Disgust made him sick, hot pressure expanding in his chest.

Two young beasts that had the appearances of human boys—perhaps five or six years of age—would soon be in his possession. The beasts were running into the same clearing they had played in for the past three days, since Johnson had first discovered they existed.

Johnson was entirely protected by his dark green suit, watching the beasts from behind the clear shield of his hood. He breathed in pure oxygen from tanks that ensured none of the airborne contaminants from those vile beasts could get to him.

The suit was similar to one worn by HAZMAT, but more efficiently designed for scientific research. The scientist and intern who accompanied him wore identical suits.

The suits had also been sprayed with a special chemical Johnson had developed for other reasons, but was perfect for what he must do now. Anything that breathed in the chemical at full strength would be unconscious immediately. After a few minutes, only remnants of the chemical would linger.

If any human, animal, or *thing* passed by, the remaining chemical signature would alter the sense of smell. How long depended on how much was inhaled and the length of time the subject was exposed to it. Johnson had ensured that this clearing had been well-sprayed daily.

He ground his teeth while he watched the "boys." Such childish innocence on the faces of heinous beasts.

Evil descendents of Eve's offspring from her affair with Satan.

The boys were laughing. No doubt mocking God.

God had willed him to find these beasts and exterminate all such abominations.

After witnessing the act that proved these tiny spawns of Satan were not human, Johnson had spent countless hours using every means available to locate possible adult beasts to ensure he exterminated all. He had found an encampment nearby filled with the spawn, all appearing as if they were human adults and children—until times when they *changed*.

A renowned scientist and a survivalist, Johnson had collected much equipment and created an extensive laboratory in a once-abandoned facility. Far below where he now stood was almost everything he needed to locate all of Satan's spawn. Satellite photos and an extremely high-tech means of examining a being's energy signature had allowed him to detect a difference between the beasts and humans.

The spawn called out to each other, using human names, and continued to laugh. To giggle.

Johnson sickened more, the pressure in his chest filled with so much hate he wanted to burn them all and be done with it.

He had no doubt that Satan's spawn must exist elsewhere and not just here in the Catskill Mountains. Whatever it took, he was going to find something that could spread across the world and eliminate all such abominations.

While the beasts laughed and brandished long sticks at each other like swords, Johnson turned his head to where Lawson hid behind a large tree and several bushes. Johnson met Lawson's eyes through the junior scientist's facemask—he needed to ensure Lawson was prepared. The junior scientist gave a slight nod and Johnson turned his attention back to the beasts.

After letting his gaze slide over the spawn, Johnson glanced to his left at his lead intern, Harkins. She gave a nod, indicating she was ready. He looked back at the beasts, the necessary chemical in his grip.

Pure disgust and anger tensed the muscles in Johnson's neck and back as the male spawn got to their hands and knees and began to *transform*.

Johnson didn't know what else to call the change from what appeared to be humans into beasts.

When he had rested on his hands and knees, one of the boys faced the direction where Johnson was standing. Johnson shook from the power of his fury as he watched the wicked thing change into a dog. A wolf pup.

The abomination's face shifted, its face elongating into a snout, clothing vanishing as hair began to sprout from its body. The other beast changed as well. Like the first, it no longer had arms. Instead they both had front and hind legs. And a tail—like Satan.

When he believed it was the right time, Johnson turned his head and looked at Harkins. Of the three of them, she stood in the perfect position where the breeze blew at her back and toward the boys.

Johnson raised his finger and pointed to the beasts. Harkins grasped the small glass chemical bottle in her hand. A couple of sprays carried to them on the wind would ensure that the spawn would be his to capture, then destroy after experimentation.

Harkins raised the bottle and pressed her finger three times. Opaque puffs of spray turned invisible and were carried on the wind to the beasts.

The abominations dropped to the ground the instant the spray reached their nostrils. They lay completely still, as if dead.

They weren't dead now. But not long and the young spawn, and others of their kind, would be completely eradicated.

ONE

Was it so difficult to grasp the concept of *by appointment only?*

I met the alpha Were's tawny-gold eyes and tried not to let irritation show in my gaze. And hoped Olivia would keep her mouth shut.

As usual, my hopes were futile.

"Your appointment is for nine tonight at the Pit, Furry." Olivia stood in front of Dmitri Kral Beketov, her hands propped on her hips, her five-two to his six-four forcing her to look up. Way, way up.

Beketov scowled.

Touched by the afternoon sunlight that spilled through the window, Olivia was as stunningly beautiful as ever. From her Puerto Rican and Kenyan ancestry, she had rich golden skin and sharp black eyes. Add high cheekbones and striking features, and she could have been a model—if she had been about a foot taller.

A petite package, Olivia was usually underestimated. But not for long. A third-degree black belt and former officer on the NYPD SWAT team, she kicked "major ass," as she would put it.

Beketov and Olivia were having a scowling contest.

Her tone had been sharp, but a wicked glint was in her dark eyes.

Uh-oh.

She looked up at the Were with total confidence and not an ounce of fear. "We don't take drop-ins, no matter how important they think they are." She gestured toward the front door where that fact was presented in iridescent purple and blue on the door's window.

NYX CIAR
OLIVIA DESANTOS
PARANORMAL CRIMES
PRIVATE INVESTIGATORS
By appointment only

When she adjusted her hands back on her hips, the movement pushed aside her New York Mets sweat jacket. The vivid green T-shirt that stretched across her melon-sized breasts was classic Olivia.

Don't make me break out the flying monkeys.

I wanted to grin but managed not to. Beketov didn't smile. He probably hadn't gotten Olivia's T-shirt. It was hard to imagine the big Were kicking back and watching a vid of *The Wizard of Oz* or sitting in the audience at the Broadway show, *Wicked*.

Beketov shifted, widening his stance. His Werewolf scent of woods and fresh air mingled with the smells of spicy Kung Pao chicken. The almost-empty cartons of Chinese takeout were perched on my desk in the midst of a bunch of bright pink sticky notes from a case I'd been working on.

"I do not have time for this." His muscular biceps,

revealed by a sleeveless beige leather shirt, flexed as he folded his arms across his chest. I had to admit the Were was mouth-wateringly delicious despite his scowl and his harsh, angular features.

Most Werewolves had emigrated from the Czech Republic hundreds of years ago. He was Slavic in appearance, his eyes deep-set, his cheekbones high, his features striking. His long hair, which fell to the middle of his back, was the most beautiful shade of bronze I'd ever seen.

I imagined him in his pure wolf form and not what he would look like at the full moon. No doubt as a wolf he would be large and sleek, with glossy fur that shone like rich bronze in the sunlight.

He slid his tawny gaze over Olivia's petite but voluptuous frame. He had that arrogant alpha Were expression down pat as he assessed her.

"Give it up, Furry." Olivia gestured to the door again, this time in a manner meant to tell him to get the Underworlds out of our office.

Yeah, we liked business, but neither one of us tolerated arrogant bastards. However, this was a client that Rodán—my Proctor, friend, and former lover—had referred to us, so we couldn't completely send the Were away.

Beketov turned to me, blatantly dismissing Olivia. She narrowed her eyes and slid her fingers along her waistband so her hand was closer to her Sig Sauer P226 that was secured in her shoulder holster.

If I didn't control myself I was going to roll my eyes or sigh. This was getting ridiculous.

"We have business to discuss. Immediately." Beketov's

Czech-accented English added to his knife-edged tone. His accent was strong, so it was possible he was over a hundred years old. That was nothing compared to Dark Elves like my father, who had lived for a couple of millennia.

Beketov stepped closer so that he towered over where I sat behind my desk. His intimidation tactic was not fair, but it didn't work anyway.

Elemental powers stirred inside me but I bade them to rest. No, this was not the time or place to use my powers. Yet. If he pushed me . . . no telling what I might do with them. Send him flying across the room with my air element, for starters. Maybe use my fire element to set his butt on fire . . .

I almost smiled at that image.

To show I wasn't impressed by his show of dominance, I kept my expression calm and my fingers relaxed on the opening of my Dolce & Gabbana gold evening clutch. It was just big enough to hold my XPhone, my Kahr K40 and my smallest Elvin-made—but very wicked—serrated dagger. I'm Drow, and I could have had either weapon in my hand instantly. I'm lightning fast when I need to be and I could have carved out his heart.

Thanks to an earlier conversation with Rodán, I knew Beketov was here for a missing persons case, but I didn't mention I already had that information. We didn't usually handle missing persons, but some of our competition did. We had bigger paranorms to fry.

"I'll determine how important your business is," I said in a cool and calm tone. "During your appointment later tonight."

He said in a guttural tone, "We are going to discuss this matter now."

Again, I tried not to grip my clutch tight, this time out of sheer irritation. Dominant males who like to intimidate people make hair bristle on the back of my neck and cause my elemental powers to stir. Not to mention said males give me the desire to draw one of my dragon-claw daggers and skewer them.

"No. We're not." I met his gaze head-on. I had to calm myself to keep the dangerous white light from flashing in my sapphire eyes.

A predatory growl rose up in the Werewolf's throat and his tawny-gold eyes brightened. It would have been a little frightening if he was dealing with anyone other than Olivia and me.

Nothing scared Olivia—not that she had ever shown— even though she was one hundred percent human.

Of course, as a Night Tracker, I had dealt with Beketov's kind for over two years. That included taking care of more than my fair share of Werewolves during the full moon. I had no reason to be concerned about his show of dominance, other than retaining a good dose of irritation.

Although . . . Beketov was an alpha. A big one. I'd never faced an alpha. Come to think of it, it was getting close to the full moon . . . just a few days.

A small shiver ran through me that I hoped didn't show. Okay, maybe I was a little intimidated at the thought of this massive man during the full moon. The only Weres that had needed to be taken care of in New York City had been rogues. Rogues were usually wannabe alphas with no pack to lead.

Deep breath. Be professional, Nyx. "Our PI firm is closed for the day, Mr. Beketov." How many times did we have to tell the big Troll? I was running out of time before Nadia would be there. I couldn't disappoint her again.

Considering I was wearing a short, black, low-cut and backless evening dress, you'd think that would have given the Were a clue. If I made it to the matinee at the Metropolitan Opera House, the Thursday performance of *L'Elisir d'Amore* was early enough that I could be in and out without going blue.

One of the things about being half-Drow is that going anywhere humans do after sundown isn't an option. I miss out on evening activities—although I can get away with a costume ball and Halloween.

"Unacceptable." Beketov's tone caused me to bristle more, my skin prickling. His gaze rolled over what he could see of me from where I sat.

Beketov braced his hands on my desk, bringing his Werewolf scent of woodlands closer, richer, as he added, "This matter is far more important than whatever you have planned."

An angry, hot flush rose from my chest. I set my clutch on the desk, managing not to slam it on the surface, but kept it close enough that I still had access to it. My elemental powers stirred harsh enough to scald my skin and I had a powerful urge to take the Were down a notch. Or several.

I slowly stood, never letting my gaze waver from his as I rose to my full five-eight height. My long straight black hair swung around my shoulders as I leaned forward, getting in his face.

"Stop trying to intimidate us," I said, keeping my voice as calm as possible. "It's not going to work."

He glared. "Don't fuck with me."

"As if you'd get so lucky." Olivia moved beside me and she leaned her hip against my desk, bumping into a haphazard pile of files on my desk. Despite my anger, I winced as the pile rocked, and hoped the files didn't slip off my desk. Olivia crossed her arms over her chest. "Nyx doesn't do furry critters."

I wanted to laugh, but held it back.

The Were straightened and his massive chest rose and fell as he inhaled, then exhaled. It must have killed him to not try to put Olivia in her place.

Beketov studied me for a long time. We had a lovely staring contest.

Finally, I saw realization flicker in his eyes. Now he understood that his behavior wasn't going to get him anywhere with Olivia and me. We weren't the type to back down, no matter how much of an arrogant jerk we were facing.

The Werewolf sighed, harsh and audible, as if letting out the anger and frustration he'd been exhibiting. He unclenched his fists and his jaw tightened, then relaxed, like he was forcing a decent look on his face.

His expression shifted so quickly it startled me into frowning. He now appeared like he was going to choke on a huge chunk of stringy raw meat because his following words were so hard to get out.

"My people's lives are at stake." He spoke in a tone that was dark, but with an almost humble quality that didn't fit him. "I need your assistance."

"My, my." Olivia's sarcastic tone brought Beketov's

attention to her. "The Big Scary Wolfman admitting he needs help." She picked up her cellphone and pretended to dial. "I'll alert the media. I think I'll start with CNN."

His gaze darkened and it must have killed him to stop yet again from trying to put Olivia in her place.

"Members of my pack are disappearing." Pain flashed through the big alpha's eyes. "Then turning up mutilated . . . and dead."

My scalp prickled and the feeling traveled down my spine in a rush. I pushed aside my clutch and slowly sat again, my palms flat on the glossy Dryad-wood desk as I stared at Beketov. "You have my attention."

Veins stood out along Beketov's neck and one pulsed on his forehead. "After they disappear, my packmates are eventually found, but always dead, their skin nearly in shreds."

My stomach churned at the image and the horror of what he was telling us. In a habit I'd developed years ago, I ran my finger along the band around my neck. The collar engraved with Drow runes announced my position as royalty among the Dark Elves—it was my one concession to my father, the Drow King.

I hadn't been informed yet on Beketov's case—just that it was missing persons. To hear Beketov now explaining the Weres were mutilated and murdered . . . The thought threatened to make my whole body shudder.

"Every time the mutilation occurred while the Were was alive." Was his body shaking? With anger? Fear for his people? Both? "This has been confirmed by our pack medical staff," he added.

"Damn." Olivia shifted her stance against my desk and one file folder landed with a plop and a whoosh, then skidded a couple of feet on the ceramic tiled floor. Right then I could have cared less about that file folder, or even the rest of the stack. Olivia also ignored the folder with its contents now scattered on the floor.

Beketov clenched his fists so hard I saw small wells of blood appear from where his nails dug into his palms. "From my pack, a total of six Weres have disappeared. All but two have been recovered and those we have found have been dead."

Chills scrabbled up and down my spine. "Here? In Manhattan?" The thought that this could be happening without Trackers or Rodán—especially Rodán—being aware was virtually unfathomable.

Beketov shook his head and a lock of his thick bronze hair fell across his forehead. "From the places we feed."

"Where do you feed?" Olivia's tone was sharp, her expression focused, all antagonism and sarcasm gone.

Beketov's intense gaze flicked from me to Olivia. When he spoke, he did so with the recognition that my partner was all business now, as was I. "The Catskills. We have changed encampments several times but it is not enough. There are only so many places we can go. We must stay close to the locations where our pack members have disappeared so that we can continue to search for the two who are still missing."

His chest expanded as he took in a deep breath. "We must also feed without endangering the wild animal population in any one area with a prolonged stay. Yet I cannot allow my people to leave."

Olivia raised her eyebrows.

"Weres rotate their feeding grounds to make sure they don't eliminate their food source in any one area," I said to Olivia. "The packs also have great respect for the balance of nature."

Beketov gave me an approving look before I swear his eyes clouded, almost misty as he added, softly, "The two that remain missing are mere pups."

My lips parted and I felt pain wash over me, as if his own was covering me in a wave. "Children?"

He looked away. "One of the pups is my son. Simon."

More chills prickled my skin and I spread my fingers on the cool surface of my desktop. My air elemental power stirred my hair around my shoulders and I had to rein the power in.

The thought of children being kidnapped and possibly murdered made me bite the inside of my cheek to control my anger. Dmitri Beketov's son's disappearance made it seem all the more real.

Beketov turned his face back to Olivia and me, looking as hardened as one of the statues in Central Park. I could almost picture the statues' Gargoyles funneling through him, exploding into the night and ripping to shreds whoever, whatever, was doing this to the Were's people.

Then in his manner and bearing, Beketov returned to being one hundred percent alpha. An alpha who was beyond furious because his people were vanishing and turning up dead . . . but also a man who was damaged from the fact that his own son was one of the missing.

And an alpha who hated to admit he hadn't been

able to help his people and was forced to ask for assistance. Likely it was even harder to have to ask two females who weren't of his kind. Weres are tight-knit and aren't crazy about letting outsiders into their ranks, much less having to ask their help.

"Have a seat." I gestured to one of the black leather chairs in front of my desk. "We need details."

Olivia moved her hip away from my desk without upsetting any more file folders. "Instead of being an ass, you could have started with that information."

Uh, yeah. It sure would have made things simpler.

"That is of no matter." Beketov scowled. "What is important is finding out what is happening to my people and getting our children back."

Olivia stepped over the folder and its contents still on the tile floor, and she rounded her desk before she sat in her black leather office chair. The wheels rumbled on the ceramic tile and the chair squeaked with the shift in weight. She arranged herself so that her forearms were on the desktop, in between her own piles of stuffed file folders and the neon-green sticky notes she used. "Tell us everything. From the beginning."

Beketov didn't sit. Instead he began to pace and growl like the animal he was when not in human form.

Fae bells tinkled at the door and I cut my attention to see Nadia, a Siren, and one of my best friends. A wash of early October air followed in her wake.

As usual, Nadia was absolutely gorgeous, but even more so in her thigh-length, glittering dinner dress that was a shade of sea foam. Strands of aquamarines sparkled in her upswept dark red hair.

My heart sank. I was supposed to be leaving now for

L'Elisir d'Amore with Nadia, but how could I go with a case this urgent? With children's lives at stake as well as adults. The children . . . that seemed to make what was happening even more powerfully wrong.

Nadia pushed a loose curl of her luxurious, thick hair away from her cheek. She looked from me to the Were to Olivia and back to me. Her musical voice sounded resigned when she spoke. "Not again, Nyx."

I grimaced. "Sorry."

Beketov stared at Nadia like she was an annoyance rather than the gorgeous woman most men couldn't take their eyes from. Of course, if they knew she could kill them with a song, they might not be so anxious to get her attention.

Nadia focused on me. When the sun disappeared in the west, Nadia worked as a Night Tracker, like me. "This has nothing to do with Demons?" she said.

Despite my show of confidence, my stomach clenched. "The Demons are definitely gone. No worries."

She looked a little green like she did when she sang her Siren's song. Which unfortunately hadn't worked on the Demons.

Time to get off *that* incredible nightmare of a subject.

"At least you have Karen and Jeanie to sit with," I said.

Nadia sighed. "But you know how Soothsayers are. If one of them has to go to the restroom, she'll *freeze* everyone in the entire Met until she's back in her seat. Goddess forbid missing the slightest bit of the opera."

A grin tried to twitch my lips but I didn't let it show as I took my XPhone out of my clutch. "Bring me back a program." I liked to look at the hot guys in the list of cast members. Even if a lot of them were gay like my friends James and Derek, they were nice eye candy.

She cocked her head. "Don't forget that you promised to go to *La Cenerentola* a week from tomorrow. Friday."

I glanced at Beketov, whose jaw was tight, his expression darker, before returning my gaze to Nadia. "I hope we'll have this case solved before then."

A frown looked out of place on Nadia, who was almost always smiling. She directed her gaze at both me and Olivia. "Whatever this is, watch out for yourselves, okay?"

"As if we need to." Olivia reached for her stash of rubber bands and erasers. "Get your ass out of here and to your opera before I nail you," she said as she fashioned a slingshot with her fingers and the rubber band, and loaded it with an eraser.

Nadia grinned, which was radiant despite the concern for us in her eyes. "You'll *never* be fast enough."

The eraser thumped the door's window. Olivia nailed the space right where Nadia had been standing, but Nadia had already disappeared out the door. Bells tingled as the door shut with a firm *thunk*.

"One of these days I'm going to get her," Olivia said before turning serious again, dropping the now empty rubber band on the small pile of always-ready ammunition at the corner of her desk.

"No more interruptions," Beketov growled as he faced us. "Lock the door."

Olivia studied Beketov, who looked beyond irritated at the delay, and she picked up her cellphone and stylus.

"Get over it and tell us everything you can about these disappearances and deaths."

I was prepared with my own phone and stylus. Olivia and I had discovered over the last couple of years that when we took separate notes, we almost always developed different angles with our cases.

Beketov dragged his hand down his face, which was roughened with at least three days' stubble. "My son and his closest friend were the first from my pack to vanish, two weeks ago. We have not stopped looking for them."

My stomach was queasy, the Chinese takeout that I'd eaten before Beketov walked through our office door not settling well. As I'd proven when ridding the city of Demons, I have a weak spot for children. That weakness had almost killed me, and I'd be dead if it hadn't been for T . . .

I was *not* going to think of T, even if he had saved my life. Twice.

And he had turned out to be something so unexpected I still couldn't fathom it. He'd vanished after we defeated the Demons and we hadn't seen him since.

"An adult female from my pack disappeared after the children," Beketov was saying. "Then two more females before we lost an adult male."

Olivia took in an audible breath as she paused from putting notes on her phone. "Damn."

Who wouldn't agree with that statement?

Beketov continued to look away from us. Then his waist-long bronze hair swung from a harsh jerk of his head when he returned his tawny-gold gaze to me. "I have sent out search teams and I have forbidden anyone from my pack to go out in groups of less than three."

"Any clues at all?" My own stylus hovered over my cellphone as I waited to write down more notes.

"Nothing matches." Beketov's Czech accent grew stronger, in tune with the growing anger in his voice. "The only thing in common is that they are all Werewolves."

Olivia tapped the end of her stylus on her desk. "Wolf or human form?"

Beketov's sigh was heavy again. "We are not sure."

"What about smell?" Olivia frowned. "Werewolves can scent anything. Humans, paranorms, and animals can't mask their scents. It just hasn't been possible no matter how many times it's been tried."

"Until now." Beketov bit out the two words like he was slicing them from the air around us. "Nothing on the Were's body when we find them. We cannot even scent anything around them."

Olivia frowned and her eyes unfocused, as if she was looking at a movie reel in her mind.

"The next full moon is only days away," I said. "How close is your pack to civilization?"

"Too close," Beketov said. "We are camped close to Devil's Tombstone, near Stony Clove Creek."

"Well, that figures," Olivia said.

I raised my eyebrows in question.

Olivia tapped her stylus on the table. "The Devil was said to have haunted that area way back when. Early settlement days. Men, women, and children were said to turn up missing frequently." She was looking at me.

"Considering what's happening, it couldn't be more appropriate."

"Nothing but superstition." Beketov's voice went deeper, closer to a growl. "We have hunted in that location for years." His huge, impressive muscles flexed as he spoke. "We go to the most isolated parts of the forest during full moon so that we are not a danger to norms or paranorms."

Olivia turned her gaze on Beketov. "Anywhere near Stony Clove is way too close to civilization come full moon."

"We may have no choice but to stay." He shook his head. "We cannot leave the area until the children are found."

"Uh, near civilization during the full moon thing— not good." Olivia held her stylus as she leaned back in her chair. "You'd be taking the chance of being seen and you might slaughter innocent people."

"Perhaps it is what's needed." He met Olivia's gaze with a hard stare. "We might take out whatever it is that is kidnapping and killing my people."

"Sure." Olivia tossed the stylus on her desktop and crossed her arms over her ample chest. "A Werewolf during full moon, a savage being not even aware of its true existence, taking care of this problem. I don't think so."

At full moon a Were transforms into a hideous beast instead of their natural wolf form. Neither man nor wolf, but a walking abomination that would kill the closest thing to it with no awareness beyond the fact that it was hungry.

Always hungry.

Beketov's expression went darker, but I headed him off. I set my XPhone and stylus to the side. "We'll solve this atrocity before the next full moon."

TWO

Tingles spread from my toes, up my body, to the pads of my fingers and over my scalp as I began my transformation to Drow.

Olivia sat on my white Sé couch as she watched my metamorphosis and she grinned. "Go, Purple Lady."

I scowled. "Amethyst."

She smirked and watched me go through my movements while I shifted, like she was enjoying a TV show. She had brought a bag of barbeque chips with her to our strategy session and while she watched, she crunched on a giant chip.

A shudder rippled through me. Olivia knew that chip-crunching caused my skin to crawl, but she was addicted to Lay's barbeque chips like some people were addicted to tobacco or alcohol.

"Wonder if there's a PCA around here," I grumbled before I concentrated completely on shifting from human to Drow. "Potato Chips Anonymous."

I leaned forward over one leg and settled myself into a hip-flexor stretch. My long hair swung over my shoulders as it started shimmering from black to a deep shade of blue. I could actually feel prickles carry the changes in my hair from the roots to the very tips of each strand.

While I switched poses and stretched over my opposite leg, my hair finished its transformation and became a rich cobalt blue.

I moved into a lunge stretch. My black leather fighting outfit felt supple and soft against my skin. I missed the feel of air on my bare flesh because I normally shifted naked. That wasn't an option with one of my friends sitting right in front of me.

The black leather of my Elvin-made suit was a dark contrast against my fair skin. My flesh slowly turned to a shade of pale amethyst marble as I moved into another martial arts warm-up pose.

With sensuous movements I limbered my body, my muscles tightening, firming, becoming more defined. My elemental powers stirred within me, growing stronger as I took Drow form.

My small fangs lowered and my mouth ached from the initial burst from my gums, and the coppery taste of blood wet my tongue.

As my thoughts flashed to Dmitri Beketov's son, anger surged through me and I pierced my bottom lip with the sharp tip of one fang. I licked the blood from my lower lip as I worked to regain focus on my shift.

When I was finished with the transformation, the air was cool in my lungs as I sucked in a deep breath. Dark Elves have more acute senses than humans and some paranorms. Olivia's freesia perfume was keener and mingled with the scents of natural lemon oil my Shifter maid, Dahlia, used to polish my hardwood floors.

I returned to where Olivia reclined on my formerly spotless white sofa that now had a few chip crumbs on it. She crunched another chip and I flinched, then snatched the bag from her.

"Hey." She reached for the chips and I held the bag behind my back.

"You're past your quota." I sank to the floor in front of the glass and steel German coffee table, and I moved into a yoga pose when I was settled. The potato chip bag made a crackling sound as I dropped it behind me and I tucked my ankles under my butt.

Olivia grumbled, her eyes narrowed, but it was a mock-serious expression.

The chip bag safely behind me, I placed my now empty hands on my knees. "I don't think there's much more to plan for the trip to the Catskills."

"I've got all the camping gear." Olivia used one hand to brush the chip crumbs from the sofa into her opposite palm. "Haven't used it since I dumped Brent, so it's still stacked in my closet."

I snorted. Olivia's version of stacked meant crammed. Where my home was designer chic, hers was Early American garage sale. I always wondered where she stashed the money she made as a PI because Rodán paid her exceptionally well, as he did me.

Olivia was also paid a very nice sum when she assisted me on various night-tracking assignments. You couldn't tell by her Wal-Mart clothing and thrift-store furnishings that she had to have a pretty hefty bank account by now. For all I knew she could have had a load of cash before working for Rodán and the GG. With

Olivia, a person never knew and I didn't feel it was my place to ask.

"Since you're taking care of the food, make sure you bring plenty." Olivia stood and started heading toward my kitchen. "I'm not into hunks of raw meat."

"Ugh." I grimaced as I pictured a Werewolf's teeth ripping into a wild animal's bloody haunch. "I'll pack enough for a week."

"We'd better have this case solved in the next few days," Olivia said over her shoulder. "I don't intend to be in the same vicinity as a pack of Werewolves at full moon."

I nodded. Taking that much food meant a quick shopping trip to the corner grocery in the morning when I wasn't amethyst and blue. Living alone, I didn't keep that much food in my cupboards.

"Don't forget the Lay's barbeque chips," came Olivia's voice as she disappeared through the archway that led to my kitchen.

I made a mental note to avoid buying Olivia anything crunchy.

With my acute Drow senses, I heard her open the cabinet door where my garbage can was tucked away to toss her chip crumbs, then the sound of running water while she washed her hands.

I shifted where I sat and reached for my cell on the nearby glass end table.

My living space was modern designer but eclectic. The designer who had decorated my entire apartment had said, "Matching is for wusses." Her words, not mine, but I liked it.

I enjoyed the contrast of the modern furniture from what I'd grown up with belowground in Otherworld. A couple of pieces of my furniture had been created by American designers, but most of the items had been imported from other countries—Germany, England, Italy, Spain, and Belgium. I liked feeling as if I was a part of the entire earth Otherworld. It was more than likely because I was rebelling from my upbringing in the Drow Realm belowground in Otherworld.

The contrast between modern and any part of Otherworld—that I've been to—is striking. Dark Elves still make everything the same way they have for millennia. Total Dark Ages look. Change in the Drow Realm? Yeah, right.

Perks of being a Drow princess—I could afford anything, so this furniture wasn't a drop out of my account. Hey, you should see the size of the diamonds that the Dark Elves mine.

"Nine in the morning, my place." Olivia scooped her XPhone off of the sofa. "That'll give me enough time to rent the SUV from Dollar and pack it, and time for you to get a week's worth of groceries."

I pointed my stylus at her. "Two weeks."

"We'd better not be there that long." Olivia slipped her phone in its clip at her waist, close to her holstered Sig Sauer. "Don't forget trail mix. The kind with lots of dried fruit."

Lots of fruit meant not too crunchy. Good. I pulled up tomorrow's grocery list on my XPhone and added trail mix. "Got it."

"See you at the Pit, Purple Girl," she said before she opened the apartment door.

"Amethyst." My stylus bounced off the door as she closed it behind her, the closed door cutting off the sound of her wicked cackle.

Flying monkeys, indeed.

The Pit was rockin' with the heavy-metal band Rodán had brought in for the weekend. Olivia and I pushed our way through the crowded nightclub until we stood by the stage at the back of the club.

"Sweet Cat?" Olivia made a face as she yelled over the blasting music. "Too bad Tragic Dance isn't playing instead."

"Hey, Sweet Cat isn't half bad." I raised my voice, too, as I scanned the stage to see if all of Cat's regular performers were playing tonight.

Olivia snorted. "But the other half is."

Iddy was on bass, Carly on guitar, and Mitsi on keyboard. Lead vocals was Adele, a Pixie with a prima donna syndrome. Adele was the reason Olivia would have preferred a different band—any band—playing tonight.

"You have to admit it's amazing what those Shifters can do with a guitar or bass," I said. "And the Nymph on keyboard rocks."

I wasn't about to mention Adele. Olivia hated her. They'd had a run-in over the same Shifter male and they both were good at carrying grudges.

"Too bad Sweet Cat doesn't have a Siren on vocals." Olivia glanced at me and smirked. "That would solve the bitch problem," she said, meaning Adele would be gone. "Sirens have the best vocals, anyway. She could entrance some of the scum in here and get rid of them."

I shook my head. "Sure. Like that's going to happen."

Sirens were rare outside of the Bermuda Triangle. Strip club owners would kill to have a cooperative Siren, but Sirens aren't known for their fondness for males in general. Especially lewd males. Sirens would sing the males to their deaths before they'd dance naked for them.

Olivia shrugged. "You have to admit it would be a great undercover assignment in a nightclub."

"Maybe." I glanced at Olivia as we bypassed the stage and Olivia tossed Adele a glare hot enough that the Pixie's hair should have caught on fire. I hurried to continue, "But not many reputable nightclub owners want their males entranced."

Olivia turned her attention to me. "It sells more beer."

I shook my head. "Every female in the place—who isn't a Siren—gets pissed off and leaves when their males get fixated on the Siren. Less clientele equals less profit. Sirens are out."

"Better than Pixies." Olivia narrowed her gaze at Adele again.

Petite beings, generally about five feet tall, Pixies can really belt it. Plus they'll do just about anything for chocolate. They even smell like milk chocolate.

Olivia continued glaring at Adele and took a step toward the stage. My partner looked ready to climb onto the stage to go after the Pixie. I grabbed Olivia's upper arm and tugged her toward the huge conference room door, far away from the stage. She stood fast for a moment, then seemed to switch mental gears and block out the thought of the Pixie as she headed with me toward the conference room.

Phew.

Smells of pipe weed, greasy hamburgers, and the yeasty odor of beer all combined with sweat from those on the dance floor and the various paranorm scents. The smells were swept through the room by the bladed fans overhead, the air still sticky with body heat despite the fans.

Speaking of Sirens, I waved to Nadia. Then I waved to Lawan, who was a Siamese cat Doppler from Thailand. My friends were walking toward the same door Olivia and I were, but coming from the direction of the far right corner crowded with overstuffed black leather couches and chairs. Most Trackers hung out in that corner until it was time to track.

A sick feeling churned in my gut. If things hadn't changed the way they had, Caprice would be with Nadia. But Caprice had been murdered by Demons so recently that the pain that balled in my chest was fresh, jagged, and vicious. I still held onto that pain and anger every time I thought of my dead friend. I could have saved her if only I hadn't been too late. If only I'd sensed the Demons sooner.

We'd never see Caprice again.

I'd never hear her call me *chica* again.

Revenge on the Demons hadn't been close to satisfying.

Doing my best to put aside the horrors I'd seen the night of Caprice's death, I glanced in the direction of Rodán's chambers.

Olivia was now one of the few allowed in his chambers, though only when she and I had extremely important paranormal assignments. This time, however, we were all meeting in the conference room with the other Night Trackers.

"Why does he want us to meet in the conference room?" Nadia hooked her arm through mine when she reached me, her fair skin pale against my amethyst flesh. "What's up?"

"No clue." Over the phone I'd filled Rodán in on my and Olivia's conversation with the alpha Werewolf, so Rodán was up to speed. "Maybe he's telling everyone about Olivia's and my new case."

Lawan looked at me with her pretty brown eyes as she leaned closer to me, her scent of tiger flowers soft and welcome. Like all Trackers, she was decked out in black leather. Each Tracker picked out whatever they wanted to wear, and everyone's suit was different. Lawan tended to dress in a modest high-necked full bodysuit that revealed only her face and hands.

She might look petite and delicate, but she knew how to use the Krabi sheathed at her side. It was a sword wielded by many in Thailand's Krabi-Krabong, a form of martial arts. I'd seen Lawan kick major ass using her skills as well as kill baddies with her Krabi. Swift and neat.

"What's going on with your latest case?" Lawan asked, her voice soft, light.

With her quiet voice, a person would never guess Lawan had a battle cry that topped any one of the seventeen remaining Manhattan Trackers. That included the big-mouthed Shifter, Ice, who preferred a pure white jaguar as his animal form. He had a roar to rival a God or Goddess if one of the deities happened to be angry. *Real* angry.

I didn't answer Lawan because we'd reached the conference room door. The other Night Trackers were talking so loudly as they made their way through that I would have had to raise my voice so that Lawan could hear me. I didn't want to announce the case to other Trackers. It was only their business if Rodán made it so.

"Where's Rodán?" Olivia put her hands on her hips as she and all of the Trackers crowded into the room.

Of course he wouldn't be in the room yet. Rodán liked to make an entrance. I just said, "He'll be here."

My smile faded as my mind touched upon our proctor. In a strange cycle, my thoughts went from Rodán to Adam. From the mistake I'd made that had caused Adam pain. I'd fallen for the NYPD detective and then screwed everything up.

I closed my eyes tight for a moment. The woodsy perfume from the polished Dryad-wood floor and conference table could be smelled over all of the various Tracker scents. We had Dopplers, Shifters, a few different races of Fae, along with Weres. All races of paranorms had different and very distinct scents.

When Rodán needed to make extremely important announcements, the room could accommodate all of the Manhattan Peacekeepers at one time, standing room only. Trackers, Healers, Gatekeepers, and Soothsayers. But not tonight.

"The way I'm treated by this bunch, you'd think I had spinach in my teeth and snot dripping from my nose," Olivia said in a sarcastic tone and I opened my eyes.

I wanted to clap my hand over her mouth before she said something that would end any chance of her being accepted by a good portion of the Trackers in the room.

With my voice lowered, I leaned closer to speak in her ear. "They're just not used to Rodán allowing a norm—or anyone else who's not a Tracker—in on one of our meetings."

Olivia rolled her eyes. "At least Lulu isn't here, not to mention the rest of the Soothsayers and whatever other Peacekeepers there are."

"Hey, some of the Peacekeepers are okay," I said. "Like Jeanie and Karen."

Olivia shrugged. "Whatever. Most of them think they're better than Trackers and you know it."

She was probably right. It was rare to have Soothsayers, Gatekeepers, and Healers in the chamber with Trackers. I'd always had a feeling it was because they considered us to be like wild animals compared to their snooty, supposed sophistication. Some of them were nice enough, but the majority needed to be taken down several pegs.

Olivia did a good job of that with Lulu whenever the Soothsayer was the one to freeze one of our paranormal crime scenes. Lulu had a serious Cinderella-of-the-Earth-Otherworld complex.

All of the Trackers took a seat around the large oval conference table. It was to the right of the room, the table big enough to seat twenty-six. There were eighteen in our group including Olivia, nineteen with Rodán, so there was still room to spare at the table.

After the deaths of three of our fellow Trackers, seventeen of us remained: Meryl, a Shifter; Kelley, a Doppler; Phyllis, a Were; Tracey, Romanian Fae—a Sânzianâ; Hades, Shifter; Ice, Shifter; Dave, Werewolf; Fere, Tuatha; Nancy, Pixie; Carlos, Were; Robert, Doppler; Gentry, Shifter; Bronwyn, Nymph; Rich, Were; and of course, Nadia, Lawan, and myself. Olivia made up the eighteenth being at the table and she was the only human.

Conversation stopped, the room suddenly silent, the air thick and tense.

I cut my gaze to the doorway, in the direction most Trackers at the table were now looking. Five paranorms that I'd never met walked through the set of doors. Two females and three males.

Immediately I caught their paranorm smells. One of the females, a petite blond with diamond-bright blue eyes and hair that hung in long corkscrew curls, was obviously a Doppler. It was easy to tell because of her tiger flower perfume, and I also scented her animal form—a squirrel.

Spices and pepper carried to my nose from the tall, umber-skinned South African Fae, an Abatwa.

A heavily scarred redheaded male was a Werewolf— he smelled of woodlands and fresh air.

The scent of amber came from one fine-looking Japanese male Shifter.

The third male's scent surprised me. Cool air and shadows. A Shadow Shifter. A cocky, arrogant one by the look on his dark features and the way he stood with his arms across his chest.

All five were dressed in snug black leather like

Trackers, and all well-armed. Swords, daggers, and fire-arms were a few of their visible weapons.

Slung across the tall Abatwa's back was her Fae race's traditional bow along with a quiver of arrows—the heads of the arrows probably poisonous and lethal.

The Shadow Shifter carried a medieval-style flail. The thick wooden handle with an iron grip had a chain attached to a spiked iron ball at the end of it. Jeez.

Ice rose from his chair, his height and bearing intimidating to most beings. The newcomers didn't look the least bit intimidated, not one of them moving a muscle. By Ice's scowl, I had a feeling the lack of any kind of response pissed him off.

"This is a private little jam session we're having." Ice's blue eyes sparked like sun on newly fallen snow and his tone was cutting. He made a motion with his head toward the door, indicating the paranorm strangers should leave the way they'd come in. "Get the hell out."

The Abatwa Fae gave a low growl, her muscles flexing. She looked like she was about to draw her bow and pierce Ice between his eyes with one of her arrows. The Shadow Shifter's gaze had grown darker than nightfall, his hand moving to rest on the handle of his flail.

Tracey glared at Ice. "Think you could possibly be any more rude?" Her race of Fae, the Sânziene, were known for their gentle sides. However, I'd seen Tracey use her spear with deadly precision when she tracked, and she used it without an ounce of hesitation.

Olivia muttered, "Ice sure gets a hard-on for antagonizing people."

I glanced at her. "Sounds awfully familiar."

Olivia glared at me and probably would have shot me with an eraser if she'd had any ammunition on hand. "Kiss my—"

Rodán seemed to appear out of nowhere, erasing the end of Olivia's sentence with his presence. Most of the tension in the room faded at once. Our Proctor had that effect on most of the Trackers, Ice excluded, even during the times us Trackers were at each other's throats. It had to be a talent, a magic Rodán commanded, although he never would tell me. It was yet another mysterious quality about him.

Seeing Rodán sent warmth through me as it almost always did, and I wanted to smile. Friend, mentor, former lover . . . he was beyond special to me.

Rodán was of the Light Elves. Despite the high probability of danger to Light Elves from the resentful Dark Elves, Rodán had braved going belowground to recruit me. He had taken the long path deep into the Drow Realm to meet with me and my father. Rodán was the reason I was in Manhattan, and I'll always be grateful to him.

A powerful man, as well as King of the Drow, my father was a difficult male to contend with. He'd started to throw Rodán out at once, not wanting to let me leave the belowground Drow Realm. But I'd insisted on going with Rodán to be a Tracker in New York City. A city my human mother had talked about since I was a youngling.

It wasn't easy wearing down the King of the Drow, but then it wasn't easy arguing with the daughter of the king, either. He'd had to relent—after all, I'd just turned twenty-five, considered an adult in the eyes of the Drow.

With appreciation, I watched as Rodán moved toward us with lithe Elvin grace. How could any woman not admire his sculpted body, broad shoulders, well-defined abs, carved biceps, muscled thighs and calves . . .

His long white-blond hair was swept away from his high cheekbones and over his broad shoulders, and his soft royal blue tunic complemented his golden skin.

Rodán was easily one of the sexiest, most sensual males I had ever met. To be honest, he was sitting at the number-one spot with no chance of anyone knocking him from that particular throne as far as I was concerned.

Even Adam couldn't compete with Rodán, not that I wanted Adam to be even the tiniest bit different. Adam was perfect just the way he was.

If only I hadn't lost him.

Our Proctor moved soundlessly across the polished wood floor until he stood between the five "intruders" and the table where seventeen Trackers and Olivia sat.

I had a pretty good idea why the five paranorms were here and doubted the males and females were really intruders.

Rodán's gaze met each of ours in a slow sweep of his crystal-green eyes before he said, "I would like to introduce you to your new fellow Trackers."

THREE

Ice settled back in his chair, his arms crossed over his chest, a smirk on his pale features that looked as if they had been chiseled from a block of ice itself. "What, no fucking Metamorphs were available?"

Tracey sucked in her breath.

Kelley snickered and I held back a scowl. Did I mention I couldn't stand Kelley?

Ice might as well have just called the group a bunch of scum-sucking underworld sloths. Metamorphs had no redeeming qualities. None.

"Why don't you find a better use for that big mouth of yours, Ice?" Nadia's beautiful skin took on a slight tinge of green with a whisper of dangerous music in her Siren's voice. "I hear one of the toilets is broken in the men's room."

Ice grinned. "I'll give you something you can use *your* mouth on, honey."

I grabbed Nadia's forearm and squeezed as she turned a darker shade of green. By the way she clenched her jaw, it was obvious she was doing everything she could to keep from breaking out into a Siren's song. At that moment no doubt she would have loved to draw Ice to her and impale him on the end of one of her slim but deadly serpent swords.

"Enough." Rodán's voice was low, but his tone and the dark swirl in his normally crystal-green eyes got his point across.

Ice still smirked, but everyone else focused on Rodán.

"The Great Guardian has been training new Trackers for all of the major cities for the past six months," Rodán said, as if Ice hadn't been making a jerk of himself.

An instant burst of heat burned low in the pit of my stomach. To keep from shouting at Rodán, who didn't deserve my anger, I had to bite my tongue so hard it hurt.

So the Great Guardian had held back new Trackers. I'd asked over and over why we weren't given new Trackers to aid us in the battle against Demons. The GG could have sent these Trackers to us when we needed them.

And Caprice might still be alive.

I bit my tongue harder. Blood, coppery and warm, flowed over my tongue from where my fangs had pierced it.

"Stop," Nadia hissed under her breath and I realized I was digging my fingers into her forearm.

"Sorry." I released my grip and tried to calm down enough to hear Rodán through the heated buzz in my ears.

One glance at the other Trackers around the table told me that most of them were thinking the same thing. The Great Guardian *could* have helped sooner and three of our fellow Trackers might still be alive.

Of course no one at the table would dare say anything about the GG aloud. Except for me, when my mouth got ahead of my brain. I hated her riddles and games.

And Ice—he was probably doomed for Underworld as it was, so what did it matter when he shot off his mouth about her?

"Introductions now." Rodán gestured toward the steely faced Abatwa and she stepped forward. "Mandisa, a tribal leader from South Africa."

Olivia suddenly looked like she was about to choke on a mango, one of her favorite fruits. "Mandisa is an African name that means sweet," Olivia said low, and I think only I heard. "If she's sweet, then I'm Barbie."

I coughed to hold back a laugh. Picturing short and very voluptuous Olivia as long-legged slim Barbie was enough to send anyone into hysterics.

Mandisa stared in our direction and I tried on a welcoming smile, hoping she hadn't heard after all. She didn't look amused.

"Angel." Rodán smiled at the squirrel Doppler whose black leather exposed more skin than my suit did. Which meant a whole lot of flesh was showing.

"Angel?" Olivia said under her breath, a laugh in her words. "Figures."

With her long blond corkscrew curls, tanned skin, tiny frame, and girlish smile, Angel looked like a petite, bouncy, and very perky human cheerleader like the ones I'd seen on the sidelines during American football games.

Rah-rah-rah.

Hades rolled his eyes when Rodán added, "Angel is

from Miami Beach." Hades's expression changed to surprise when Rodán added, "She graduated from Harvard with a degree in astrophysics. She started her training as a Tracker after an internship in astrobiology with NASA at Goddard Space Flight Center."

I saw the glint in Angel's blue eyes. Oh, yeah, she might not look it, but she was dangerous. A cheerleader with a brain—one who could use the barbed whip at her side to squeeze the breath out of a being while slicing the being up with the barbs without an ounce of remorse.

All while wearing a neon-orange string bikini.

"Wouldn't want to be on the wrong side of *her* whip," Nadia said close to my ear.

I managed not to smile. Siren's song didn't work on females, but Nadia could handle herself just fine, male or female opponent.

"Nakano," Rodán said as the slender but clearly muscular Shifter stepped forward. "From Japan. He is of the elite Ninja warriors."

Nakano bowed, but didn't smile. His samurai sword was secured in a black sheath at his back, the sheath decorated with intricate gold patterns. His black outfit looked like traditional Ninja gear, but when I concentrated, I saw gold Japanese symbols on the hems. Probably a warding of sorts.

Rodán inclined his head toward the big, scarred auburn-haired Werewolf who was armed not only with a pair of throwing knives at his belt, but a mean-looking Beretta, too. "Max, who left the Bronx pack to join us," Rodán said.

Max's dark brown gaze studied us as he stood with

casual male arrogance. Nothing like a roomful of alpha male Trackers, to a one.

Sheesh.

"And from Down Under is Joshua." Rodán indicated the cocky but fine-looking Shadow Shifter. "He was a mechanical engineer before being recruited as a Tracker."

"Australian accents are so sexy," Olivia said loud enough that I lightly punched her arm.

"Quiet, before Rodán kicks you out," I said under my breath. "Or I do."

"Try it," Olivia said with a laugh in her whisper.

"Don't tempt me."

Olivia flipped me off—like only a best friend could get away with.

"Find a seat." Rodán held out his hand toward the table, indicating the newcomers should fit in among us.

What fun, I thought with a mental grimace. *Thanks, Rodán, for making things really uncomfortable by not preparing everyone beforehand.*

Considering the eighteen of us were spread out, the five new Trackers had to separate and each find a seat between other Trackers. Mandisa, the Abatwa, took the chair beside Ice—I was absolutely sure she did it deliberately. I think she was seriously considering taking one of her poisoned arrows and jabbing it into his heart.

Of course Ice gave her his trademark unrepentant and almost evil grin.

When everyone was seated, an uncomfortable and tense silence blanketed the room. Most of us looked at Rodán as he took his chair at the head of the oval table. Once he was seated, that left only two empty chairs.

"Your full attention. Now." Rodán's commanding voice had all of our gazes riveted on him at once. Even Ice seemed to involuntarily fixate on Rodán.

"Three of our new Trackers will rotate and train with every one of you over the next couple of weeks," Rodán said. "I will designate your assignments shortly." He paused to look around the table. "There are pressing matters at hand."

"Not Demons." Nadia shuddered, her delicate shoulders shaking. I had to repress a shudder myself at the thought of what we'd all just been through

"Not Demons," Rodán repeated her words, only with confidence rather than concern. "At least not that we're aware of, and not here in the city."

"What, then?" Ice leaned back in his chair, an arrogant expression on his face and insolence in his voice. "Pixies?"

Olivia snickered under her breath.

Nancy, a Pixie, glared at Ice.

Rodán fixed his stare on Ice, indicating with his gaze that Ice was way out of line. Of course Ice didn't even flinch.

Our Proctor turned his attention back to the group, meeting each of our gazes, one at a time as he spoke. "The Manhattan Werewolf pack needs assistance." He gestured to Olivia and me. "Nyx's PI agency will be on the case. Nyx and her partner, Olivia, will need backup."

Ice smirked. "Why do a bunch of Werewolves need babysitting?"

Personally, I thought Ice could use a fist to the face. Might just be mine if he kept up the routine he'd been doing all night.

"What's stuck up your ass, Ice?" David said with irritation in his voice.

"Not your dick, that's for sure," Ice said, and David gave a low growl that only a Werewolf could do in human form.

Rodán chose to ignore Ice and the exchange. Instead, he started providing the details I'd given him earlier, about the Werewolves vanishing, then turning up mutilated and dead, as well as the still-missing children.

The room grew quieter, the tension thicker. Ice's expression darkened as he listened and I could see in his eyes the focus that made him an excellent Tracker. "Where?" he asked, his tone even. "Not Manhattan."

"The Catskills." Rodán folded his hands on the table. "Unfortunately, the events are keeping the Weres too close to civilization and they refuse to move on until their pups are found. The next full moon is within days."

Fere whistled through his teeth.

"This better be dealt with before then." David shook his head. He should know. Being a Werewolf, he had to take to the mountains during the full moon, as far away from norms and other paranorms as possible.

Palpable energy stretched around the table as if each of us was ready to stand up and fight something. Anything.

"Nyx and Olivia are leaving in the morning," Rodán said. "I want three of you to accompany them."

Shock rippled through me and I felt it mirrored in Olivia. Why was he doing this? Olivia and I always worked alone. Always. Well, there had been T hanging around—doing things like saving my life—during our battle with the Demons, but I was so not going there.

In answer to my unspoken question, Rodán said, "Olivia and Nyx will need backup considering the danger involved. An unseen enemy with no scent is far more dangerous than anything we've dealt with before."

"Except Demons," Nadia muttered.

"Maybe more so than Demons," Rodán said even though Nadia had spoken so low it should have been impossible to hear. But Rodán was Elvin and, like me as one of the Dark Elves, his acute hearing gave him an advantage that most others didn't have. "A threat one can't see or smell, and doesn't leave signs of any kind, makes it difficult to determine how to fight it, or even find it."

Nadia gave a slow nod. "I guess you're right. At least with the Demons we knew what we were facing."

"For the most part," I said. There had been a lot of unknowns, puzzle pieces Olivia and I had to fit together before a virtual Armageddon could have been unleashed.

"Nyx," Rodán said. "Along with Olivia, you will take two of the new Trackers, Angel and Joshua." He kept his eyes fixed on me. "Ice will also join you."

The tension in Olivia's body was so powerful that I knew she was about to say something we both might regret. I grabbed her forearm and pressed my fingers into her skin hard enough to make her grimace and glare at me.

Before any of us could say anything, Rodán continued. "Ice is our best scent tracker. Joshua is virtually invisible when he shifts into shadow." He looked at Angel. "As a squirrel, Angel can serve as sentry and travel through the trees in a way no one else can."

I had to admit, his logic was spot-on.

"Of course," Rodán said, "Nyx and Olivia are the best PIs in the state of New York and are needed to solve this situation." He looked directly at Olivia. "And they are *both* excellent Night Trackers."

For once Olivia didn't seem to have some smartass remark as she realized Rodán had referred to her as a Tracker. It was obvious she was stunned. For that matter, so was everyone else at the table.

"I guess I need a tight leather suit to go along with my Sig," she said, and Nadia grinned.

"Nyx, Olivia—I want you and your team to stay and discuss your plans. Bronwyn, you take Ice's territory while he's gone."

Bronwyn, currently a rover, nodded. "Got it."

"Nadia, this week you're with Mandisa," Rodán said. "Kelley, you'll be working with Nakano. Carlos, you'll partner with Max."

Everyone gave a nod of agreement, but Nadia looked a little green. "She's bigger than I am," Nadia mumbled, "and she has poisoned arrows."

This time I grinned as I looked at my friend. "You're an even match. Have fun."

"Oh yeah, fun." Nadia put on a brilliant smile and faced Mandisa.

Mandisa didn't smile.

Rodán gestured with his head toward the door. "Everyone but Nyx and her team get out there and get to tracking."

The Fae Trackers' movements were silent as they made their way out, but everyone else seemed to make an inordinate amount of noise as they left the room.

"Ice?" Olivia scowled as she looked at me. "Can't you get us out of this, Nyx?"

I shrugged.

"What's your problem, norm?" Ice wore a smug expression as he looked at Olivia from across the table. "Intimidated to work with me?"

Olivia gritted her teeth before she said, "I'll intimidate your ass."

I put up both hands, indicating they needed to shut up. "Save your energy for the real problem."

The "Down Under" Shadow Shifter, as well as the Doppler cheerleader with Stephen Hawking's brains, moved to other seats so that they were closer to me and Olivia.

Rodán stood and bowed. "I will leave you to it," he said before exiting the room.

Great. Two newbies and Ice, all accompanied by a good dose of arrogance, not to mention Olivia, who personified attitude all by herself.

Dream team. Not.

When everyone on my newly assigned team was seated and the door had closed behind the last of the Trackers and Rodán, I folded my hands on the table. "We're headed up to Hunter Mountain in the Catskills in the morning. You'll need camping gear and enough food for two weeks."

"What's your master plan, Blue?" Ice said with a skeptical expression.

I tried not to clench my teeth at his reference to my hair, obviously trying to get a rise out of me.

"The master plan is to make sure you end up as one of the missing once we get there." Razor-sharp irritation snapped in Olivia's voice. "Shouldn't be too hard, considering you have the intelligence of a potato."

Before a small war started, I cut in, fast. "Like Rodán explained, we don't know what we're facing." I folded my arms on the table and leaned forward, doing my best to project full confidence in my voice that I didn't completely feel. "We will do reconnaissance, interview the Werewolves, and track down whatever or whoever is kidnapping, mutilating, and murdering the Werewolves."

I looked at Olivia, Angel, Ice, and Joshua. "This is not a situation where I simply tell you what to do. I'd like you to offer up your own ideas on what is happening and what you believe could possibly lead us down the path to solving this case."

"No scent . . ." Angel pursed her lips, and her expression looked like she was running a million options through her mind like a human computer.

I shook my head. "Unbelievable considering how sensitive Were noses are."

One of Angel's corkscrew curls fell over her shoulder as she moved. "Hawking suggested folding space to travel from one galaxy to another. It hasn't been accomplished or even proven by humans, but I believe it's possible. Perhaps a similar method is being used to take the Werewolves."

Interesting. Trust our Harvard grad to come up with that option. I pursed my lips. "Perhaps it's an unidentifiable scent that is the problem. Your suggestion would make sense in that regard, too."

"What about the Great Guardian?" Angel pulled on the loose corkscrew curl and it bounced back up to her cheek. "She should know."

Ice snorted and Olivia rolled her eyes.

"Don't bother," I grumbled. "All we'll get are riddles and cryptic messages from the GG."

Olivia snorted. "No kidding."

Ice smirked. "We don't have the time to screw around with the Guardian's games."

The two new Trackers looked interested in but non-judgmental about our back-and-forth about the GG. Neither said anything.

"Don't follow our example," I said to Angel and Joshua. "Out of all of the Trackers, the three of us are going to end up in Underworld. We're the GG's least biggest fans."

"Since I'm human, it'll be Hell for me." Olivia leaned back in her chair. "I don't know which would be worse—Hell or Underworld."

"Hell." The Shadow Shifter caused us all to swivel our heads toward him. His expression was even, but yellow-orange flames danced in his almost black eyes. "Believe me—Hell is far worse than Underworld."

FOUR

Usually I reveled in tracking and enforcing paranorm laws. But this morning it felt good to be home instead of out still hunting down bad guys. Maybe it was because I'd be leaving in a couple of hours for Goddess knew how long and wouldn't have my home as a refuge.

After the team's brainstorming session, I'd headed out to track. Thank Anu it had been a slow night because my mind had been on the upcoming assignment.

And Adam.

I stared at my duffel on my bed and fingered the soft black leather of one of my fighting suits as I pictured Adam. I imagined looking into his eyes that were the beautiful color of alder wood . . . running my fingers through his rich sable hair . . . and seeing the passion in his expression that had once been for me.

But not anymore. Not after blowing it big-time.

"Stop it!" I gritted my teeth and scooped up a week's worth of Victoria's off my comforter and threw them into my duffel. Thank goodness Kali hadn't shredded all of my bras and panties. Dahlia, my Shifter maid, was going to feed Kali while I was gone.

The blue Persian had curled up my pillow as if she was a queen on her throne holding court. I frowned. Kali's tail moved up and down in a lazy movement.

I shook my finger at her. "Do you think you can leave the rest of my panties and bras alone while I'm gone, your highness?"

Kali gave me her usual regal yet annoyed look before she raised her front paw and started licking it in delicate swipes of her tongue.

If I was gone for more than a couple of days, she was bound to finish off what I had left in my drawers. "I really need to buy a safe just for my panties and bras," I grumbled for probably the five hundredth time since moving to New York City from Otherworld.

Kali ignored me.

I returned the favor.

Last night while I tracked, a debate had ping-ponged in my mind so hard it had given me a headache. I wanted to tell Adam that I would be gone. But I didn't know if he even cared. I didn't know if he'd forgiven me. If he'd ever forgive me.

"Don't delude yourself into thinking that." I moved away from the bed. "After what you did, there is no more Adam and Nyx."

It had ended before it had really started.

My head hurt more as I went to the shelves in my closet. I grabbed my black leather Elvin boots and a couple of sets of the Elvin-made black leather half-tops and pants that I wore at night when tracking. The pair of jeans I was wearing now felt different than my usual designer skirts and slacks, but I liked the feel of the brushed cotton against my thighs and the snug fit around my hips and at my waist.

The hardwood floors were cool beneath my bare feet as I made my way to the bed and shoved the outfits into the expensive leather duffel. Maybe I spoiled myself too much. Nah.

But right then I'd have traded every designer shoe and handbag to have Adam forgive me and to be back in his strong arms.

Two weeks had passed since our last time together and it was still so difficult trying not to picture his boyish smile and his quarterback build and remember every brush of his skin against mine. I shook my head and forced thoughts of Adam from my mind. Or tried to.

Guns N' Roses's *Welcome to the Jungle* belted out from my purse, the current ringtone for my XPhone. My long hair swung across my face as I leaned across the bed and reached for my purse. I shoved my hair over my shoulders with one hand when I had the phone in my other.

"Olivia," I said out loud when I saw the caller ID screen. I pressed the *on* button with my thumb and brought the phone to my ear. "What's up?"

"How long is it going to take your girly ass to get ready?" Olivia said, almost sounding amused. Why she'd be amused, I had no idea. "You're going to be late, but you'd better not be too late."

"What's with you? I'm never late." I rolled my eyes and smiled. "But thanks for checking up on me, Mom." I brushed my palms on my jeans, then adjusted my light brown sweater over my breasts, enjoying the softness of the cashmere against my skin. "Almost finished dressing and packing."

"Think you can live without your designer clothes on this case?" Olivia said with good-natured sarcasm in her voice. "I don't suppose you'll wear practical Levi's or T-shirts on an outing like this."

"I'm bringing practical clothing." I'd wear my Elvin-made boots I used for tracking. That made sense. The other turtle-necked cashmere sweaters I'd packed would of course be practical for this kind of case during the day. They were even colors that would blend in when I was in the forest. Double practical.

The black Burberry jacket and the cashmere sweaters would keep me warm in the extreme chill of the Catskills this time of year. Because I'm Drow I don't get very cold, but I liked the snuggly feeling of a nice coat. "I'm more than ready to spend some time in the woods," I added.

"Uh-huh." I could swear Olivia was holding back a laugh.

I pulled the phone away and scowled at it before I put it to my ear again. "I'll be there by nine, so don't worry about it."

"Oh, you're going to be running late," Olivia said, but didn't sound annoyed, which was odd. So was her insistence I wouldn't be on time. "Just not too much, got that? I'll give you an extra thirty minutes, tops."

What was she talking about? I narrowed my brows. "I'm not going to be—"

Olivia severed the connection at the same time I heard a loud knock at my front door. The following knock was loud enough that it reverberated through my head.

While still gripping the phone in my hand, I walked to the door. What was with Olivia? And who was making my headache worse with all of that knocking?

I unlocked the door and yanked it open. "It's not necessary to—" I dropped my phone and it landed with a clatter on my hardwood floor. My heart jerked.

Detective Adam Boyd.

Adam.

He strode through the door, forcing me to step back as he closed it behind him.

His sable hair was adorably tousled by the wind, but his expression was grim and his eyes a shade darker than normal.

"What's wrong?" I asked just before he grabbed me by my upper shoulders, pulled me to him—

And kissed me.

Startled was too mild a word for how I felt, but I regained my senses fast enough. Fast enough to wrap my arms around his neck and press my body against his.

Goddess, how I'd missed his scent, coffee and leather and masculine spice. Zeus must have been throwing bolts of lightning the way the sensations zinged through my body as Adam's muscular chest flattened my breasts.

I couldn't get enough of his taste, his touch, his scent. I didn't even pause to think why he was there because all that mattered was that I was in his arms.

Adam placed his hands on my ass and pulled me upward so that my feet left the floor. I gasped against his mouth and crossed my ankles behind him. With my thighs hugging his hips, I felt the hard ridge of his erection against me, even through my jeans. I held onto him, my arms wrapped around his neck.

He explored my mouth with his tongue, and it felt like he was trying to learn every detail again. I did the same, nipping his lower lip, then running my tongue over his teeth and further into the warm depths to explore every part of his mouth I could.

Adam raised his head, breaking our intense kiss. He stared down at me and so many emotions seemed to travel across his face. My head was spinning too much to even try to figure any of this out, much less the emotions that might be simmering under his surface.

He focused on me with his beautiful alder-wood brown eyes and I licked the taste of him on my bottom lip, savoring it. "What—"

"You were going to leave without saying goodbye?" Adam gripped me tighter to him and he frowned.

"I didn't think you cared anymore." More surprise caused my eyes to widen. "You said—"

"I can't stop caring for you, Nyx. I should have given you a chance to explain." Adam shook his head, his expression almost harsh as if he was angry with himself. "Although I just can't—" His jaw tensed. "It was none of my business what you did before we slept together. If it had been after, then yeah, I couldn't forgive that. But that wasn't what happened, was it?"

"No." I swallowed hard and he set me on my feet before bringing me to him so that my head was lying against his chest. "Rodán was my lover, but I'd stopped seeing him when I started feeling the way I do about you. Even though you and I hadn't done more than work together."

I drew away and looked up at his face. "That night I spent with Rodán a few days before you and I . . . got together . . . it was the night Natalie was murdered." Adam's features seemed to grow softer as I spoke. "Rodán and I comforted each other in the only way we knew how. But I never would have been with him if you and I had started seeing each other. *Never.*"

"I'm sorry, Nyx." Adam took a deep breath and brushed my cheek with his knuckles. "I should have known better than to judge you like that."

"How could you have?" I moved my face back and forth against his fingers. The memory of what he'd told me after finding out about Rodán traveled through my mind. *"Nyx, I can't see a woman who's involved with another man."* Adam had said the words with pain in his eyes. *"Been there already and not going there again."*

"It wasn't right of me to assume that you were having a dual relationship with Rodán," he was saying in the here and now.

"You went through something terrible." I reached my hand up and cupped the side of his face. His stubble was rough against my palm. He hadn't shaved that morning. "Someone hurt you badly and that day brought back those memories."

My voice was soft as I continued. "I'm not going to ask what happened, but I can make a guess why after what you said. I won't ever hurt you like that, Adam. I could never hurt you."

Pain flashed across his face, pain from the memory of the way some other woman had hurt him. The strong urge to track her down for what she'd done to him made my body ached. I didn't know what I'd do with her when I found her, but I wanted her to know how badly and how wrong it had been to hurt him the way she had.

He shook his head again. "What happened in the past is no excuse to treat you the way I did."

"Enough." I tipped my face. "Now is what matters." I brought my mouth to his and placed a gentle kiss on his lips.

"Where are you going with Olivia?" Adam held me close and it felt like his body was burning as much as mine was. "It's dangerous, isn't it." It was a statement, not a question.

I drew my brows together. "Did Olivia call you?"

Adam had a puzzled expression. "I had a feeling. It was strange. I knew you were leaving and it didn't feel right. Something about where you're going. What you're doing."

Even through his concern he looked a little sheepish as he added, "So I called Olivia." He shook his head. "I couldn't believe it when she told me you were leaving the city on some kind of assignment. How could I have known that?"

Rodán's words flashed through my mind. *"Each liaison has latent psychic ability. A psychic version of stem cells . . ."*

When the Demons were capturing key human liaisons, the shock of Rodán's statement had reverberated through every Tracker at the strategy meeting. That information was yet another thing that had been kept from the Trackers, as well as from the human liaisons themselves. I was so tired of the Great Guardian's—and sometimes Rodán's—secrets.

I gave a slight shrug and smiled. "Coincidence." It probably wasn't a good idea to go into that with Adam and tell him he had some kind of psychic ability that was apparently making an appearance. It didn't really feel like it was my place to say anything.

"We have some kind of connection." He leaned his forehead against mine. "I don't know what it is, but it's powerful."

"I'll miss you." My words were soft and low. "I've missed you since that day we had the . . . the misunderstanding."

"I want to go." Adam raised his head. "I've got a shi—boatload of time coming." He always tried not to curse in front of me and it made me smile. "I haven't taken a vacation from the NYPD in God knows how long."

The desire to have him with me was so strong I wanted to shout "Yes!" But the truth was he'd be in as much danger as anyone else in the Werewolf camp.

I couldn't meet his eyes and instead I looked at the back of my hand as I moved it over his pecs. "I can't take you."

"You mean you won't." Adam's voice was hard enough to make me snap my head up. "You're protecting me just like you have been for the past two years. You know how I feel about that."

I clenched my fist in his T-shirt that was beneath his worn brown bomber jacket. "I brought you in during our final battle with the Demons."

"And I'm still here." He was starting to look a little angry.

I drew a card he couldn't argue with. Well, he might anyway.

"The Werewolves will not accept another human in their camp." I gripped his T-shirt tighter and wanted to shake the stubborn look off his face. "They're already having a real problem with Olivia being there. The Weres don't want humans anywhere near them. They don't trust norms."

Adam turned his head and looked away from me for a moment. I could see the battle raging on his features as his jaw tightened and his brows drew together.

When he looked back at me he let out a frustrated breath. "I swear to God if anything happens to you they'll have to turn me into hamburger to stop me from going into that camp."

I grimaced. "Now that's an image I don't particularly want to remember."

His eyes went a darker shade of brown. "The only reason I'm not climbing into that SUV with you as soon as you're packed is because I don't want to make things more difficult for you with the Weres."

"Thank you." I kissed him again and he tightened his arms around me.

"That doesn't mean I'm letting you leave without saying goodbye," he said as he started to walk me backward to my room. "Properly."

FIVE

I almost couldn't believe that I was with Adam again. That I'd *really* be with him again. The fluttering in my stomach was nothing compared to the desire flowing beneath my skin.

Sunlight slanted through the sheer curtains and I blinked as we passed through the rays. Briefly I felt the sun's warmth as Adam guided me backward into my bedroom.

"Olivia says I can't have you all day." His smile was both sexy and mischievous as he sat me on the middle of the bed. "I'm afraid she'll take a battering ram to the front door if I keep you too long."

"She would." I sent a small whirl of my air elemental power to Adam and hugged his shoulders with it before pulling him down to me at the same time I lay back on the bed. "But I can handle her."

"Hey." Adam grinned as I drew him on top of me so that he was between my thighs, his weight on my upper body. "How'd you do that?" He pushed himself up and braced his arms on the bed to either side of my head.

I grinned back at him. "That's nothing compared to what else I can do."

"Hmmm." He raised his brows. "I think that statement might be worth exploring a little farther. A lot farther."

With another tug of my elemental air magic, I brought his head down so that his mouth was close to mine. "Let's start here."

"Fine by me," he murmured before he kissed me.

I could have kissed Adam forever. His kisses were warm and sweet and delicious. He used his tongue and teeth and lips in ways that made me sigh and moan. Every inch of my body quivered in anticipation of having him inside me again.

I circled his neck with my arms and brought him as close to me as I could. A sigh of pleasure came from me as he pressed his hard body on my slim frame and his even harder erection to my belly. My jeans didn't feel so comfortable anymore and I ached to get them off and feel his skin slide against mine.

"Damn, Nyx." Adam pressed his forehead to mine. His breath was warm on my face as I met his brown eyes. "Is this okay? Do you want it as bad as I do?"

I gave him my best innocent look. "Want what?"

"You *know* what." He reached between us and easily unfastened the top button of my jeans. "Tell me if this is too soon."

"Shush." My zipper was down and I was shimmying my jeans and panties over my hips before he had finished his sentence. "The only thing I regret is that we don't have time to stay in bed all day."

Adam stared at me as he stood, then helped tug my jeans to my knees. "Every time I look at you I can't get over how beautiful you are."

"Just come inside me." I pulled my sweater over my head and had my bra off fast enough it might have set a record if I was human. "Now."

He continued to study my features as he unfastened his belt, then undid the top button of his jeans. "I want more time with you."

"Can't have it." I sent a draft of my air element toward him and used it to tug his jeans. I grinned the moment I saw his Looney Tunes Marvin the Martian boxers. "You *do* have Marvin."

"Of course." Adam shoved his boxers down and my attention went instantly to something far more appealing.

His erection was so thick and long, and a burst of need shot through me. I didn't give him time to pull his jeans off. I used my air magic to draw him down to me. This time he didn't act the least bit surprised. No, we were definitely on the same page because he thrust into me in a rush.

I cried out. "That's good, that's good, that's so good." My breath was suddenly coming in short, harsh gasps.

Adam grunted and I looked up and met his gaze as he took me with one powerful thrust after another. "Can't go slow this time, Nyx."

"Don't want you to." I said each word in between breaths. "Want it just like this."

His intense expression was hard to decipher, but I really didn't need to know what he was thinking at that moment. I just wanted him to take me like this. Just like this.

As he rocked with each thrust, his boxers and jeans rubbed my thighs and his bomber jacket slid along my bare chest. I loved the feel of his clothing scraping my soft bared skin. I loved the feel of my jeans around my knees as he slid in and out of my core. I loved the smell of his sweat mingled with his other familiar scents.

I loved him. I loved Adam.

The thought didn't surprise me, but I kept it to myself and felt blessed in this incredible moment with Adam.

Everything, every thought and feeling, swirled through my head and my body at the same time the intensity of my oncoming climax twined inside me. Memories of all of the human/paranorm cases Adam and I had worked on and what little time we'd had when we finally came together had led up to that incredible surge of love I felt throughout me.

I looked up and held Adam's gaze with mine as he continued to take me with solid thrusts that seemed to fill me from my core to my belly.

The love I felt for him was like gold sunshine brimming in my heart while at the same time a blanket of the moon's silver light caressed my skin. I was from two worlds—day and night, aboveground and belowground—and each world inside me loved Adam on every level possible.

For a moment I wondered if Adam could read the love in my eyes. But he said nothing as he took my arms from around his neck. He clasped my wrists in one of his hands and pinned them above me, stretching my arms. He lowered his head and took my nipple into the wet warmth of his mouth.

The pleasure of his light bites and pressure of him sucking first one nipple and then the other had me crying out. I wanted to shout my love for him, but no. I would keep my feelings to myself until—*if*—Adam said he loved me. He'd have to go first. It just seemed right. He needed to figure it out at his own pace, without pressure, and that was good enough for me.

The sun's and the moon's rays within me collided in a spectacular explosion of gold and silver in my mind. I gave a cry that I didn't recognize as my own as the exquisite pleasure filled me. The rays traveled to every part of my body, warming me—yet a cooling sheen of sweat on my skin followed the warmth. Like daylight followed by moonlight.

Adam made carnal sounds of pleasure deep in his throat as he came. His cock pumped inside of me, throbbing hard as the walls of my core gripped him tight and I took his semen. Being part Drow, I couldn't get pregnant unless I wanted to, and I couldn't get STDs. I reveled in the sensation of being able to feel him completely.

A few drops of sweat from his forehead trickled into my hair, joining my own sweat that prickled on my scalp.

"Jeez, Nyx." Adam's weight felt good, not suffocating, as he rested on top of me. He raised his head and pressed his lips to mine. "You have something special inside of you that makes me want you in so many ways."

He released my wrists and I brought my arms around his neck again. I smiled. "Ditto, sexy."

His laugh was soft as he eased off of me and out of me before lying beside me on the bed. "Sexy?"

"Of course." I moved one hand to his chest, over his

T-shirt. "I wish we had time to do this again and again. Only this time with you naked."

Adam circled one of my sensitive nipples with his index finger and I sucked in my breath. "I should have taken you slow," he said. "Forget Olivia and her battering ram."

"But then I would have to pay for a new door." I think I managed to look serious.

"I'd have paid for it." His lips were so soft and warm as they met mine. "You're worth every penny and far more."

My smile turned into a grin. "I cost a lot more than pennies."

"I bet." His expression became mischievous but intent, too. "Forget Olivia. I've got to have you one more time."

And he entered me again.

"An hour and a half late." Olivia was beside a Jeep Wrangler in the alleyway behind her apartment building, checking her watch and frowning. I was pretty sure it was a mock frown. "Good thing you weren't any later or I would have dragged your naked ass out of your bedroom."

My smile was firmly settled on my face and no amount of teasing from Olivia was going to take that away. I didn't think my body would ever stop thrumming from the short time I'd been able to spend with Adam.

Delicious and decadent sensations swirled throughout me and it was as if I could still feel him inside me. Even with Manhattan's usual odor of pollution along with its myriad of other smells, I could still scent the smell of our sex—despite taking a quick shower with Adam. I gave a little shiver of pleasure at the thought of our fabulous morning.

Mmmmmm . . .

"I couldn't stop at the grocery store until after a friend's unplanned visit." Total innocence was in my voice as I set three green cloth eco-bags of groceries on the asphalt.

Olivia snorted. "Sure. If a friend is what you want to call a hot detective who wants to get into your pants every time he sees you. And no doubt did a good job of it this morning."

"No ice since Beketov said they keep plenty on hand." My cheeks did heat a little as I looked into one of the cloth grocery bags while making a point of ignoring Olivia. "I bought your extra-fruit trail mix and those pepper-Jack cheese sticks you like so much. Of course hot dogs, buns, condiments, et cetera."

"Nathan's?" She grabbed two of the grocery bags and swung them into the rented Jeep that was close to forest green. Our personal vehicles wouldn't begin to handle a trip like this—all we had was my Corvette and her old GTO.

"Of course Nathan's," I said as I eyed her T-shirt. "Is there any other kind of hot dog?"

"Better be regular mustard and none of that Dijon crap." Olivia propped her hands on her hips, one hand near her holstered Sig Sauer. "Did you get the barbeque chips?"

"Oh, darn." I think I did a credible good job of look-ing innocent. "I forgot."

Olivia gave me a wicked grin and I groaned when she said, "Don't worry, I grabbed plenty."

She scuffed her brown Keds over the pebble-covered asphalt. The T-shirt she was wearing today, a brown shade that matched her Keds, was a new one.

A friend will help you move.

A real *friend will help you move a body.*

I looked from her shirt to her face as I handed her the last grocery bag. "Heh. We've done both of those."

"That's why we're *real* friends." She stuffed the bag between a tent and a small kerosene lantern in the back of the Wrangler. "Damn. I forgot to bring body bags. An extra-large one for that big asshole of a Werewolf."

"I'm not helping you move Beketov's body if you decide to take him out." I wiped my palms on my jeans as she closed up the back of the Wrangler. "I'm not that much of a real friend. He's too big."

She gave a shrug. "I'll make a new friend."

I smiled and headed to the passenger side while she went for the driver's side door. Gravel in the alleyway crunched under her Keds while my boots didn't make a sound.

My seatbelt was on and I was gripping the "Oh shit" handle above the door before Olivia was in the car. My stomach was churning already. "Think you can back off trying to compete with the yellow cab drivers? These things flip over fairly easy, you know."

"Hold on" was all she said before she peeled out from the alleyway and maneuvered the Jeep down the small side street.

Daggers and my elemental powers at the ready, I could track dangerous beings and Demons without hesitation. However, riding in the same vehicle with Olivia when she was driving was putting my life in her hands and not being able to control the outcome.

I sucked in a deep breath and closed my eyes as Olivia spun the Wrangler into New York City traffic.

SIX

The drive from Manhattan to our isolated destination in New York's Catskill Mountains should have taken close to two and a half hours. With Olivia behind the wheel we made it in less than two.

The Wrangler made it easy to bypass the last campsite in the Devil's Tombstone campground and keep on going, but I still gritted my teeth and kept a tight grip on the "Oh shit" handle as the Wrangler rocked back and forth. I swore she almost rolled it at least ten times. I touched my collar with my free hand, as if it had the magic to make sure we didn't find ourselves upside down.

Way up high, snow capped the tallest peaks of the mountains. Such a beautiful sight I wasn't familiar with because Otherworld didn't have snow and I'd never been out of New York City before.

I'd have to change that and do some traveling.

A kaleidoscope of color from trees and bushes turning to their fall shades greeted us as we made our way further into the mountains.

My lips parted in awe. "We don't have change of seasons in the Elvin part of Otherworld," I said. "This is unbelievable. So beautiful."

"That scarlet patch is sumac." Olivia pointed with one finger toward a shrub.

My heart leapt as the Wrangler jerked harder on the trail. "Don't let go of the wheel!"

Why did she always have to ignore me? She pointed to a tree. "The lemon-yellow leaves are on the poplars and black ash, the purple-leaved trees are white ash and that golden-orange over there are sugar maples."

I gripped the handle tighter. "How about you give me a lesson when we're not about to roll over the side of a huge gulch?"

Olivia gave me a wicked grin. "Because this is more exciting."

I closed my eyes tight and said a prayer.

When we came to a hard stop, I jerked back and forth against my seatbelt and opened my eyes.

"Can't go any farther with the Jeep." Olivia frowned. "Too bad. This was fun."

"Yeah. Fun." Thanks to Olivia's driving, I was probably three shades of green when she turned off the engine. Green doesn't nearly fit my complexion as well as amethyst—it looks better on Nadia.

My legs were a little shaky when I climbed out of the Jeep. Instead of kissing the ground in thanks that we'd made it to our destination alive, I paused to scent the air.

"Almost as good as Otherworld." I filled my lungs and my sensitive sense of smell caught signs of the humans who'd passed nearby in the present and the slightest scent-memory of those who had been here in the past.

"We need to get moving." Olivia glanced up at the sky and I followed her gaze to see dark storm clouds gathering. "I'd like to have camp set up before the rain gets here."

I saluted her. "Yes, ma'am."

"And I'd like to get there before you go purple and freak out the natives." Olivia opened the back of the Wrangler and started pushing things aside until she found what she was looking for. She brought out two large forest-green backpacks. "Start packing the gear."

It didn't take us long to get the gear stowed, and I then fastened my weapons belt around my hips. I normally only wore it while tracking at night, but we were heading into a potentially dangerous situation.

Lightning and Thunder, seventeen-inch-long, two-inch-wide, Drow-made dragon-claw daggers, had been designed just for me and settled at my thighs in a way that felt comforting. I fastened my double-bladed oval buckler, Storm, like a belt buckle at the front of my belt.

My Kahr had its own sheath, as did my XPhone, which would probably be useless as a cell phone in the Catskills. I had never worn my weapons belt with my civilian clothing before, but I didn't expect to run into any civilians. Also, I could use a glamour to hide it if I needed to.

Olivia had her Sig in its shoulder holster, along with a dagger sheathed at one hip and a couple of other knives hidden in her clothing.

"How do you manage to get that much into the backpacks?" I asked while shaking my head.

The small tent actually fit into hers, pots and pans into mine, and our sleeping bags were rolled up and secured at the bottom of the backpacks so tightly they looked like trussed-up roasts.

"Talent." Olivia looked up at me with a smart-aleck grin. "You forget your partner is brilliant at everything."

I rolled my eyes to the treetops.

After she drove the Wrangler as far down an incline as she could, and into some heavy brush, we locked it up. We hid the Jeep by covering it with plenty of branches thick with leaves and pine needles, along with plenty of brush.

Olivia and I shrugged into our backpacks, then headed up one of the less traveled trails not too far from where we'd hidden the Jeep. Beketov had given us detailed instructions on the Werewolf pack's location the night we took on the case.

I have an excellent memory, so it wasn't hard to figure out where to cut off the trail into dense forest where no human could possibly see a path.

"Are you sure this is the trail?" Olivia kept her voice low even as an oak branch with maroon leaves slapped her in the face. She grimaced but didn't complain. Olivia never did when it came to pain, no matter how bad it was. If she complained, it was only her way of lightening the situation. "If you call this a trail," she added before she dodged her head beneath a poplar branch.

"You forget your partner is brilliant," I threw back at her and she made a noise of disagreement.

I sensed and scented the Werewolves even though the sign was faint, and I saw the barest disturbance of brush from those who had passed through.

Only Elves, Fae, Weres, and Shadow Shifters have that skill. No other beings that I know of are completely silent when they move. Weres are only that silent when in their Were form, though.

Definitely no human can begin to track a Werewolf.

"Wonder where Ice and the two new Trackers are." My tone was whisper-soft as I gazed in sheer amazement at the beauty of the tree leaves and bushes turning to their fall colors.

Damp tendrils of Olivia's dark hair curled on her forehead as she looked over her shoulder at me and shrugged. "You need to teach me how to make these damned bushes part like the Red Sea, same as they do for you."

"You're not bad for a human." The vegetation barely skimmed me as I walked, branches moving aside without touching me and giving way for me to move through. "But to Werewolves and Fae, you might as well be clomping into a library wearing combat boots with all the noise you make."

Another branch slapped Olivia's face, this time nailing her right on the nose. "Bite me," she said.

I grinned. "I won't, but the Weres might."

"A certain alpha Were had better watch his ass while we're here," Olivia said. "Who needs a body bag?"

Deeper and deeper and higher and higher we hiked into the forest, making our way through the thick foliage, over fallen trees, and around moss-covered rocks of all sizes. The air smelled even better here, sweet and fresh. The fall scents were a pleasant change from breathing Manhattan smog and other city odors on a daily basis.

The heaviness of my backpack didn't bother me even though Olivia had packed it as though she'd been stuffing everything into a black hole. My cashmere sweater felt soft against my skin and the light weight of my jacket was comforting.

I didn't mention it to Olivia, but I sensed four wolves

minutes before two of the Werewolf sentries slipped out of the brush. The wolves blocked our way and bared wicked-looking teeth. My senses told me there were human weapons nearby.

Their thick coats shone in what little light the foliage overhead allowed. The female Were had a rich lightly streaked deep blond coat and the male's was a glossy dark brown. Growls rose from within their chests and with their protective stances, neither of them looked too friendly.

"Welcome to Oz," Olivia said under her breath as she moved her hand closer to her Sig.

The Werewolves growled louder and looked even fiercer as their hair rose on end. I'd kept my hands at my sides. I can look relaxed but I never let down my guard.

I shot Olivia a look, and she moved her fingers away from her handgun. Instead she gripped her hand into a fist as she casually loosened the rest of her body into a martial arts stance. She didn't take any situation for granted. She would remain prepared until she was positive we were safe and she made sure the opposition knew it.

"I'm Nyx Ciar and this is Olivia DeSantos." I gestured to my partner, then dropped my hand to my side. "Dmitri Kral Beketov is expecting us." I showed my respect for their alpha by my formality, even if I did think Olivia might have had the right idea when it came to eliminating one big pain in the ass. Well, not really, but if he acted like he had in our office all the time, the idea would be tempting.

A heavy pause as the two Weres continued to assess

us. No doubt the fact that members of their pack were being kidnapped, mutilated, and murdered didn't make it easy for either of them to trust strangers.

While the female wolf held her position, the dark-haired male was the first to take human form. I tried not to wince at the popping sounds of shifting bones and the thought of the pain the Were must have been masking as his muscles rippled and his nose, forehead, and cheekbones shifted.

His coat shimmered and transformed into a light-weight brown tunic and breeches, but he had no weapons or shoes. In a blur of movement, as soon as he was in human form, he snatched a rifle from under a pile of leaves. A nasty-looking rifle. If I had it right, it was a Czech SA Vz 58 assault rifle. Since the Weres had emigrated from the Czech Republic before settling in America, I wasn't surprised they preferred Czech weapons.

Then the male Were was standing. His features were strong and handsome, his hair short and deep brown. His eyes were the shade of aged oak, his gaze unreadable, and he had to be at least six-two.

"Hands up." He kept the weapon trained on us as we obeyed.

"This is bullshit." I could barely understand Olivia's low words because she spoke as though she was gritting her teeth at the same time.

I wanted to kick her ankle to get her to shut up, but I managed to keep my feet still.

The male spared a brief glance at the other Were while keeping us pinned by the rifle with the obvious ease of a trained professional. He gave an almost inde-cipherable nod to the female.

The popping of bone as the female Werewolf shifted didn't seem as loud, but I doubted it could be any less painful than the male's transformation must have been. Even though they were unquestionably used to it, such an extreme change still had to hurt.

When she rose, her own tunic was a light taupe. Her face had shifted into the stunning features of a beautiful woman and her hair was long and shimmer-ing. She didn't reach for a weapon. Instead she took a step toward us, her bare feet silent on the rich loam.

"I'm Kristen Abbatiello Neff." She gave all three of her names in the Werewolf tradition. She gestured with a slight nod over her shoulder at the male. "Jason Ray Taylor."

"You're late." Taylor held his rifle in a military posi-tion so that it wasn't pointed at us, but would allow him to be prepared for anything.

The two Werewolves were obviously young compared to the Weres who had emigrated centuries ago from what is now known as the Czech Republic. By their American accents and names that weren't even close to being Slavic, these two had to be part human, possibly as much as half. Maybe it wasn't as rare as I thought for humans and Werewolves to mate.

"Come." Neff turned away from us, her walk easy and graceful as she moved through a virtually invisible path.

Tingles ran along my spine as Taylor moved behind us to take up the rear of our little party.

Neff glanced over her shoulder before looking forward again. "Your friends are already here."

"Friends?" Olivia started walking and looked at me. "You expecting any friends?"

I did kick Olivia's shoe this time as I fell in step beside her. "The Doppler, Angel, probably traveled all the way through the forest as a squirrel, which is why I didn't identify her over the scents of normal squirrels," I said as we followed Neff. "No doubt Ice decided on a Werewolf form, which would keep me from scenting him, too."

"And the Aussie, Joshua . . . Can you smell a Shadow Shifter?" Olivia said while we stepped through what seemed like a minefield of rocks.

"Pretty impossible, even for the Fae or Elves." I glanced at Olivia and smiled. "When they're in shadow form, it's like trying to capture a breath of clean air in the middle of a polluted Manhattan wind or distinguish it from a fresh mountain breeze."

"That's almost scary." Olivia hitched up her backpack. "Wonder how close that bunch got to the Werewolf camp before they met up with the Weres."

Neff's spine seemed to stiffen as she walked ahead of us, and I guessed Ice, Angel, and Joshua had gotten a lot closer than the Werewolves had expected. Or appreciated.

When we reached the pack's camp, it looked like any other large group of campers someone might run across. Tents of all sizes, shapes, and colors squatted around the clearing, Coleman lanterns hung from tree branches, ice chests sat near tents, and assortments of other camping supplies were arranged everywhere.

Male and female Weres in either human or wolf form moved around the camp, most ignoring us as they did their chores. A couple of Weres did eye the daggers sheathed at my belt. Six wolf pups played well within the circle of tents.

Smoke tendrils rose from rock-contained campfires scattered in the center of the clearing. The encampment smelled of smoke from the fires, kerosene that filled the lanterns, and also of raw meat from a couple of deer strung up from wooden poles to one side. The scent of the Werewolves was hard to distinguish since they always had the scent of woodlands and clean air.

"Ugh." Olivia made a disgusted sound and I looked in the direction her eyes were focused on.

I held back my own squeamishness as I watched a couple of male Weres in human form ripping raw meat from bone with their teeth. Blood smeared their lips. It looked like they each had a haunch of a very large deer. I turned away, deciding the upper branches of the trees were far more interesting. The black storm clouds we'd seen earlier hovered right on top of us now.

The tent we were shown to was an average size compared with those around the camp. I frowned when I saw the two male Weres standing near the entrance. One on each side, they were obviously guards. Why would we need guards?

Neff pulled aside the blue tent's entrance flap. "Dmitri said you should go right in when you arrive. He'll be here when he's available."

"When he's available?" Olivia grumbled. "He'd sure as hell better not make us wait."

This time I elbowed her.

"Thank you." I nodded to Neff, who inclined her head in return.

I glanced over my shoulder at Taylor, who also gave a nod, only his was almost too slight to see. He looked like one tough, protective guy, which was what the pack needed.

Olivia ignored them both and I heard her say, "Oh, great," as she slipped into the tent.

Not good. I ducked inside to head off anything that might set Olivia off. I almost stumbled as I ran into her backside.

Angel, Joshua, and Ice lounged on top of rolled-out sleeping bags. In the middle of the tent sat two large half-full platters of food. One platter held cooked hamburgers and hot dogs in already toasted buns. The food smelled so good my mouth watered.

Ketchup, mustard, relish, and mayo had been placed on a tray nearby. Slices of cheese, onions, lettuce and tomatoes were piled on the other platter along with apples and grapes. An open ice chest was filled with bottles of Michelob, Foster's, different flavors of Mike's Hard Lemonade, and plastic bottles of water.

Darn. No vodka.

"What did you do, walk all the way from Manhattan?" Ice said before he took a swig of a bottle of Michelob. Next to him was an empty paper plate with smudges of ketchup and mustard on it.

I pushed Olivia down on a sleeping bag, hard, to keep her from opening her mouth. She glared at me as she landed half on her butt and half on her backpack.

Rain started to plop onto the canvas tent in big fat

drops. A stronger chill crept in through the partially open flap and carried with it the clean smell of rain.

"We're late because something came up this morning." As if I was going to tell them about Adam. I sat yoga-style on the remaining sleeping bag after I eased out of my backpack straps and set the huge pack aside.

Olivia had removed her backpack and now grabbed a paper plate, then a hot dog, and started loading it with condiments.

I had to arrange myself so that I could sit with two seventeen-inch daggers belted to me. "Fill me in on what's happened so far." I eased out of my coat as I spoke and tossed it onto my pack. The chill didn't bother me.

Normally, my favorite hamburgers were char-burnt with everything on them. I chose the first hamburger that looked fairly well-cooked—good enough—and put it on a paper plate. My stomach rumbled as I started loading the burger with two slices of cheddar cheese, onion, tomato, and lettuce.

Angel studied me with blue eyes filled with so much intelligence it was easy to forget she looked like a poster girl for a cheerleader magazine. There had to be a magazine for cheerleaders, right? Everything else on earth had a magazine.

"Each of us was ordered to go to this tent as we arrived." She pushed a corkscrew curl behind her ear. A half-full bottle of water was beside her. "I arrived first. When I shifted in the middle of the encampment they freaked." She gave a grin that was totally unrepentant. "Werewolves are so easy to piss off."

It just didn't seem right to have a word like "piss" come out of her pretty mouth.

I couldn't help a grin in return. "Most Dopplers couldn't have pulled that off."

She gave a delicate shrug of one shoulder. "I'm not most Dopplers."

"Bloody hell, you're right," Joshua said, his Aussie accent sounding exaggerated as his dark gaze settled on her full breasts. "With a set of world-class bazooms like that, you'll drive all the Weres daft."

I narrowed my eyes. Looked like Joshua might be Trouble with a capital T. As if we needed another pain in the ass like Ice.

Angel's expression didn't change and her tone was pleasant. "If you speak to me like that again, you'll be a mere *shadow* of yourself when I get through with you. I know your weakness, Shadow Shifter."

Joshua looked intrigued as he raised an eyebrow in a sexy, mouthwatering way. "Fascinating, Sheila." He used the name most men used to refer to women in Australia.

I gripped my burger, almost squeezing out the contents. "Stop it. We're a team." I narrowed my eyes as my gaze met each team member's, one at a time.

First, Joshua. "No lewd remarks. And her name isn't Sheila. Same goes for any other female you meet."

My gaze met Olivia's, and I could tell she was trying to hold back a grin. "No smartass comments."

I focused on Ice. "Stop trying to tick off everyone on the team. Show a little teamwork. Maybe a little class if you can find any."

"Ouch." Ice gave me a lazy smile. "Do those statements apply to team leaders?"

I tried not to glare at him, I really did.

Then I had to say something to Angel since I'd just reprimanded the rest. "Keep your knowledge of a species' kryptonite to yourself. And don't use it."

Angel stared at Joshua with a wicked expression. "Unless they deserve it."

"Not even then." I shifted on my sleeping bag to get into a more comfortable position. After I took a really big bite of my hamburger, chewed, and swallowed, I said, "Okay. Time to start planning."

Lips turned into a sarcastic expression, Ice opened his mouth. I pointed my finger at him before he could speak. "Shut up, Ice. I need you to be serious. Not an ass. We don't have time for that."

He grinned, then took a swig of beer. Unbelievable. He'd actually listened to my order.

Had the Lord of the Underworld started cultivating flower gardens?

The tent flap opened with a loud snap.

A hulking mass appeared outside the entrance.

SEVEN

As the large being crouched at the entrance to the tent, a rush of cold wind blew water droplets inside, and I rubbed off some that had spattered my face.

The six-four Beketov ducked into the tent. His very muscular mass made the space instantly feel too small for all of us to be in there at the same time. He bent on one knee inside the entrance as the tent flap fell behind him, the flap blocking the rain again. Not that much could get past his bulk.

With Joshua and Ice in the tent, too, it was a wonder the space held us all. Both the Shifter and Shadow Shifter were pretty impressive themselves in size and height.

Beketov's wet hair appeared more mahogany than its normal bronze shade. The long strands hung to his waist in waves. Droplets of water rolled from his tanned arms, the hair on his forearms pressed against his skin from the wetness.

Each member of our team assessed him without comment—thank the Goddess for that blessing. It was the first time any of them had seen or met Beketov, with the exception of Olivia.

"This is Dmitri Kral Beketov," I said before anyone did decide to open their mouths. I set my plate with my burger on the sleeping bag beside me after a quick look of longing. "The pack's alpha."

"Thanks for the drinks and lunch." Angel inclined her head toward the ice chest and half-eaten platters of food. "Nice way to start the afternoon." Her smile was pleasant, her eyes assessing the gorgeous alpha the same as she might look at any other male. If she thought he was hot, it didn't show on her face.

Beketov's tawny eyes studied her before resting on each of us before he spoke. "It is rare for a Werewolf pack to allow non-Weres into our midst." His gaze was cool, and not really what I'd call welcoming. "You are the first to be brought into ours."

"Lucky us." Ice drawled the words and Beketov narrowed his eyes at the Shifter.

"We're all here to help." Why did I always have to head things off with this team? You'd think they'd have at least some manners. "We were just starting to discuss the case."

"Case?" Beketov growled the word as he scowled. "We speak of my peoples' lives."

"I understand." I leaned forward and looked at him intently. "Would you prefer that we refer to the tragedies you and your people have faced some other way?"

Beketov pinched the bridge of his nose, the movement hiding his eyes. When he lowered his hand, the combativeness in his expression was gone.

"Case . . . That is . . . acceptable for you and your team." Beketov sighed, a deep sigh edged with pain. Pain that filled him from the loss of many of his people and his son. "It does no justice for our travesties, but if it is easier for you to refer to it as such, then do so."

My stomach rumbled but I ignored it. Now was not the time to eat. "Do you have any more information that might help us?"

"Nothing." Beketov's gaze turned dark with fury, his normally tawny eyes like bronze glass. "It makes no sense. How can we not scent whatever it is that is taking my people? How is it possible that whatever is causing this disappears into nothing?"

Olivia grabbed a bottle of Michelob from the cooler and cracked it open. "Do you think something is coming from Otherworld, taking the Weres, then dumping their bodies?"

I shook my head. "I grew up in Otherworld. There is no being, no beast that would do anything like that."

"Underworld?" Joshua said with his eyes focused on me.

"No." I wrapped my arms around my knees and brought them close to my chest as I spoke. "Anything in Underworld would just eat whatever they took."

Beketov growled and my face heated.

"I'm sorry." I hadn't meant for my words to come out so callously, like they must have sounded to him. "I shouldn't have said it quite like that."

Angel rescued me. "If a creature in Underworld was capable of coming through at all, we'd have an even bigger problem. That would mean any foul thing that inhabits Underworld could escape."

"And whatever came from Underworld wouldn't be returning to that place. Not by choice." I reached for a bottle of water and twisted off the cap. "We would have another threat to keep Trackers more than busy."

The bottle chilled my palm as I swallowed a long drink. The water felt cold all the way to my mostly empty stomach.

Olivia furrowed her brows in thought. "What, then, if not Otherworld or Underworld?"

I met Beketov's gaze. "That's what we're here to find out."

"Sir!" The tent flap was yanked open by a soaking wet young male, about sixteen, who slammed into Beketov's back. The boy looked too frantic to apologize as Beketov turned his head and glared. "They found Alois."

The alpha whirled, and even in a kneeling position, he did it with surprising grace. The boy was so close to Beketov that the alpha's shoulder hit him and knocked him out of the tent and into the rain.

Beketov looked like he was trying hard to maintain the composure of an alpha. "Does he still live?"

"Barely." The boy got to his feet, Beketov following him out of the tent. "Dr. Zeman is with him."

"Where?" Beketov said, hands balled into fists as he stood. "Is Alois in the camp?"

Heart pounding, I dropped the water bottle next to my hamburger plate and followed Beketov. The rest of my team hurried out of the tent behind me, into the pouring rain.

"Dr. Zeman wouldn't let anyone move him." The boy pointed toward the east. "Over by Bear Rock."

Beketov took the boy by the shoulders. "Have you been there, Vilem?"

Vilem shook his head. "But I want to go. I want to help."

Beketov gave Vilem a firm, don't-go-against-my-word look. "Stay in camp. You have an important job here. Make sure the little ones do not stray."

"Yes, sir." Vilem looked disappointed, obviously a boy wanting to be a man. He turned away and started jogging to a larger tent in the campsite, his shoes splashing in the mud.

Beketov said nothing to us. I heard the crack and pop of bone, then looked to see Beketov shift into an enormous wolf with fur the same shade of bronze as his hair.

He was already bolting from camp before I caught my breath.

When I glanced over my shoulder, I saw a shadow that passed my feet, a squirrel that darted up a nearby tree, and a pure white wolf, all taking off after Beketov.

I met Olivia's gaze and we ran after the others.

My boots practically sailed over the mud as I tore through the forest. My weapons belt was secure at my hips and I didn't feel its weight. I had no problem keeping up with the others.

Olivia might have been short, and considerably slower than a paranorm, but she was fast for a human. She wouldn't be far behind.

I arrived in a small clearing just a moment after the others. Beketov had shifted back into his human form and was already bent beside a man who looked to be about thirty. Another man knelt beside Alois, probably the doctor—he had an open bag next to him with what looked like medical equipment and he wore surgical gloves and a mask, even in the rain. Three other Weres stood a few feet from Alois like sentries. Their faces were hard, but I saw pain in their eyes.

The moment I saw Alois, I wanted to throw up.

Alois was nude, his wet skin flayed everywhere on his body. It was hard to find a spot that hadn't been cut open. In some places Alois's flesh was black or looked gangrenous. In other places the cuts looked fresh, the flesh pink or red.

Beketov refused the surgical mask the doctor tried to hand him. The alpha removed his own shirt, leaving himself bare from the waist up. He laid his shirt over Alois, the shirt covering the male from his shoulders to his upper thighs.

Alois's entire body trembled so hard it looked like he might come apart. He held his hands to his chest, fogged eyes staring up at Beketov, who was speaking to him in a low, soothing tone. I didn't think Alois could see, but Beketov's voice seemed to ease the male's shaking.

The Were's lips were black. His tongue was still pink and I thought he was trying to talk. I heard nothing. Beketov leaned closer.

"Do not come too close, Dmitri." The doctor's tone was gentle. "We do not know if he is diseased with some kind of contagion."

Beketov's face flickered with pain. I got to my knees in the mud and grass near the alpha. Alois's throat worked and he looked like he was trying to push words out.

The Were managed to say something, his lips vibrating. I couldn't hear a word but Beketov's eyes widened.

Then Alois's head lolled to the side, his face turned from Beketov. The Were looked upward like his fogged eyes might see something. Alois shrieked, a horrifying, painful sound. Then his body slackened, his eyes staring into the rain.

The doctor closed the male's eyes with his gloved fingertips.

Heartbreak tore across Beketov's face. The alpha started to place his palm on the dead Were's forehead, but the doctor stopped him.

Beketov lowered his head, now his big hand covering his own face.

When he removed his hand and raised his head, I wasn't sure if teardrops were rolling down his cheeks, blending with rain.

My words were almost lost in the sound of the rain hitting the ground. "What did he say?"

"Only . . ." Beketov's throat worked and he didn't look at me. "My son is alive. And yet unharmed."

An ache pushed behind my eyes and my throat hurt. "We'll find whoever, whatever is doing this, Dmitri. And we'll get your son before anything happens to him."

He didn't respond or meet my gaze.

I got to my feet and faced my team members, who were all a few feet away, in human form. I gave a slight nod toward the forest and the five of us walked away from the clearing.

When we were under the cover of trees and well away from the Weres, I spoke. "The Were told Beketov his son is alive and well." I swallowed, the ache in my throat making it difficult. "Nothing else. No clues that would help us find the boy. Nothing."

"We've got to find his son." Ice shocked me with his explosive words and the caring his anger showed. His expression was harder than I'd ever seen it. "We can't let whatever it is hurt the kid, too."

Angel pushed soaked corkscrew curls away from her wet face. Joshua was somber, and Olivia stared up into the rain falling through the treetops.

"We'll get back before anyone disturbs the scene more than they already may have." As I gave the instruction, the others nodded. "The Weres aren't Trackers or PIs, so all of the past scenes may have been too disrupted for them to catch any clues."

"I don't understand why I smell nothing near the Were they just recovered." Angel pursed her lips. "I didn't even smell Alois. I've had a difficult time scenting much of anything."

"You're right." I frowned as what she said sank in. "I was so concerned about the Were that I didn't notice until now."

"It's hard to smell the forest or the rain," Olivia said, her eyes dark and thoughtful.

Joshua looked around us. "Bloody hell. She's right."

"Whatever or whoever it is is fucking with our sense of smell." Ice's face was unnaturally red, contrasting with his white hair. "Won't be any pieces left when I'm through."

"We have our first clue." Angel peered into the forest as if searching for something. "And it's a dangerous one."

I started toward the small clearing. "We'll fan out starting from Alois's body and search for more clues."

We were a dead serious group when we returned.

Trackers didn't screw around when it came to our positions on this earth Otherworld, working to make right whatever was wrong.

When we reached the body, Beketov was standing. "Test your sense of smell. Is it hampered?" I asked.

Beketov frowned and nodded. "I have been able to scent the bodies of my murdered people before, but nothing else." He glanced at the Were's mutilated body. "This time I do not even scent Alois."

"Don't let your males move from here until I say." I gestured to the Weres acting as sentries. "They might disturb the scene more than they have."

I was betting it was difficult for Beketov to take orders from anyone, much less a female of any race, including a female Were. Saying nothing, he inclined his head and turned to speak to the sentries.

Olivia, Angel, Joshua, Ice, and myself took positions around Alois's body. "Thirty minutes," I said. The others nodded and we started our search, slow and methodical, covering all of our territories.

My sense of smell was shot as I moved through my area. The fan of my territory grew larger and larger. I didn't see Ice or Angel, both of whom had been to either side of me when we left. I wondered if they searched in animal form. Probably. Their sense of smell could be better, if it wasn't hampered like it had been in human form.

Thirty minutes later, we each returned, and it was easy to tell no one had good news. Frustration was on each Tracker's face.

"Found what could be a trail leading from the edge of this clearing," Angel said and everyone looked at her.

"Broken twigs, muddy but smeared prints that could have been a bear. With my sense of smell shot, I couldn't tell if it was an animal or something else. I lost it about fifteen minutes into the search."

"Animal trails everywhere," Joshua said. "But nothing leading away from here."

Olivia and Ice nodded. The fury on Ice's face hadn't lessened. The fact that I hadn't given a thought to Ice being that concerned about a child, or anyone else, made me feel a little chagrined. I'd seen him fight with intensity and anger, but I never thought of him doing it because he cared.

"Looks like Angel's lead is our best." I started walking to her territory.

"This time I'll go high." Angel shifted into her squirrel form and scampered toward the territory. She didn't take to a tree until we were all at the trail. I wondered how often Angel could shift within a certain time period. Most Dopplers had to have time to regenerate—usually twelve hours.

A large shadow passed me, followed by Ice in wolf form. Olivia and I worked as a two-person team as we searched the trail, too.

The five of us returned to the tent and slipped inside. We were all drenched, and I was happy to see a pile of thick cotton towels, one for each of us.

All of the used paper plates and beverage containers, along with the platters of food, had been removed. My uneaten hamburger and the rest of Olivia's hot dog was gone, too, and I was grateful for that.

After seeing what I had, the smells would have made

the urge to vomit even stronger. The Weres probably realized that because they had had that same reaction every time they discovered one of their family members or friends brutalized and murdered. Like Alois.

We changed into dry clothing, Ice and Joshua actually giving the three of us girls a little privacy by turning away. Their grins were on the wicked side, though.

Olivia picked the perfect T-shirt, although both males seemed amused when they turned back and saw it.

Attitudes are contagious. Mine might kill you.

Heh.

We spent some time going over what might have been a short trail that wasn't by an animal, but it had been too hard to tell, especially with the incessant rain.

Well into our conversation, my skin started to tingle. "The sun is setting soon," I said more to myself than my team. "I need to shift."

"Can we watch the show?" Ice asked with a smirk.

I was going to break every one of my rules and kill Ice along the way. The thought of his caring for the child immediately cooled my anger.

My skin tingled more and more and I didn't want to transform in front of an audience. I ignored Ice and hurried to tug out my leather tracking outfit from my backpack. My weapons belt and daggers shifted on my hips as I shoved my way past the tent flap and into the almost-night.

Rain slapped my face and immediately soaked my hair and clothing again. "I need to relieve myself," I said to the two males guarding our tent.

Guarding . . . Why in the Goddess's name would

Beketov put guards in front of our tent? Probably Ice's big mouth. That would do it. Nah, more than likely it was because of the disappearances.

All I cared about was the fact that I had to pee and I needed to shift, both very badly.

I walked past the guards and marched behind the tent. Not far into the forest, mist had begun to gather close to the ground.

"You cannot leave the camp without accompaniment," one of the guards said from behind me in a thick Slavic accent as he followed. I glanced over my shoulder, and his sour expression told me he could care less about my safety even as he added, "It is dangerous to leave alone. We go in groups of three by orders of our alpha."

I gripped the now wet leather suit and tightened my fist. "I'm a Tracker. I'll be fine."

The guard gave a low rumbling growl. "Do not argue, female."

Female? My skin tingled even more, and I knew I had to give in despite the fact that I didn't like this Were's arrogant attitude. I'd had to put up with that kind of male Dom mentality on a daily basis in the Drow Realm.

"Fine, *male*." I gritted my teeth and started toward a thick clump of trees in the forest. "But I have to hurry."

"Cermak. Lida." The Were guard called out with irritation in his voice. "Join the *guest*." He said *guest* like it was a nasty word.

I didn't look over my shoulder again until I found what I thought was the perfect place to change and shift. A nice circle of trees not too far from the camp. The haze rose higher, growing thicker, which made for better cover, too.

I turned and faced the two Werewolves in wolf form who crouched behind me. "I'm going to change in private. Don't follow me around the bushes."

One of them stepped forward. His coat was gray and he was way bigger than Neff and Taylor were.

The change to my body was already happening and I could feel the roots of my hair starting to turn blue. I held up my hand, palm facing him. "Give me privacy. I'll be right here."

Thank the Goddess they didn't insist on watching me. Still, instead of my usual stretching exercises while shifting, I let my body go through its changes while I stripped off my clothing, then pulled on my leather pants and top. I'd never shifted this way—while changing clothes and not focusing on the transformation.

It was a bit weird and the shift was a little painful because I wasn't doing my usual stretching into the change. My muscles strengthened and became more defined. My gums even ached more than usual where my small incisors dropped. Maybe I should have shifted the right way regardless, but I didn't want to literally get caught with my pants down by my "guards."

After I relieved myself and covered it with loam and plant matter, I fastened my weapons belt to my leather pants.

I shook out my arms and rolled my neck from side to side. I did a couple of deep stretches now that I was dressed, then picked up my discarded jeans and soft cashmere sweater. I took a deep breath in of fresh air, pleased my sense of smell had returned.

Rain continued to soak me, the feel of it pleasurable

on my skin, especially my bare midriff and arms. But the mist . . . something about it felt eerie and wrong and took away some of the pleasure.

Water was one of the four elements I used in magic, but I hadn't been able to control mist. Mostly because I'd never had much training with it. When I'd tried to contain and control mist in Otherworld, all the fog had ever done was swirl around me and become thicker.

"Come out, female," said the male from the other side of the bushes.

"My name is Nyx." My voice was hard as I stepped in front of the two Weres. "Not 'female.'"

They were close enough that we could see each other fairly well through the thickening haze. Both had shifted into human form.

The two guards each widened their eyes when they saw me, blue hair, amethyst skin and all.

"What are you?" the female Were said with a frown.

"I'm half human, half Drow." When both Weres continued to look puzzled, I said, "Drow are Dark Elves."

The male Were scowled and appeared ready to say something when I jerked up my head and swiveled to face the fog that now almost completely shrouded the trees behind me.

A sound came to me, muffled by the mist. Then another sound.

Something wasn't right. I could feel it with my water elemental magic—the rain carried the message to me despite the heavy fog.

"One of the Weres, maybe two, are in trouble," I said

to the guards as the knowledge came to me as clear as if I was already there.

I bolted away from the guards before they had a chance to blink.

EIGHT

The pounding of my heart thudded in my ears as I ran through the thick mist of forest, dodging trees, jumping over logs and bounding over rocks. I used my air element to propel my natural speed and to guide me through the fog so that I wouldn't run into anything.

Normally, with the grace of the Elves, I could avoid anything I saw the instant it came into view. But the haze was becoming so thick, that talent was almost impossible. Soon I had to rely on my air element to act like sonar to make my way without bumping into anything, or tripping, or falling.

From in front of me, both my air and water elemental magic brought to my ears sounds that didn't belong. Strange. But they were muffled and I had no idea what it could be. My adrenaline kicked up a notch. Just a few more seconds and I'd be there.

I came up short when I reached the outskirts of the location where I was certain the sounds had come from. I stopped close to a tree to get my bearings and avoid rushing into the middle of something I was unfamiliar with.

Near silence pressed against my ears like the fog

pressed against my body. Only rain pattered on the leaves and ground. I drew Lightning, one of my dragon-claw daggers.

Muffled noise broke the silence and echoed around me, ping-ponging through the mist. Goose bumps crawled over my skin at the eeriness of what sounded like low inhuman wails.

My muscles remained tense and I tried to use the rain and air to identify where the sounds originated. I kept my other hand close to my Kahr since I didn't know what to expect.

I should have been able to identify the location the wail was coming from. It was as if something was purposefully sending out the low cry in all directions to keep its true location from being identified.

Yes, that was it. An unnatural object, possibly human-made, was emitting the unearthly sound that echoed in the mist. I tried using my air element like sonar to pin down the location, but somehow the sounds were confusing my ability. I smelled nothing, and I should have been able to scent whatever was there.

Then beneath the wail, my rain and earth element brought to my ears a faint scraping sound. So faint I could have imagined it. But I knew I'd heard it, and it wasn't a sound that belonged in a forest. While the low cries echoed from all directions, the scrape came from one specific location.

In wolf form, the Werewolves reached me and stood like silent sentries to either side of me. The mist was so thick I couldn't see them—I could only sense that they were there.

I crouched and reached my hand out until I was certain the back of it was beneath one Werewolf's muzzle. It licked my hand and I knew it understood what I was going to do. With a slow movement I felt down the wolf's chest and drew a circle in his fur before reaching back up and very gently pushing its muzzle to the right, in the direction I wanted it to go. The wolf went immediately to circle around to the right.

Then I reached out to my other side and repeated the sequence with the other wolf. When that wolf left, I prayed to the Goddess that I hadn't just sent either wolf into a trap—and that I wasn't about to walk into one myself.

The inhuman wail continued as I stayed low and crept closer to where the scraping sound had come from. My hair hung in soaked ropes around my face, and I wiped the back of my hand across my forehead to get it out of my eyes. I gripped my dagger tight in my other hand but kept my body loose. I sensed more Werewolves arriving in wolf form, as well as a squirrel and a Shifter's faint amber scent, but I didn't stop moving.

The scraping sound didn't repeat and the wail grew fainter. Whatever was emitting the sounds was slowly losing power and I was able to identify where it was coming from. A few more steps and my "sonar" showed me where the thing was—something round and as big as my fist on the forest floor.

I sensed no presence, just the object. I kept low to the ground, relying on my senses as I reached the thing. My magic and senses told me it was harmless, simply a sound emitter. With a very slow movement I inched my hand toward the small object and touched it with one finger.

Electricity and pain pierced my body and brilliant blue light exploded from where I had touched the object. The jolt of electricity was so powerful it rocketed me backward, and it was so unexpected that I didn't have time to protect myself.

My back and head slammed against a tree. More pain whipped around the electrical pain still surging through me. My whole body jerked as if I'd been struck by lightning.

I couldn't breathe, my vision was black, my face contorted with pain. It took all my training not to cry out from the excruciating electrical charge racking me. I hadn't had time to use my air element to prevent the thump of my body slamming against the tree.

Someone bent down beside me. The faint tiger flower scent of a female Doppler neared me and I knew it was Angel who had shifted from her squirrel form.

My body continued to jerk and my eyes ached so badly tears would have been flushing down my cheeks if Dark Elves had tear ducts.

"Shit," Angel whispered and I felt her cool fingers against my neck. She raised her voice so that it carried through the fog. "Don't touch whatever made that noise—Nyx is down."

With her fingers, Angel applied pressure a half inch below the base of my skull. Pain vanished as my body went slack and I passed out.

My temples ached in a way they had never ached before. I shook my head, only to discover two things: The movement hurt as if my skull had served as a trampoline for about a hundred kids, and my head was on a large pile of leaves. Fortunately the rest of me was attached, and I rested on flat but springy loam.

An explosion of blue light flashed through my mind and I knew what had happened. I'd been electrocuted by the emitter when, like an idiot, I'd touched it with my finger. From my senses, and brushing it with my elements, I'd been so sure it was safe. But it wasn't the first time I'd been fooled.

Scents of fallen rain and forest surrounded me but the rain had stopped.

Voices gradually pierced my hearing as it returned from muted to clear. Beketov's furious bellow rose above Olivia's and Angel's angry responses. Bless it, their fighting was going to sever my head from the pain it caused.

I pressed my palms against my forehead and gritted my teeth before I yelled, "Shut up!"

My own shout just about split my head open.

"About time." Olivia's voice was below shout level when she responded, but I still winced. Leaves scrubbed the ground as she crouched beside me. "Stop screwing around, Nyx, and get your ass up. We need you."

I would have smiled if I could have. Instead I opened my eyes. At first Olivia's features were a little distorted, but once I blinked a few times I could see her better in the silver moonlight. Clouds no longer shrouded the now clear sky.

Olivia was trying to hide it, but I could see concern in her eyes.

"You're supposed to be on the job, not playing Sleeping

Purple Beauty." She grasped one of my hands and lightly tugged, but didn't force me upright. She waited for me to start to push myself up before helping me sit. "You've been letting us do all the work for the past six hours. It's after midnight."

"Amethyst." My head spun a little and a remnant of electricity snapped in my body, causing my muscles to have involuntary spasms. "It's after midnight?"

"We need your purple ass up and helping figure this thing out." Olivia's dark eyes examined me from head to toe. "You'll live."

This time I managed what I think was a smile, at least a partial one. She released my hand and I braced my palms on the ground to either side of me to keep myself in an upright position.

The haze was so faint now that I could see we were in a clearing. Moonlight touched everything in the small area, including all beings, but it made things look a little distorted through the remnants of mist. About twenty feet from me sat the small white object, and I shuddered before scowling.

I reached for my Kahr that was sheathed in my weapons belt, even though my arm ached at the movement. "I'm going to shoot the piece of—"

"As much as I'd like watching you use that thing as target practice, it *is* a clue." Olivia pushed my hand away from my weapon. "The second clue this pack has had after the smell thing. And you were the lucky one to find it."

"Yeah, lucky me." I rubbed my temples with my fingers. Thankfully my headache was starting to ease even though Beketov was pacing and shouting orders. "What happened after Angel put me out of my misery?"

"The pack, the Trackers, and I pressed in as a circle until we knew nothing could be between us and that thing." Olivia looked over her shoulder at Beketov.

I followed her gaze and watched the pack's alpha. "What did you find?"

"It took hours until the mist got light enough to see so that we wouldn't disturb the scene or kill each other," she said. "We did find a third clue. In one spot the leaves and wet dirt are disturbed." Our eyes met again. "It's the first time any sign has been left at the scene of a kidnapping. Other than the possible trail Angel found. And that trail isn't even close to here."

I frowned. "Beketov never mentioned any kind of noise emitter."

"That's because it's never happened before," Olivia said. "We think whatever it was figured out you got here before it had a chance to finish the job, so it used that thing to throw you, us, off balance."

With a shake of my head, which didn't hurt as much this time, I said, "Whatever it was shouldn't have been able to sense me unless it's clairvoyant."

Olivia took my hand again, this time to help me stand. "Or it has equipment that can identify approaching threats."

"Whatever is doing this to the Werewolves is human, isn't it." I meant it as a statement. Now that my head was clearing, it seemed the logical thing. "Certainly nothing supernatural would have something like that."

"Unless it was stolen." Olivia walked with me to-ward the object that glowed in the moonlight. We kept a healthy distance from the thing. "But I seriously doubt it."

Beketov approached us, veins standing out on his neck and a big one pulsing on his forehead. His size and the storm of emotions on his features was almost scary. "We know now who is missing. One of the females and her pup."

Anger matching my own flashed across Olivia's face. "Damn," she practically shouted.

I pressed my hand to my belly as a sick sensation churned inside. "But this is so far from the pack's camp."

"Kveta must have been lured." Beketov dragged his hand down his face. "I do not know how, but there is no other explanation. Every pack member knows that at least three adults must travel in any group that leaves the security of the camp."

My body heated with fury as I walked away from Beketov and Olivia to study the spot where the wet dirt, leaves, and pine needles had been disturbed. I ignored the Werewolves who stared at me. No doubt they weren't used to a blue-haired amethyst-skinned woman with small fangs.

When I reached the exact location where the disturbance had been, I knelt, settled on my haunches, and braced my hands on the ground away from the spot. I brought my face close to the ground and took a deep breath. Nothing. My sense of smell—what in the Goddess's name?

The scent of a female wolf should strong, the pup a little lighter scent. All children and adolescents have a varied smell from the adults of their species.

If Beketov's face grew any darker he was going to

implode. "Kveta is pregnant. We must recover her and Petra."

The news made my stomach churn from more anger at the female being stolen. "How far along is she?" I tilted my chin to look up at him from where I was kneeling. "When is the pup due?"

"Pups." Beketov scrubbed his hand over his face again. "Triplets."

Olivia's hand was awfully close to her Sig, like she wanted to shoot something.

I wanted to shoot something. Better yet, take my dragon-claw daggers and slice something up. Daggers were more personal.

Somehow her being pregnant made it seem even more urgent. We had to find the pregnant female and her pup, and *soon*.

"Did anyone scent something I didn't?" I asked, try- ing to control my shaking.

"Same as last. No one can smell much of anything. And it's worse this time." Olivia jerked her thumb to- ward Ice, who was a good distance behind us, then pointed with her index finger at Angel and Joshua on the other side of the clearing. "The dream team didn't come up with anything more."

"I heard a scraping sound." I stood from where I'd been kneeling and looked at Beketov. He narrowed his eyes in obvious surprise at my statement. "It was faint because of the noise emitter, but it was there," I added.

"No other has mentioned a sound such as that." Beketov continued to study me with intensity.

My gaze held his, and I knew my expression was

equally intense. "I barely heard it, but that's what drew me to the emitter."

"I will inform my people." Beketov's bronze hair glowed in the moonlight and he looked almost like a god ready to strike down whatever was in his way. "Perhaps it will aid them in their search. We must find Kveta and her pup, the wee Petra."

My stomach churned again at the thought of this pregnant female and her daughter having been kidnapped before I could reach them. It hit me as if an iron mask had been slammed onto my face and throat, nearly strangling me and taking my breath away at the same time.

I'd lost friends in the battles against the Demons. Losses that I still blamed myself for because I hadn't gotten there in time.

I wasn't going to let it happen again.

While I was trying to breathe and calm my racing pulse, I examined the clearing, for the first time getting a really good look at it. It was small, mostly surrounded by trees so thick they swallowed any moonlight close to them. A rocky wall took up one side of the clearing, about six yards from me. The rocks started out smooth at the base but grew craggy and dangerous as the wall soared into a steep part of the mountain.

"I want to examine this area first." I returned to a crouch and looked up at Olivia. "Have you gotten everything that you can from here?"

She gave a short nod. "With the exception of the emitter. We'll have to find a way to collect it and send it back to Manhattan to have fingerprints run on it. If there are any."

"Good luck with that," I grumbled. "Unless I got all it had. Somehow I doubt that."

"I'm not planning on touching it to find out." An evil expression crossed her face. "Why don't we tell Ice to—"

"Don't you dare." I held back a grin. "We need him on this mission."

"You always ruin my fun," she said with a wicked light still in her eyes.

With my gaze, I started examining the ground surrounding the disturbed wet leaves and dirt. "Thanks for not trying to kill Ice."

"Yet." Olivia patted her holstered Sig. "I'll probably end up killing him eventually."

I just shook my head. "Maybe there's a trap door to an underground cavern."

She nodded. "My thoughts, too."

"Let me get to work." With my hands at my sides, I closed my eyes and took a deep breath. My power over the elements should tell me something.

At twenty-seven, I was extremely young among Dark Elves. Most Drow are centuries if not millennia old, like my father. Because I was so young, using elemental magic always weakened me and I had to be careful not to leave myself exposed.

Right now there were enough beings around me that I felt secure enough to allow myself to lose sense of place and time and concentrate on finding the missing Weres.

I reached out with my earth magic first. I let the element flow into me, drawing the magic and gathering it like a giant fist of power.

With slow, even breaths, I released the power in a smooth wave. I reached into the earth, plunging into it, diving down, down—

Then my magic slammed into something solid.

Pain exploded in my head.

NINE

Like a star going nova, the pain burst in my head despite the fact that my physical body was nowhere near whatever it was my elemental magic had slammed into.

The pain lessened and I explored with my earth magic. It was bedrock. A layer so thick my senses couldn't even reach through it.

I could master earth and move rocks, boulders, and other things with earth magic, but I couldn't do anything with unyielding stone or other things like solidified lava rock.

All I could do was spread my power throughout the earth above the bedrock. I sent feelers of magic along the top of the stone, exploring every possible fissure that might allow me to dig deeper with my power.

As far as I could tell, there was no cavern beneath the stone. I didn't sense any hollow sensations and the bedrock seemed to go on forever. Every crack I tried to go into went deep, but I always ended up coming to an abrupt stop and couldn't go any farther.

A scream of frustration threatened to tear from my mouth as I came back to my physical body. My knees gave out the moment I returned to myself and I sat hard on my backside. I shook my head and Olivia was frowning at me when I looked up.

"Unless whoever is doing this has figured out a way to travel beneath an incredibly thick layer of bedrock," I said as I tried to catch my breath, "there's nothing down there other than the rock."

Olivia looked up at the stars in the now clear sky. "Beam me up, Scotty."

As she looked back at me, I cocked my head as I stared at her, thoughts churning in my mind. "There are countless beings that exist on earth and in Otherworlds and Underworlds that norms aren't aware of. I suppose there could be alien life too, on other planets in earth's galaxy."

She reached out a hand. I took it and let her help me stand again. "I hope not," she said. "It's bad enough trying to keep track of all of you paranorms."

"No kidding." I shrugged, dismissing the possibility that aliens were stealing Werewolves. That idea just didn't feel right. Something else was going on.

It was even colder now, our breath coming out in puffs of fog. I studied Olivia. She was the only human on the case, and despite her coat, the cold had to be getting to her.

I was glad to see she'd put on a pair of leather gloves and secured her insulated coat rather than leaving it open. She probably had pocketed her Sig first, of course, to make sure she could get to it as fast as possible. Still, her face was unprotected.

Olivia's skin was dark, so it was hard to tell if her nose was turning blue. I put my hands on my hips.

"Put on your balaclava now or I'm going to have to hurt you."

"Try it," she said. But Olivia must have been really cold because for once she didn't argue. She unzipped her jacket a bit and jerked her facemask out of her inside pocket, then pulled the balaclava over her head before zipping her jacket closed again. The facemask covered everything but her eyes. "I'll kick your ass if you don't watch it," she said, but the words came out muffled.

I grinned. "Bonus points for making it harder for you to mouth off."

Olivia narrowed her exotic eyes, but I walked over to Beketov. Olivia was probably wishing for ammunition on hand stronger than rubber bands and erasers. If I wasn't careful, she might come up with the idea of using rubber bullets. Knowing her, she would do it if she thought of it. I certainly wasn't going to help her in that department.

"Haven't come up with a thing yet," I said to Beketov when I reached him, then explained about the solid bedrock that had stopped my magic from searching any deeper. "I'd like to take a look at that rock pile now," I said when I finished telling him of my non-discovery. "If it's not solid, and there's something behind it, I might be able to tell."

He nodded, his lips thin, and his expression looked like he was trying to decide if it had been worth bringing us in on this case. A layer of irritation coated my skin. I'd already proven myself by finding the location and the emitter—even if I had gotten myself knocked out.

I concentrated my anger against whatever took the female and her pup while I moved toward the base of the rock wall. "Maybe the scraping sound was made here." I frowned again as I looked over my shoulder. "Even though it sounded more like it came from the location the emitter is at."

"That thing could have blocked the real direction of the noise and thrown you off." Olivia came up beside me and I was tempted to grin again at the sound of her muffled voice. "Maybe there's a cavern behind these rocks where there wasn't one below."

"Let's find out." I shook my limbs, easing some of the tension that still gripped my body from the electrical charge. "I'll blow the place apart if I have to."

"Don't bring down the whole damned mountain with whatever it is you do with your earth magic." Olivia stopped me before I reached the pile of rocks at the base of the cliff. "And try to avoid ruining any clues."

I rolled my eyes. "I've been a PI for over two years now."

"That thing over there could have fried your brains." She crossed her arms over her large breasts. "I'll be keeping an eye on you."

"Yeah, yeah." I strode the couple of steps to the rock face.

Three Werewolves in human form were at my destination. Neff was examining the leaves at the base of the rocks. "Nothing." She shook her head and looked up at me. "No imprint, no scents. How could they disappear like that?" She gestured to the rocks. "We haven't had any luck there, either."

Another Were glanced at me with wide blue eyes that

were red from crying. "I am Radka Noemi Cermak. Kveta is my sister, Petra my niece. We must find them."

Radka's words compounded the hot anger that had been with me ever since it was discovered who was missing. This made it all the more real. All the more personal.

"Let me see what I can do." I tried to look reassuring and gestured to the three Weres to move back.

When they were out of my way, I focused my earth elemental magic on the rock face. I closed my eyes and searched for something, anything, that would give me a clue to where the missing Were and her pup had disappeared.

Weakness from using so much of my earth magic earlier made it harder to try to reach the earth behind the rocks with my power. I swayed and had to bring some of my concentration back to my physical body to steady myself.

I could do this. I had to do this. Again I pushed at my earth elemental power and reached between the rock, sliding my magic over the boulders, through the crevices, until I finally reached earth.

My breathing came easier and the earth strengthened me for now. There wasn't much earth to use before rock blocked me from reaching out with my magic any further. It was almost like running into a steel barrier, but it was simply more blessed rock.

Tingles ran up and down my physical body. The sensation was distant and I was surprised to realize that so much time had passed since I first sensed the missing Were and her pup being taken. The sun was about to rise and I had to find someplace private to shift.

I gathered up what strength I had left and returned to my physical self. Exhaustion seeped through every pore and I was grateful to find Olivia holding me by one arm when I opened my eyes.

"Find anything?" she asked from behind her balaclava as she steadied me. I shook my head and she added, "Then what good are you?"

I smiled but the tingling grew stronger and she released me as I drew my arm from her hold. I hated having to hurry into a bunch of bushes to avoid being watched when I shifted. I glanced up at the sky.

"Be right back," I said as I turned toward the dense forest.

"No way." Olivia jogged and caught up with my longer strides. "I've seen you change, baby, so you know you are comfortable around me. Not to mention you aren't going anywhere alone after tonight."

"Since it's you, all right." I dodged around a bush while Olivia waved off a couple of Weres.

"Pee break," she called out, but two male Weres followed as far as the edge of the treeline.

The shift didn't hurt but added to my exhaustion, something that had never happened before. The entire time I leaned back against a tree with my eyes closed.

"That charge must have really gotten to you." Olivia's voice didn't sound muffled anymore and I opened my eyes to see she'd taken off the balaclava. "I've never seen you like this."

I shrugged, which in itself was tiring. "Must have been that electrical charge and using my elements." I was used to long days and nights since I worked as a PI by day, Tracker by night. So it was unusual for me to just want to crawl into bed. "I could use a really long nap."

"Let's get your purple ass back to camp," Olivia said, but when I pointed to my now pale arm, she added "Correction. Your white ass."

"This white ass is going to bed." I pushed away from the tree. "And sleeping for hours."

Ice, Joshua, and Olivia were all snoring like cars at a drag race when I woke. We were in the tent we'd been sent to when we arrived and I was snuggled into a warm sleeping bag, lying on my side and facing Olivia. I still wore my leather fighting suit since I'd crashed as soon as we got back to camp this morning.

"Unconsciously I think they're having a competition to see who can snore the loudest." Angel's amused voice came from my left and I rolled onto my back and pushed myself up so that I was sitting and facing her. "They've been going at it for hours." Angel looked as beautiful as she had the first time I saw her, with perfect corkscrew curls and blue eyes clear of any traces of exhaustion.

"How do you look so perfect first thing when you wake up?" I yawned and imagined my black hair was a total mess and an imprint of my sleeping bag had made a red mark on my cheek.

"That's the nice thing about being a Doppler." She twisted one of her curls around her finger. "All I have to do is shift into a squirrel and then shift back."

"I need a comb." I ran my hand through my hair and snagged my fingers in a snarl. "Not to mention a toothbrush and paste." I made a face as I reached for my backpack. "Yuck. Morning breath."

Angel reached into a brown backpack and dug out her own toothbrush and paste. "I'll go with you." She scooted to her knees, then moved up and unzipped the tent flap with her free hand.

I glanced at the still snoring Joshua and Ice, who had backpacks near them, too. I followed Angel out of the tent where she paused and took a deep breath.

She stretched her arms over her head, her scoop-neck white T-shirt rising up to expose a strip of her tiny, flat waist. She looked so perky, petite, and beautiful in the T-shirt and jeans she wore. Her small bare feet were even cute, with bright pink polish on her toenails.

Angel gave each of our Werewolf guards a brilliant smile. I swear the males salivated as they stared at her. Or rather they were staring at her breasts. Joshua had been crude last night, but right, about how the Werewolf males would respond to the sight of her cleavage.

I cleared my throat, barely holding back a grin at the males who appeared almost incapacitated with lust. "How did you and the guys get your stuff here?"

Angel turned her attention to me as she lowered her arms and the T-shirt slipped down over her waist. "Rodán had our backpacks sent ahead so that we could travel in our natural forms."

"Don't let Olivia know that little fact because we had to carry ours." We turned away from the guards and I waved one of the males off when he started to follow us. "We're not going anywhere and there are two of us," I said to him.

But the male whistled to someone across the camp. "Lukas."

I glanced over my shoulder as I walked away. "Oh goody, company."

"Let's lose him." Laughter was in Angel's voice.

I grinned at her. "Shouldn't be too hard."

She took three steps and shifted into a blond squirrel as she moved, her plastic bag with her toothbrush and paste dropping to the ground.

Dopplers are amazingly fast when it comes to transformations. It's equally amazing how their bodies can shift into animals far smaller than their human forms.

Angel the squirrel scurried up the closest tree trunk and disappeared among the branches. I dropped my own toothbrush and paste and I laughed as I bolted from the camp and into the forest. Elves are faster than almost any being, and even in my human form I possess the same speed as I do in my Drow form.

Werewolves are quick, but didn't stand a chance against Angel and me, especially with the head start we had.

Shouts behind me only made me smile more. Angel kept pace with me as she scampered from one tree to the next. My long black hair whipped around my face and the cool morning breeze brushed my bare midriff. The morning dew wet my bare feet.

The air smelled delicious—of pine and loam, as well as the clean scent of last night's rainfall. I was so glad to be able to smell again. How bizarre was that? Something was being used to mask smell and inhibit one's sense of smell.

Angel and I made no sounds and didn't even startle

wildlife as we kept our distance from a whitetail doe and her fawn, a flock of wild turkeys, and even a lone black male bear.

I hadn't consciously planned on returning to the site of the Were kidnappings last night, but that's exactly where we ended up. I pushed my hair away from my eyes as I came to a stop in the middle of the clearing. Angel walked out of the forest and joined me, wearing her T-shirt and jeans again.

Every paranorm being has magic, no matter how little, and all types of beings that can shift have the gift of being able to transform completely back to the form they were in to begin with. That is magic that I certainly don't have.

Angel slipped her hands into the back pockets of her jeans and surveyed the area along with me. "There can only be a logical explanation for these kidnappings."

My attention was on the place where the noise emitter had been last night. It was gone. "Who managed to take that thing?"

"I did." Angel was digging her bare toes into the leaves and pine needles where she was standing. "I isolated the electrical frequency with rubber."

Surprise flickered through me. "Rubber. Of course."

"I had a couple of Weres return to camp and bring back a spare tire from one of their older SUVs." She spoke about it casually as if coming up with the idea had been the logical thing to do. "I used the tire tube to contain the emitter and the tire itself to serve as transport by having it rolled back to camp."

I tried to picture how she'd managed it. "How did you get the emitter into the tube?"

"Cut it open, made a sort of chute on one end, then used the excess strip to scoop and push into the opening of the tube." She shrugged. "I only had it put into the tire as an extra precaution."

"Fantastic." I grinned. "I was going to shoot it to put it out of our misery, but unfortunately that wasn't the rational thing to do. That, and Olivia wouldn't let me."

Angel laughed. "Olivia is one tough female."

"You have no idea." I turned my gaze to stare at the rock wall. "Even though I didn't find anything with my earth element I can't help but think there's something behind all of those rocks." I frowned as I met Angel's eyes. "Or beneath the bedrock. Where else could the Weres have been taken?"

She looked thoughtful. "A geologist who's familiar with this area could give us some information."

"The geologist might be able to tell us if it's even possible that something could be here." I stretched my arms and my legs while I spoke, trying to limber up. I'd missed not stretching into my changes last night and this morning, and my muscles felt a little tight. "Any other ideas?"

"I heard Olivia's 'Beam me up, Scotty' comment," Angel said with one of her brilliant smiles. "Considering I interned with NASA, you'd think I would consider life out among the stars." She stared up into the sky. "People on earth are alone in this galaxy." She returned her gaze to me. "But they do have us paranorms, they just don't know it."

"Olivia was kidding about the *Star Trek* reference. I think." I winked at Angel before walking over to the rock wall and putting my hands on my hips. "Nothing makes sense but something being behind here or below ground."

"Or both," Angel said.

"Or both." I was almost absent-minded as I repeated her words and reached out to run my fingers over one of the smoother stones at the base of the wall. "They kidnapped another child, Angel," I said even though she already knew that information. "And a pregnant female. Pregnant with three babies."

Anger surged through me, somehow hotter and harsher than it had before. How in the Underworlds could the mother and her pup have disappeared like that, with me not far away?

I gathered my earth magic, ready to release it and use the earth at our feet to move aside some of the rocks.

Shock bolted through me. Remnants of the electrical charge were still in my body, as if they had been hiding, wrapped around my spine. But now they were free and I fought to control something I had no idea what to do with.

Too much anger, too much magic was inside me to release my elemental magic. I shook with the power of my earth elemental.

Have to stop, have to stop it!

Everything went crazy, as if the world was spinning. My air power joined with the earth magic that had twined with the electrical charge and magnified.

My power slammed into the pile of rocks at the base of the cliff.

The ground trembled and shifted beneath my feet as

if an earthquake had struck. I almost lost my footing and stumbled to the side. The pile of rocks started flying away from the base of the cliff—

And the wall started to come down on Angel and me.

TEN

My entire body shook and the earth seemed to act against me. I anchored my feet like steel had clamped them deep into the ground.

"Nyx!" Angel dove for me as I was nearly deafened by the rumbling and crashing of boulders shooting down the side of the mountain.

She body-slammed me from behind, forcing me to the left of the landslide. Her surprising strength sent us both tumbling into the forest.

"Up!" Angel grasped my hand and jerked me to my feet before I had a chance to get my bearings on my own. "Dammit, Nyx, run!"

Her words jolted my brain. Just as a boulder the size of my kitchen rumbled toward us at amazing speed, I found my wits and ran. Angel jumped to the right, landing in her squirrel form and scampering up a tree. I flung myself to the left, twisted in the air, and back-flipped six times through the trees and bushes before I came to a stop.

It was like a knife fight where the moment seemed like it lasted forever but was over within a couple of minutes. My breaths were harsh, but not from exerting myself. It was from surprise and fear.

Dust clouded the air and filled my nostrils. My head swam with remnants of the magic that had left my body in such an overwhelming, almost devastating rush.

"Angel!" What if a boulder had slammed into her tree? Or what if she'd been injured even as she saved me? "Are you all right?"

A blond squirrel skittered down a nearby tree, and then Angel stood in the squirrel's place just a few yards from me.

I wasn't sure if it was anger or concern in her blue eyes. Maybe both. "Damn, Nyx." Angel gestured in the direction of the rock wall, and when she spoke her lips were thin. "What were you thinking?" Apparently it was mostly anger she felt right now.

I leaned over and braced my hands on my thighs, trying to slow my breathing, and I shook my head at the same time. Silt slipped out of my hair onto a small clump of grass beneath me. "Some of that electrical charge was still in my body. I had no idea until it was too late."

The anger on her features relaxed, but only a little. "You were pretty pissed when you started to use your magic. Are you sure that didn't have something to do with your loss of control?"

I straightened and inhaled deeply one more time as my breathing returned to normal. "You're right. I was angry, but normally I wouldn't have a problem control-ling that anger. It would never have happened if it wasn't for that charge."

She nodded, a slow movement, and I saw from the look in her eyes that she was churning over and considering something in her mind. "Is more of the electricity in your body?"

"I don't feel anything." My hair was sticking to my face, which felt as if it was covered in dust. When I pushed my hair aside, more silt made a nice little shower on my shoulders and the ground around my feet. "But then, I'd had no idea it was still inside me until that moment."

"Let's hope not." Angel gazed in the direction of the landslide for a long moment before looking back at me. "We can't afford for that to happen again."

"No kidding," I snapped at her, suddenly irritated with her talking to me like a child. I calmed my tone. "I'll have to watch out in the future, to make sure it isn't going to interfere with my elemental magic again. I'll deal with it, Angel."

She gave a deep sigh. "That just scared the crap out of me. I'm concerned that some of the electricity that was in your body might remain and something like that could happen again."

"Same here." I rubbed my face on my arm, but that didn't do any good because my arm was covered with dust, too, and my face felt even dirtier. "Now that I'm aware of the possibility, I can be on guard."

Angel put her hands in her back pockets. "Sorry to act like a bitch."

"You're fine. You're just concerned." I wanted a blessed bath instead of having this conversation.

Then like an idiot I remembered the Elvin word for "clean" and I rolled my eyes.

"Avanna," I said and immediately all of the dirt and filth was erased from every part of my body, and from my clothing.

Angel's features returned to her natural good-natured appearance. "I was wondering when you'd get around to that."

"Must have gotten hit on the skull." I smiled back at her. I didn't feel a single injury, thanks to Angel probably saving my life. "Of course your shift left you looking as terrific as ever."

"As long as I'm not seriously wounded, it's no problem when I shift." She stretched her arms up like she had earlier before settling on her heels. "Now let's see what kind of mess we left."

I appreciated her use of the word "we."

It took a bit to get back to the rock wall because I'd back-flipped so far to make sure I got out of the way of the landslide. When we reached the clearing, it wasn't so clear anymore.

"Oops." I winced at the amount of damage I'd caused as I stepped my way through a heavy layer of rock covering what was once a dirt and grass clearing.

"Doesn't look good." Angel walked ahead of me. "There are a lot more rocks than before at the base of the cliff."

We reached the wall. I stomped my foot. "Like we need any more roadblocks with figuring out these disappearances."

Angel gave me a teasing smile. "This could definitely be considered a roadblock."

I was about to answer when I saw something glint in the sunlight behind one of the boulders. Rocks didn't shine like that. No, it was a metallic glint. I was sure of it.

Only a few more steps in my bare feet through rocks brought me to the bottom of the sheer wall. I'd had to climb over boulders that hadn't been here the last time. Rocks shifted behind me as Angel followed. She didn't usually make noise, but she must have been in as big a hurry as I was.

My heart thudded with excitement and I felt a sort of high. A lift of my spirits in knowing that this could be it. This could be all we needed to solve this case.

It didn't take long to get as close as I could to what I could see more clearly now. Rough stone scraped my skin as I pressed myself against the final boulders. I couldn't squeeze between the giant rocks, but I could reach through an opening with my arm.

And I touched it.

"This had to be at least four feet behind the rocks." A smile of satisfaction spread across my face as I ran my fingers along a smooth metal corner. "I may have torn down the place," I said louder to make sure Angel could hear me, "but I found something. I'm pretty sure it's a door."

The more dirt I brushed away, the larger the corner became. I was so into examining the metal and brushing what dirt and rocks I could from it that it took me a few moments to realize Angel hadn't said anything.

She should be as excited as me. I turned to look over my shoulder—

It took one second, one second too long to comprehend what I was seeing. Angel's unconscious features, followed by a mess of corkscrew blond curls, disappearing into a forest-green body bag. A silent plastic zipper completed its task by a man wearing a matching HAZMAT-looking suit.

In that single second, I processed several things.

The suit itself.

No scent. Even with my sensitive sense of smell, I couldn't scent the suit, and the Werewolves obviously hadn't, either.

It was also why no scents had ever been left at the scene of a Werewolf kidnapping or body dump.

The body bag was of the same material as the suit.

And in that same second, I realized a man stood within my peripheral vision, who must have been the one making the noise on the rocks behind me. Not Angel.

He held a perfume-sized bottle—and was pointing it at me.

One second too late I started to reach for my Kahr.

Unscented spray hit me full in the face.

Darkness took me instantly.

I dreamed of Superman.

The comic book hero lay on a cold, sterile floor in a pristine white room. His body was crumpled, useless.

His muscles wouldn't respond to his attempts at movement. His heart barely continued to beat. His sense of smell was all but gone. He couldn't open his eyes, but he knew *it* was there.

Somewhere beside him.

Stealing his strength.

Stealing his hope.

Somewhere beside him was his kryptonite.

* * *

My mind was sluggish. Images of Superman kept coming to me and I didn't understand why I'd be dreaming and now thinking about a superhero in blue tights, a red cape, and a big shield with the letter "S" on his chest.

In my world, superheroes came out at night, wore black leather, and carried swords and big-ass guns, as Olivia would put it.

Gradually I started to drift away from my dreams of a make-believe hero and was able to start concentrating on my new reality.

Reality.

What was reality?

I touched my collar and flashes of memory came to me. My blood must have stilled completely in my veins as every bit of my memories came rushing back to me.

Finding the metal corner of a door.

A man wearing a facemask and a green HAZMAT suit zipping Angel into a body bag.

Another man in one of the green, sterile suits spraying me in the face with something that felt like powder when it touched my skin.

Then I was gone.

Angel and I had been taken by the very people—or beings—who had been stealing away the Werewolves. One mystery solved in part. Although I sure as the Lord of the Underworld didn't like the way it had come about.

How had I not sensed them? It had to be something about the HAZMAT suits, which looked like they were used to perform scientific experiments. No, it was more than that.

The spray.

My sense of smell was shot, much worse than it had been before when I'd been to the scene where Alois was found and had died, and the scene where Kveta and Petra had disappeared. It was much, much worse, like cotton balls had been stuffed up my nose.

The side of my body I lay on ached from being on something very hard and cool. It felt like polished marble on the parts of my skin that were bare. My fighting outfit was snug on my body, and I was still bare foot.

I opened my eyes and sterile white walls and a recessed light above were so bright they nearly blinded me. I looked around the room. It was like my Superman dream, except no glowing green kryptonite. Four flawless, spotless white walls, white floor, white ceiling.

Panic seized me like a fist around my throat, as if my collar was strangling me. I was trapped in some kind of room. I scrambled up and the cold of the floor shot through my bare feet. My black leather fighting outfit was the only relief from the intense white of the room.

I put my hands to my waist—my weapons belt was gone. Lightning and Thunder, my dragon-claw daggers, along with my buckler, Storm . . . gone. Of course my Kahr was missing along with my XPhone.

Rational thought exited. Something about the room made my heart nearly explode. A scream tried to claw its way out of my throat, making it feel raw even though nothing came out.

Urgency within me grew so intense that I ran to one of the walls. I searched every part I could reach with my fingers and the rest with my gaze. The walls were thick, so thick I couldn't sense any earth beyond them. It was as if the room had been carved out of solid granite that went on forever.

Finally I found one area in a wall that had the barest break in the smoothness. I ran my fingers along the nearly invisible separation. It was a small block that could be moved, I was certain. Something that could be opened only from the outside, though, because no matter how I tried, there was no way to move it. I shuddered. It must be an opening that food could be shoved through for a prisoner.

Next to the single movable block, I found a door. A door fitted so tightly into the wall that it might as well have been just like all of the other walls.

Then it hit me.

I never thought Drow could hyperventilate. The way my breath jerked in my chest and my vision threatened to close in on me, I was almost positive I was going to pass out. I braced my palms on my thighs and took deep breaths as I ran through everything in my mind.

A windowless, solid room with walls so thick I couldn't feel earth; recycled air—the oxygen pumped into it had no traces of magic; no water—not even a toilet or sink; and no fire within reach, not even static air that had magic of any kind. I had no way of grasping any of my elements and using them to fight or even save myself in this room.

This was my kryptonite.

In here I was helpless without the elements.

Flashes of men and women in green suits flowed through my mind. Faces hidden behind sterilized suit masks while the men and women poked and prodded me. I had been strapped to a metal table and I had faded in and out of consciousness. Not understanding anything until now. I didn't even know if any of the elements could have saved me then if I had been truly aware of anything.

A sick feeling settled in my stomach like foul sewage and I looked at the inside of my elbow. A bandage secured a cotton ball.

They didn't. No, they couldn't have.

Oh, my Goddess. I tore at the bandage, flung it away, and it landed on the pristine white floor. A small dot of blood spotted the cotton ball. My gaze jerked to my arm and I saw the tiny pinprick of dried blood that was barely visible in the skin above one of my veins. I slumped against the wall with the door and slid down it until I was sitting on the floor.

Whoever kidnapped me and Angel now had a sample of my blood and no doubt hers. When examining the blood, they would have known instantly that I'm not completely human, and that Angel wasn't human at all.

The only relief I could feel was that I still looked human with my pale skin and black hair. At least I hoped I hadn't been knocked out so long that I'd gone through the change in my sleep.

My fingernails dug into my palms and I ground my teeth at the combination of the pain and the knowledge that I was in deep, deep trouble.

I looked up at the ceiling and saw a small vent through which the oxygen was being pumped. A much smaller white circle was nearby with a tiny glass lens within it. They had a camera trained on me. I tried to reach out with my senses, hoping to find some weakness where the air vent and camera were, but without my elements, my senses were useless. Both the vent and camera were so small I didn't think there was anything that could be done with them anyway.

The fact that they were watching me—whoever "they" were—made my stomach feel even sicker than it already was.

Transference . . .

The thought came to me from somewhere in my head, as if someone old and wise had spoken it. As if it were me when I grew older, telling myself I could do it now.

I frowned. My father had always said I wouldn't be able to use the transference until I was much older. Perhaps fifty at the youngest. At twenty-seven, I hadn't developed my full powers, unlike most Dark Elves who had lived for so long, many too many years to count. I'd worked to prove my father wrong and tried to use the transference so many times, but had failed with my countless attempts.

With a deep breath, I touched my collar and ran my fingers along the Elvin runes, as if for strength—or luck. I put my hands down, to either side of me, and tried to relax.

And focused. Focused with everything I had.

I pictured myself in the forest, in the Werewolf camp where I could get help now that I knew where to look for whoever, whatever, had taken Angel and me.

Again and again I attempted to pull myself into that image. Take myself to the last place I'd been. At one time I thought I felt darkness coming for me, the darkness of a transference, but that thought slipped away. Maybe not, but it had probably been my imagination.

I stayed trapped within four white walls.

Giving up was not an option. I touched my collar for comfort before trying again. This time I pictured an empty room. Something nearby that I could get to through stone. But I had no idea of what surrounded me and it made the image in my mind vague.

A distant grating sound, like stone scraping stone, grabbed my complete attention and I no longer focused on the transference. The noise vanished and I held my breath. Something was happening. A much harsher sound echoed in the room.

The door was opening.

ELEVEN

As the door scraped open beside me, I scrambled to my feet. I moved to the side so that I could see out the door. With just the right position, I could take down whatever came through that door and make my escape.

But when the massive door opened, I saw only another thick stone door behind a person wearing a facemask and a green sterile suit. He wore a thick yellow armband and I had an image of red and blue armbands on green suits. I mentally shook my head.

The door he had come through was on the far side of an equally white stone room about six feet high and four feet wide in each direction. Obviously the person entered that room and then closed the door before opening this one. My senses told me that door was just as impenetrable as the one to my prison.

Through the individual's facemask, I couldn't tell if it was a man or a woman because the person was a good six feet away from me. He or she was close to five-eight, my height, but was considerably larger in girth than me. The person held a small glass bottle similar to the one that contained the spray that had knocked me out. The person had the sprayer aimed at me.

My eyes narrowed and my lips twisted into a scowl. I backed up, wanting whoever was hiding behind the mask to walk in, to get close enough that I could use my fighting skills and neutralize him or her. I didn't need the elements or my weapons to take him out in a one-on-one fight. No bottle of spray was going to stop me.

I saw a man's face on the other side of that mask when he walked into the room and the bright light made it easier to see him. Clean-shaven, pudgy cheeks, faint eyebrows, and small blue eyes with no lashes that I could see.

I waited for him to speak. I didn't have to ask questions now because when I got through with him, he'd be spilling everything he knew within a couple of minutes.

With a hard shove he slammed the door shut behind him. It made more grating sounds and then a reverberating noise when it settled into place. My heart sank a little that there was no visible means of escape, that my elemental magic was useless. I pushed those thoughts away. I remembered the camera but didn't look at it.

"I'm Dr. Lawson." He looked at me for a long moment before he spoke again and then his words came out with a nasty edge to them. "You look human, but your blood sample shows foreign bodies that tell us you're not." His voice came out through a microphone, sounding tinny and strange. "Bizarre combinations of red and white blood cells . . . Almost completely unlike the Werewolves as well."

Almost?

My body tensed as Lawson's grip tightened on the bottle he was holding. "Tell me what you are and what the beast is that was with you."

Beast? I rarely cursed, except in Drow, and I had to bite back a long string of words telling him what he could do with himself and that bottle. I wasn't about to use my native language, which would prove to him that I have a background not entirely human. The language of the Dark Elves is deep and guttural and unlike any earthbound language.

Lawson dug his free hand into a pocket of his suit, and a long needle caught the light when he pulled out a syringe. His pocket must have been reinforced for the needle not to have pierced it.

My heart beat a little faster as he raised the syringe so that it was eye level to both of us. A drop of fluid glistened at the end of the needle. I still had no sense of smell and I caught no odors.

"This is a special truth serum created in our lab. It has been most useful with the abominations that call themselves Werewolves." He practically spat his last words.

The way Lawson referred to the Werewolves as abominations made my skin burn hot, and anger crawled all over my body.

If I had been in my Drow form, Lawson would never have taken his next step. He would probably been intimidated and would have exercised more caution. But

I look like a fragile human, unlike how I appear when I change. I don't look dangerous at all in my human form.

Lawson took that step.

His mistake.

With a roundhouse kick, I hit both of Lawson's wrists and knocked the spray bottle and the syringe from his hands. The bottle hit his shoe, which cushioned the fall before it clattered as it rolled across the floor. The syringe landed a few feet away.

Lawson cried out in surprise and didn't have a chance to react to my lunge forward as I sent my fist straight for his facemask.

The clear material shielding his face didn't so much as crack. Adrenaline pumped through me so fast I barely noticed the pain from the impact of my knuckles against the unbreakable material.

I didn't stop to think because I immediately followed my right punch with my left fist straight into his gut at the same time I hooked my ankle behind his and jerked.

Lawson screamed behind his mask as I pulled his leg out from under him and he fell on his backside.

The grinding sound of the stone doors opening told me Lawson's backup was coming in.

My knees hit the hard floor as I dropped beside Lawson's head. He reached for me but I was too fast for him. I had my arm wrapped around his neck and I jerked him up so that his back was to my chest. I settled my elbow against his Adam's apple as I pulled him tight to me with a small dose of my inherent strength.

He gurgled and no doubt his face was red behind his mask. He was lucky I hadn't crushed his windpipe. But I needed him and I needed answers.

Before the door fully opened, I used my strength to tear off his facemask and he gave a strangled scream. "No!" He tried to shout but my hold was too tight on his neck. "You'll contaminate me!"

Several more Drow curse words came to mind and I jerked harder against Lawson's neck. I wondered if he'd be spitting up blood if I wasn't careful. His thin gray hair that had probably been combed over his balding head stuck up like wisps of smoke, and this time I thought I might have caught the smells of sweat and terror.

I was using my free hand to reach behind me, trying to grasp the syringe, when the door opened. My whole body stilled as a man in one of the green suits stepped through with a gun.

My gun. Pointed straight at me.

This time I knew it was a man by his build, broader shoulders and the masculine way he carried himself as he walked through the door.

"I'll break his neck," I said in a low, furious voice.

"Lawson is now contaminated," came a mature masculine voice through the microphone in his suit. His voice told me he had to be at least in his sixties. "He is useless now."

"No!" Lawson tried to get out despite my stranglehold on him.

The man stepped closer, aimed the Kahr—and shot Lawson through the side of the head.

Blood and brain matter splattered the floor to the

side of me and on my right arm. Horror spread throughout me as Lawson's body slumped in my lap. I looked up at the man.

He studied me. He was close enough that I could see the sharp angles of his features and his calculating brown eyes.

I shoved Lawson's corpse away from me and it landed with a thud on the formerly clean floor. Lawson's blood was brilliant scarlet against the white stone. The smell of it—now, unfortunately, my sense of smell had partially returned—made me want to gag.

When I started to get to my feet, the man shook his head in a slow movement and kept the gun trained on me. "I am Dr. Johnson."

Better choices than *Johnson* came to mind but I kept my mouth shut.

"You will start talking." Johnson's angular features were hard behind his facemask. "And keep talking."

I glared at him.

"I won't kill you," he said, surprising me. "But I have no problem shooting you in places on your body that will make you suffer. I will do so until you tell me what I need to know. I can make you suffer in ways you cannot imagine . . . as I have done to several of the Werewolves."

My skin went unbelievably cold and I had to suppress a shudder.

Johnson looked at Lawson's body, then back to me. "Obviously we underestimated you and should have sent in one of the interns with Lawson." He shook his head. "Lawson was one of our most talented junior scientists." Johnson's gaze met mine. "Once you contaminated him, I had no choice but to dispose of him."

The coldness in his voice was enough to chill my skin even more. I was sitting on my haunches and tired of looking up at him. No doubt he wasn't letting me stand because he wanted that intimidation factor of his height over my position on the floor.

Sometimes I really hated males.

"So does that mean," I said, putting the most thoughtful expression on my face and consideration in my tone, "that once I rip off your mask you'll have to shoot yourself?"

Johnson scowled and pointed the barrel of the Kahr at my thigh. "You're an abomination, like the Werewolves and that other beast we captured with you."

I clenched my hands into fists and bit my tongue hard to keep from screaming at him. Abominations? There was that word again. And he had called Angel a beast. Had she shifted into a squirrel?

The dangerous flash in my eyes would only give him more reason to fear and want to exterminate my kind, so I had to control it.

"According to our blood tests, it is something different than the Werewolves." Johnson scowled as he spoke and my spine went rigid as he referred to Angel as an *it*.

"She is not an *it*." I dug my nails tighter into my palms. Soon I would cut my own flesh open from the power I was exerting. "You'd better not hurt her or I'll kill you in the *most painful* way possible."

Behind his mask he smirked and my nails broke the skin of my palms as I clenched my fists tighter. Stinging sensations radiated through my arms and warm blood touched my fingers.

Johnson glanced at the camera and said, "Send the techs in," before returning his gaze on me. He said nothing. I wasn't inclined to speak, so we just held each other's gazes. I could stare him down all night if he wanted a staring contest.

The door scraped open, giving him an excuse to glance toward it. Two individuals came through the door, whom I assumed were techs. They wore the same type of masked green outfits as Johnson and Lawson, with the exception that each suit had a thick blue armband.

What really held my attention was the shiny metal chair they were rolling in. Metal cuffs dangled from thick-linked chains at the arms and legs.

Johnson intended to strap me to that chair and force me to talk. My palms grew even bloodier from the power I was exerting by digging my nails deeper. It seemed to be the only thing grounding me at that moment.

"Marton, Terrence, set it there." Johnson nodded to the center of the room and the techs set the chair down with a thump.

No way in all of the Underworlds would he get me in that chair. I might not have my elemental magic, but I had my Drow strength. I'd taken out the other scientist, and I'd take Johnson out, too.

Blood dripped down my palms and a spot splattered on the floor. I didn't even feel the sting of the cuts.

Behind his facemask I could see Johnson scowl. He looked at the camera again. "Jenkins, Harkins. When you come in, bring sterilized cleaning supplies. It is bleeding. The techs are going to clean up this creature's blood as well as Lawson's mess when you bring in what we're waiting for."

A hot, hot flush burned my cheeks as Johnson referred to me as an "it" like he had referred to Angel.

"I. Am. Not. An. It." As I slowly enunciated each word to him, I got to my feet.

Johnson didn't stop me from standing this time, but continued to point my own gun at me. He merely looked bored as I spoke. "You are not human, therefore you are nothing short of an animal."

It took everything I had not to lunge for him.

Another string of Drow curse words threatened to come out. Instead, I couldn't hold back a human curse. "You bastard."

This time he had an amused expression behind that mask and I wished I had one of my dragon-claw daggers to pierce his sterilization suit and sink the blade deep into his heart.

Johnson was the one responsible for all of the Werewolf kidnappings, mutilations, and deaths. I knew it with every one of my senses that I had within me. Gut instinct and my heart told me, too.

I glanced at the chair. I could easily rip away from nylon or leather straps, but metal cuffs would be much harder without my elements. Only elemental-magic-treated cuffs of other materials could contain me.

"You're not putting me in that chair." My words were strong, definite.

"No, I am not." Johnson gave a brief nod to the camera before meeting my gaze. "I have better things in mind."

Before I could respond, if I could have thought of a response, the distant noise of the first door grating open met my ears. It was followed by the sound and the movement of the door to my prison.

Two more green-suited people came in, this pair wearing scarlet armbands instead of blue. Interns, he had called this pair when he ordered them to come in.

The interns carried Angel's limp body by her feet and her upper arms. Her head lolled to the side and her corkscrew curls were a tangled mess.

Blood from a cut on her cheek and more from her temple had dried a dark brown. Blood stained her now dirty white T-shirt. That, and the bruises on her other cheekbone and on her chin, as well as her black eye, caused a horrible sick feeling to settle in my stomach like pure acid. When I saw the purple bruises around her neck, more acid rose inside me. At the same time fury rode my veins and I shook with it.

"What did you do to her?" I asked as the acid invaded my words.

"The interns will strap the creature in and then the questioning of this beast can begin again." Johnson watched me and ignored the interns, who didn't have any trouble doing exactly that with the petite Doppler.

With a tone that was almost absent-minded, Johnson added, "You'll recognize junior scientists by yellow armbands, interns by red, and techs by blue." He glanced at one particularly tall man with a blue armband before glancing back at me. "You especially will not want to mess with the techs. They are highly trained specialists. Each is well-versed in some form of martial arts or hand-to-hand combat. Most are former Special Ops from different branches of the military."

I'd battled Demons. I wasn't afraid of these men. Not really.

"You said the questioning can begin *again*." I looked at the bruises on Angel's face and imagined that beneath her bloody T-shirt and beneath her jeans that she had even more bruises. "You tortured her."

Johnson shrugged. "Unfortunately, nothing worked. Not even our truth serum. I thought perhaps you could be persuaded before I start shooting your friend."

His certain death was behind every one of my words when I looked at him. More human curse words spilled out. "You evil sonofabitch. You will die for everything you have done to her and to the Werewolves."

Johnson's features turned storm-cloud dark. "You would be among the dead already if you weren't an unknown species. First, I need information on the rest of your kind before I dispatch you and eradicate the rest."

Eradicate. Many, many more of Olivia's human curse words came to mind but I held them back. I was unique. Alone. Johnson wouldn't find any of my kind in this earth Otherworld, but I certainly wasn't going to share any information with him.

When Angel was strapped into the metal chair, Johnson stepped farther away from me and pointed the Kahr at Angel. I sucked in my breath and a ringing sound started in my ears. He didn't have to say a word about what he was going to do. He was going to shoot Angel if I didn't cooperate.

"Harkins." Johnson pointed to one of the interns, a woman, I thought. She was one of those who'd carried Angel in and the intern had cloths hanging out of her back pockets. "Give Terrence and Marton the cleaning supplies."

"Yes, sir," Harkins said with a slight bow of her head.

Johnson glanced at the two techs who had brought the chair in. "Clean up the mess, including this creature's blood."

"Of course, Dr. Johnson," Marton said at the same time Terrance said, "Immediately, sir."

By the stiffness of their stances and words, Terrence and Marton weren't pleased about their orders. Harkins pulled supplies from large pockets on the legs of her suit—a couple of spray bottles, then the cloths from her back pockets—and handed them to the two techs, who left to clean up the "mess."

"Wake it, Jenkins," Johnson said to the other intern who had carried Angel into my prison with Harkins.

"Yes, sir," said Jenkins.

It. I let every one of Johnson's hateful words and references add fuel to my anger. I would get Angel and myself out of this. Dear Goddess, I had to.

Jenkins took a syringe from his pocket, found a vein on the inside of Angel's elbow, and slid the needle into the vein.

Angel blinked awake almost immediately. The drugged expression on her features vanished and she fought against her metal restraints as if she was going after Johnson. "You sonofabitch," she shouted. I don't think she had noticed me. Her entire focus was on Johnson.

Johnson's finger tightened on the Kahr's trigger as he aimed it at Angel. She froze, her gaze locked on him. He glanced at me. "Just to show you I'm serious."

He squeezed the trigger.

Angel screamed.

TWELVE

"No!" I shouted as a red spot expanded at once in the jeans material covering one of Angel's thighs.

She didn't make another sound but her lips were drawn back in a grimace, exposing her teeth, and her jaw was clenched tight.

Fury raged through me, hot and wild. I would have gone after Johnson, but I was afraid he'd shoot Angel again. He might not kill her because he'd want to experiment on her, but he'd probably mutilate and maim her.

Johnson looked at me in a casual manner, weapon trained on Angel. "If you want *it* to remain intact, let's start with you. What are you?"

There was nothing I could do about it. I stared at the blood soaking Angel's jeans. I wouldn't let him hurt her anymore. I'd kill him later, anyway.

I kept my gaze steady as I focused on him. "Like Werewolves, I'm a paranorm. I'm half Drow, half human."

Johnson narrowed his brown eyes behind his mask. I noticed the two interns and both techs had gone still as they looked at me with curiosity and disbelief.

Johnson's voice was distorted through his microphone when he shifted his body to face me completely. "Drow. What the hell are Drow?"

"Dark Elves." My voice was strong and filled with venom.

He snorted behind his mask, a strange sound through the microphone. "Elves. So you are saying you are part of a mythical race of beings?"

"We're not mythical." I straightened. "Much of human mythology is based on fact."

Johnson jerked his attention to the two techs who were supposed to be cleaning. "I want that mess out of here. Now."

"Yes, Dr. Johnson," came a deep voice through one of the tech's microphones before the pair started scrubbing blood and whatever else had splattered across the floor.

"When you're finished, get that cadaver out of here. It stinks." Johnson made a face like someone walking into a public restroom at a gas station. "I don't want a drop of any contamination left when you are finished." Both techs nodded and didn't meet his eyes.

Johnson looked back at me. The sneer on his face told me he didn't believe what I'd told him. "Explain."

"A couple of millennia ago, Dark Elves were Light Elves. We were all just *Elves*, no distinction between Light and Dark." As I spoke, my mind continued to run through options that would help save both Angel and me. How could I get us out of this room? Best option would be to take Johnson as prisoner once the two techs left with Lawson's body.

"Drow were banished belowground in Otherworld,"

I continued, ". . . due to differences of opinion and life-style."

"If you come from some other world, why are you here?" he asked. "Where are the others of your kind that live and breathe our air?"

"Live and breathe *your* air?" My tone was sharp as my temper rose. "It's our air just as much as it is yours. Dark Elves are everywhere. You would never begin to find us all."

That wasn't, isn't, true. I'm the only one of my people in this Otherworld because I'm the only one of my kind. Full-blooded Dark Elves never leave Otherworld's be-lowground realm because they can't be in sunlight—or they fry.

What is true is that I am the only half-human, half-Drow who can be in sunlight during the day as a human, and shift to Drow at night. All other half-human, half-Drow have been born with their human half completely dominant. They live as humans, never knowing their true birth origins.

I didn't plan on telling Johnson any of that.

"What about Light Elves?" I continued. "Plan on get-ting rid of them, too?" Rodán was actually the only one of the Light Elves I knew in the Earth Otherworld, but that wasn't something I planned on volunteering, either.

Johnson was scowling. "This is beyond absurd." I went rigid as I saw his fingers tighten on my Kahr. "I do not believe your fabricated story. Elves are mythical beings."

"Who could make up something like this?" I raised my arms and let them drop by my sides. "You saw the bloodwork."

"We'll get back to whatever you are." He gestured with his head to Angel. "What is *it*?"

Angel glared at him as she spoke to me. "Don't tell him."

"Your other thigh is next." He spoke with a cruel, calculating intensity. "I can experiment on you no matter what your condition. I can keep you alive until I'm finished with you."

Angel's eyes were clear, defiant. "What will you be experimenting for if you don't know what I am?"

Another shot rang out, the sound hurting my ears, a powerful ringing noise echoing in the stone prison again.

The interns standing behind Angel flinched.

I had shouted at the same time as Angel as her other thigh began to bleed through her jeans. She twisted against her bonds, the metal making grating sounds against the chair as she struggled.

"I can't let him do this to you." My voice went deadly low. I relaxed my hands before clenching them into fists again and causing my palms to sting more. "He won't live through this, anyway."

A light flashed in Angel's eyes. The same determination I felt inside me was reflected on her features now.

Johnson aimed the gun at me. "If you threaten me one more time, I will start putting bullets into you."

"She's a Doppler." I saw death in Angel's eyes, death for Johnson. "Dopplers are paranorms who take different animal forms," I continued, "unlike Werewolves, who always change into wolf form."

"Not to be mistaken with Shifters." Angel surprised

me by volunteering information. "Shifters can choose whatever animal they want to transform into. Dopplers are born with one predetermined animal form."

A confused light was in Johnson's eyes for the first time and he didn't speak, as if trying to digest a fantastical story. He looked like he was attempting to gather himself as he cut his gaze to the pair of techs who were now carrying Lawson's corpse toward the stone door.

"Take the body to cold storage for now." Johnson made a motion to the camera. "After you bag it."

The door opened, scrubbing the floor with a loud grating sound that made my skin crawl. The outer door scraped open next.

Johnson turned back to me. "How many of you *paranorms* are there?" He said *paranorms* like the word itself was a virus.

"We're everywhere." I took one step closer to him as the stone door shut with a thunderous sound behind the two techs. "We hide in plain sight. Humans don't know how many species of paranorms there are. You can't eradicate us all."

I didn't take another step as an insane expression crossed what I could see of Johnson's face behind his mask. A smile. He was smiling? Yes, and it was maniacal.

"Upon studying the blood samples from both of you, we discovered you beasts and the Werewolves have a single matching mutated gene." As he spoke I felt sudden tension ride my shoulders. "This gene gives you one common vulnerability that humans do not share."

The tension I'd been feeling in my shoulders spread

throughout the rest of me so fast that every part of me ached. Angel stiffened in her chair, her bruised features still.

Johnson's smile grew. He paused as if savoring what he had to say next. "The mutated gene has a predisposition to be susceptible to virus. My team of junior scientists and I simply have to find the right virus that will exterminate every one of you abominations."

He looked so pleased as he added words that sent chills through me. "I believe we are close enough that we can soon begin the eradication."

"That's impossible. You're lying." The words slipped out heavy with horror, showing weakness I hadn't planned or wanted him to see. I mentally cursed myself because I couldn't take back the words or the fear in my voice.

His arm was probably tired but Johnson still looked alert as he slowly lowered the gun. A breath of relief escaped me.

"Fascinating, isn't it?" he said.

My fingers twitched, aching to grip Lightning and Thunder tight in my palms. I would slice him to shreds with my dragon-claw daggers with no remorse.

Maybe I'd even feel pleasure. Satisfaction at killing the man who had murdered so many Werewolves, a man seeking a way to destroy what he considered abominations. If every paranorm shared that one gene, not just Angel and me, he could erase us all.

I wanted to rub the growing chill from my arms but I wasn't going to show any more signs of weakness.

Johnson shifted on the heels of his rubber-soled boots and they squeaked on the stone floor. "What other disgusting beasts exist that I am unaware of?"

"There are no disgusting beasts." My words came out like a whip as I thought about his plan. Well, Metamorphs could qualify as disgusting, but their race didn't deserve to be extinguished. I could live without Zombies. I ignored those thoughts and continued. "We all are beings who have just as much a right to exist as humans do. Most paranorms were here long before humans."

Johnson's face went red behind his mask. "God created man. You abominations are a result of Eve's unfaithfulness to Adam. That is why you possess the weak gene—so that one such as I can punish Eve's ill-begotten children. Children who are the spawn of Satan."

My head almost snapped back in shock at what he'd said and the fervor in his tone, the fanaticism, and the disgust that accompanied it. We were dealing with a crazy man. Worse yet, a crazy scientist.

"Tell me," Johnson all but screamed as he pointed the gun at Angel again. Spittle splattered across the inside of his face shield, but I don't think he noticed.

"Okay." I held up my hands, my palms facing him in a gesture meant to tell him I didn't want him to hurt Angel again and would comply. "Whatever you want."

"You know what I want." He lowered the gun again. Good, his arm was becoming weaker from training the weapon on us for such a long time.

"Yes." I gave a slow nod. Maybe I could shock him into thinking there was no way his plan would work on all of us. "There are so many paranorms it's hard to know where to start." My list ought to give him nightmares. I almost shuddered myself at the thought of Zombies again.

I started ticking off the various beings on my fingers. "You know there are Light Elves and Dark Elves as well as Dopplers, Shifters, and Werewolves."

"Hurry up," he said in a snarl.

"This is going to take a while," I said, but I did rush to continue my list. "Vampires, Necromancers, Incubae, Succubae . . . Zombies." I took a breath before I went on and had to start counting on my first, then other hands again. "Metamorphs, Magi, Demons, Gargoyles, Shadow Shifters, Witches and Sorcerers."

The scientist's eyes looked like they were going to cross behind his mask. I didn't give him a chance to speak—I was on a roll.

"Then Fae—almost too many to count." I was tempted to use my bare toes as well as my fingers. "Pixies, Abatwa, Brownies, Dryads, Faeries, Gnomes, Nymphs, Sânziene, Sirens, Tuatha, Sidhe, Goblins, Dwarves, Undines, and Sprites." I cocked my head, trying to look deep in thought. "I may have forgotten something, but that's pretty close."

Johnson shook his head like he was in a dream. "You are fabricating this story."

It was my turn to shrug. "You asked."

He swallowed, his Adam's apple bobbing. It was easy to tell he was working to control his reaction. "God has given me this task, to destroy what does not belong in this world." He tipped his chin up and straightened as if sucking up his courage. "I am most certainly up to this challenge."

Johnson couldn't have looked more distracted than he did at that moment.

I wasn't close enough to lunge at him. I bunched my muscles, took one step, and forward-flipped toward him.

Anger fueled my motion. As I came down, I landed on my left foot while hitting his gun arm hard with my right. I'd break his wrist.

He reacted faster than I expected and jerked the gun toward me. I missed his wrist, but my leg came down hard on his forearm. Enough power and fury was in my motion to knock the gun out of his hand despite his tight grip.

A shot rang out at the same time my leg hit his arm. Pain exploded in my knee. My leg almost collapsed under me but I shifted my balance to my other leg in time.

The weapon clattered to the stone floor and spun away.

Pain magnified my rage. With a knife-hand strike I hit his neck. Too low. My shot knee had me off-balance and I nicked his collarbone.

Johnson shouted, a loud sound of pain, but strange and distorted through his microphone. The blow would have snapped his neck if I had hit him correctly or had been in my Drow form.

Unable to bear weight on my right knee, I had to rely on my fists. The scientist lunged to punch me. I blocked it with my left arm. I jabbed him in the solar plexus with my right, then left fists before sending a third punch to a sensitive spot between his jaw and skull, below his ear. His suit cushioned most of my blows, but the last one got him enough to knock him out.

A muted cry, then he was facedown on the floor.

It was over in seconds.

Angel shouted, "Behind you!"

I had been ready for the two interns. Of course they would come after me to help Johnson. They hadn't had any visible weapons, but I had been prepared for anything—except getting shot in the knee.

Jenkins had a bottle of the knock-out spray aimed at me. I clasped my hands into one fist and swung at the intern's arm. My blow was so hard that the bottle flew from his hand, sailed across the room, and hit the far wall.

Sounds of shattering glass and Angel's cry of "Oh, damn" seemed distant, as if from another place.

I ignored the pain in my knee and concentrated on taking out the man in front of me. Damn the mask because it kept me from ramming the heel of my palm into his nose or my fist into his eye.

The fury inside me came from everything these people were doing to paranorms and the horror of what they planned to do next.

The intern shrieked when I punched him hard enough to crack two of his ribs with one fist, then another rib with the next punch.

Continuing to balance on my left foot, I grabbed the tech's shoulders, jerked him to me, and head-butted him just above his protective facemask. He sucked in his breath in a deep gasp. I released his shoulders and he hit the floor.

I hated head-butting when I was in human form. Stars sparked behind my eyes. It didn't matter, though—I was still completely alert, on guard.

Now for the other intern. I started to go after the female—but she was passed out on the floor. What?

I jerked my attention to Angel. She was still cuffed in the chair but she was out cold, too.

The powdery feel of the spray used on me when I was first kidnapped touched my skin.

The broken spray bottle. The fumes had traveled from the wall to where we were.

I was out before my body hit the floor.

THIRTEEN

I didn't think Superman had ever been stupid. At least he had that going for him.

Apparently, I didn't.

My head ached this time when I woke and opened my eyes. Being very careful not to move my shot knee too much, I pushed myself to a sitting position. Pain still made me grind my teeth. I felt dizzy, too, as if I'd been kicked in the head.

Same room as before. I really hated this room.

I eased up and leaned against the wall. I was so glad for its support because I probably would have fallen onto my side without it. Even the back of my head hurt when it touched the wall.

My brows narrowed—which caused my whole head to hurt more—and I frowned. I reached up, touched my temples and my cheek, and winced. I'd been hit or kicked in the face.

I ran my fingers all over, wincing every time I touched something painful—which was just about everywhere on my face. Judging by how swollen and bruised it felt, and by my split lip, my head had been somebody's soccer ball.

It was a little late in coming, but I realized my eyes hurt and it was hard to see. Johnson or his techs or his interns, or all, had even kicked me in my eyes.

I wasn't surprised he'd stoop so low. And what did he care if I was seriously hurt? If I was blind, deaf, and dumb, it wouldn't matter to him. As long as I was alive for him to test and abuse.

More pain started to shout for attention. My whole body had been used as a kicking target. And my knee . . . blood coated my leather fighting pants around where my knee had taken the bullet. Neither Johnson nor his techs had bothered to bandage or disinfect the wound. My kneecap was shattered. I was screwed until I shifted.

And then I felt the first tingle.

Olivia's favorite phrase seemed to be perfect for every bad situation, and this was definitely not good.

Oh, shit.

My internal clock told me the sun was going down aboveground and I was about to shift into my Drow form.

Well, that ought to freak Johnson out.

I'd heal during the shift, but the last thing I wanted was to be recorded as I changed forms.

A sick sensation filled my belly and I held my arm to that part of me that ached, too. I looked up at the camera and then gazed around the sterile white room. It was the only camera I could see. Didn't mean I wasn't missing something, but I could hope. Without my elemental magic, I didn't have the full ability to discover what secrets, if any, that room held.

The more my body tingled, the more my heart raced

and the more urgency filled me to get out of the camera's range of sight. Like a peeping Tom it stared at me, taking away my privacy.

Even though I tried to keep my weight off my bad knee, pain made me lightheaded as I pushed myself up. I wavered, trying to balance myself as I stood. The tingles ran along my skin and the roots of my hair prickled with sensation.

I limped toward the same corner as the camera, biting the inside of my cheek as I hurried the best I could. Goddess, I hoped the camera had a blind spot at the back side of it. When I reached that corner, I settled where the two walls met, closed my eyes, and touched my collar as if it would give me strength. Maybe it did, maybe it didn't, but I couldn't tell with such wrenching pain.

Not only did the change hurt because I wasn't doing my usual stretches, but the healing process had me doubling over. My bruised and battered face and body felt like I was being punched all over again. I hadn't realized my wrist was fractured and a rib was broken until the bones started knitting themselves back together.

It was my body's idea of healing my shattered kneecap that had me biting back cries and shouting out prayers. Who knew that healing could bring someone so close to passing out? It occurred to me that I'd always taken my elements for granted when I shifted after being injured. When I normally stretched and moved during the shift, I used air along with the transformation to heal.

I clenched my teeth as my muscles strengthened and became more toned. Blood filled my mouth as my incisors pierced my lip because I had my teeth welded so tightly together.

When I knew the change was complete, I opened my eyes. For the first time ever after a change, I was breathing in harsh gasps. Even though I was now healed and the pain had vanished, I felt like I was hyperventilating just like the first time I'd discovered myself in this awful room.

I took deep, steadying breaths as I raised my arm and looked at my more defined muscles and my amethyst skin. Strands of my cobalt blue hair lay over my shoulder.

A screaming noise filled the room.

It pierced my head like a Drow blade.

Pain screeched through me. I grasped the sides of my head. Bent double as the scream went on and on. So like the one from the forest.

Only ten times louder.

My head was going to explode.

Everything wavered and I felt like I'd been beaten again.

Through the sudden haze behind my eyes I saw the stone door open. The shrieking was so loud I couldn't hear the door scraping the floor.

Twelve techs and interns wearing green suits with red or blue armbands came into the room. They had earphones on and were pushing a steel gurney.

I'd taken on as many Demons as the number of techs entering the room. Demons that had been evil beings with a weakness so difficult to get to that saying it was a challenge to kill them was a joke.

Yet here I was facing mere humans and I could barely

stay on my feet, the screeching so intense that my body wanted to collapse in on itself.

But no way was I getting on that gurney. No mere humans were going to get the best of me.

It was so loud I couldn't hear the rattle of the gurney's wheels across the stone floor. My vision was even foggy. So foggy that I didn't see the spray bottles until the interns and techs were within fighting range.

My muscles were already bunched, prepared to fight on autopilot. I deflated the moment I saw those bottles. My head hurt too much and my vision was too bad to tell for certain, but I think every one of the techs was carrying a bottle. Yay for me that I merited twelve bottles of spray.

The techs surrounded me. Gloved hands grasped my wrists and cuffed them in front of me. I felt rubber from their gloves on my bare arms and bare midriff when they picked me up and settled me on the gurney. Dropped onto the gurney was more like it.

My breasts were smashed down as they strapped me in with so many thick nylon straps that it was overkill—or would have been if I wasn't Drow. I'd wait for the right moment . . . when I'd be in touch with my elements again.

I wanted to beg them to make the screeching stop, but I bit the inside of my cheek to keep myself from saying anything.

Twelve pairs of eyes stared at me for a moment after they had me completely strapped down. I could imagine what they thought as they saw an amethyst woman with unblemished skin and blue hair. A woman who only minutes ago had been fair with black hair, and had bruises and cuts all over her swollen face along with a shattered knee.

The screeching noise stopped. My body went limp with relief. My ears still rang.

"Let's go." Harkins—I recognized the intern's voice, which sounded loud now that the noise had stopped. "Dr. Johnson wants it in the examination room now."

It. Like I was nothing. Maybe a bug on the floor for her to smash under her rubber soles. If I could figure out a way to get out of this mess, I might choke her before I took care of the other eleven techs. That was after I killed Johnson, of course.

I clenched my fists and tested my restraints. Could I get out without my elements? Maybe I would have access to them wherever they moved me.

The techs and interns talked around me like I wasn't even there. "This will be an interesting case." Marton this time.

One of the techs within my line of sight gave me a look of pure hate from behind his mask. "You call this freak interesting? More like demonic."

"It even has fangs," another tech said.

My body started to shake with fury. Every one of them would be "dead meat," as Olivia would say.

Lights seemed brighter thanks to the sensitivity to my eyes brought on by the noise. The gazes of the techs behind the masks were distorted, almost eerie. Like they were some kind of aliens from a distant planet doing tests on beings from earth, rather than the reverse.

The gurney's wheels rumbled over the floor, down huge hallways, all brightly lit by fluorescent bulbs that made me want to keep my eyes shut. I kept them open, though, hoping to see something that might aid me in escaping and allow me to help Angel and everyone else who might be here. Like the pregnant female and the Werewolf pups. Assuming they were still alive.

While they moved the gurney, the techs and interns continued to talk about me. I only half listened in case they said something that might be important. The only thing they were doing right now was talking about all of the "subjects" and making me want to take an underground Troll's club to them, one by one.

I focused most of my attention on trying to grasp my elemental magic. To examine what I had available to me.

Air—it still wasn't fresh, but recycled. The natural elemental magic inherent in air was gone, completely gone in this place.

Earth—I was surrounded by stone and couldn't feel earth at all.

Fire—the electricity here was different . . . generated somehow underground. I didn't feel the power that electricity normally has that I could twist into fire. No, here they used AC power, which doesn't contain magic. And not a bit of static with magic in the air.

But water . . . there was a waterfall somewhere underground—fresh water from the mountains. And it was close. A powerful element filled with magic that I could make use of.

The time and place would have to be right. Water isn't an element easily contained in a place like this and I could end up flooding it and drowning us all. I'd have to learn more about what kind of facility I was in. A facility that appeared to be built far underground within stone.

Unfortunately, the water used in the facility had been run through a filtration system and a water softener. It was useless to me.

I'd figure out what to do with the waterfall when I didn't feel like I'd been trampled by a herd of Gargoyles.

Hallway lights continued to flash overhead and hurt my sensitive eyes. We passed several rooms that I couldn't see well because of my entourage of techs and interns. I couldn't smell again. I wondered if there was long-term damage from too much spray.

"Haven't been out of this goddamned place for six weeks," Marton spoke and my attention perked up. "I'm going fucking stir-crazy."

"Watch it, Marton." Harkins's voice had a sharp, nasty edge to it. "You're lucky Dr. Johnson hired you."

Harkins was at the foot of the gurney with Marton. A tech or intern pushing the gurney from behind whispered, "Harrison, you're new, so I'll let you know rule number two. Watch out for that bitch, Harkins. She's Johnson's pet."

"What's rule one?" another tech said behind me, presumably Harrison.

"Never fuck with Johnson." The first tech lowered his voice. "You heard what he did to Lawson."

Harrison cleared his throat. "Yeah."

"That could be you next."

Harrison made a nervous sound while clearing his throat again.

Terrence said in a sarcastic tone, "When are Dr. Johnson and his juniors coming back from Manhattan?"

When I heard Terrence's question, I had to keep from widening my eyes. Johnson had left the facility? I wasn't sure if that was a good or bad thing. I needed to take him out, but when was better? Here, or after I tracked him down in my city?

"Probably day after tomorrow," a female intern said.

A male tech with a smartass voice said, "Did you hear about Jenkins? The dipshit is laid up with a bunch of broken ribs. Freak here did a number on him and the doc."

Harkins looked over her shoulder at the tech. "Shut up."

The tech saluted Harkins. "Yes, ma'am."

Light burned my eyes and I blinked several times as the gurney was maneuvered into an enormous room. That at least was easy to tell even with the techs crowded around my fun little means of transportation.

"Into examination room four," Harkins said as the gurney rattled across the floor.

The pounding of my heart ratcheted up several notches. Goddess, how was I going to get myself out of this mess? Without my elements did I have the strength to break all of these nylon straps holding me to the gurney? I was starting to feel better physically, but I didn't have my full strength back.

"Hold." Harkins said and the gurney came to a full stop. "Interns will take it from here."

The intern or tech who'd been talking to Harrison moments ago kept his voice low when he said, "My fucking pleasure."

Eight techs walked away from the gurney, including the two who'd been behind me, leaving only four interns. Nice. I liked those odds a lot better.

I could see now without all the bodies around me.

Banks of computers, monitors and workstations along two walls. I frowned as I saw monitors showing the forest along with huge screens with satellite images on them along with a panel that I believed was from heat-seeking radar. On a green background, forms that were yellow, orange, and red clustered in some areas.

Then I noticed one group of solid red forms. Was that how Johnson was finding the Werewolves? I imagined they had different energy signatures, like we'd discovered Demons did.

My breath burned my throat when I sucked it in as I turned my head. Cages lined the third wall. The top cages were empty.

Inside a bottom cage was a Were I assumed was Kveta. Angel was in one of the smallest cages next to the pregnant Were. Panic gripped me when I saw there were no Werewolf pups. Not one of the three were there.

Angel was lying on her side, her wrists cuffed to one of the metal bars of the cage. Her knees were bent because the cage was too small for her to stretch out her legs.

Something snapped inside me when I saw that her jeans were even more soaked with blood than before. She had to be weak from loss of blood. Her face was pale behind her bruises, but her blue eyes did not reflect a fraction of hopelessness. No, they were filled with rage and intelligent calculation as she stared at the interns pushing the gurney.

Angel's gaze met mine and she gave a slight nod as if acknowledging some secret way that we were going to get out of this situation. Now might be a really good time to possess the gift of telepathy.

I frowned to myself as Harkins typed a code into a numeric keypad before placing her face up to a protruding white eye scanner. A glass door whooshed open.

The interns shoved the gurney through an opening in a glass wall that was just high enough to allow the gurney through. A sucking sound, then air pumped in with fresh oxygen washed over my skin and dried my eyes.

The gurney rolled into a brightly lit room that smelled of antiseptic and strange odors. The gurney came to a complete stop a couple of feet from where it had been pushed in.

For the first time since I'd been strapped onto the gurney, I was alone. The nylon restraints felt beyond tight against my skin as I tried to shift my body. The interns and techs had done a good job, restraining me with about ten straps—not a bit of wiggle room.

Still, I strained against the straps. My muscles tightened and I gritted my teeth as I tried to move. They must have used some kind of advanced-design nylon straps, because I couldn't budge them or even stretch them. Not even a fraction. It didn't help that my elements weren't with me.

With my teeth clenched in frustration, I turned my head and took in the room. A large sterile area filled with medical instruments, possibly close to every kind imaginable. A bank of computers and other sophisticated equipment made it look like a high-tech laboratory. It put my friend James's lab to shame.

Noise came from the general area I'd just been pushed from. The four interns were in an airlock area stocked with red sterilized suits that looked like they were made of the same material as the green suits everyone wore around this place. The interns were changing into the red suits and tossing the green ones they'd been wearing into a big container in one corner.

A scream of complete and utter frustration rose in my throat, trying to force its way out.

A glass door slid open and the four red-suited techs walked into the room. All of them paused as they studied me. My heart beat faster and faster. With a sucking sound, the door slid shut behind them.

"This one ought to be fun." Harkins sounded amused. "Look at it. Purple skin. Blue hair. Fangs."

Amethyst, popped into my mind. *Not purple, amethyst.*

For Anu's sake, there was a lot more that I should be concerned about right now than the color of my skin.

Rage, frustration, helplessness roared through me as they neared me. I bared my fangs and felt the dangerous white flash in my eyes.

Three of the interns came to an abrupt stop. Nervous-looking.

"Come on." Harkins continued toward me, and I could see a look of confidence on her face behind her mask. If only I could rip away that mask, I would tear her head off.

The interns went to various parts of the examination room, each looking like they had done this before. No doubt they had with the Werewolves, and maybe Angel, too.

One of the interns pushed a wheeled metal table beside the gurney and panic started to run through my veins. On that table were test tube bottles along with the rubber strap and needle used to collect blood.

Next to the test tubes were several instruments, including a razor-sharp slim knife. A wrist blood-pressure cuff, an ear thermometer, a stethoscope, bandages, cotton balls, even a tongue depressor—as if they'd get that thing into my mouth.

What made my skin crawl the most were the numerous syringes filled with clear fluid. What was in those syringes?

I turned my head to look out the glass walls and saw the cages with the female Were and Angel.

My Drow collar seemed to grow hot against my skin.

Transference. The word jumped into my mind again with the ageless, intelligent voice. As if it was my own voice talking to me from my distant future.

Yes, transference. I had to do it.

My focus grew so intense it felt like my entire body was a beating heart. *Thud, thud, thud.* I hadn't been able to do the transference in the stone room, but now . . . Again, I told myself my father was wrong.

I concentrated. Imagined my body leaving the gurney and this room. I pictured standing on the outside of the glass walls looking in at the shocked interns. And I saw myself opening the cages and setting Angel and Kveta free.

The magnitude of my focus doubled. Tripled. My body began to shake, visibly. I saw the interns frown with the exception of Harkins.

"What's wrong with it?" came a faint voice.

"Faking." Harkins. "It wants to throw us off so that we'll stop."

"Are you sure?" said another intern.

"Shut up." Harkins approached with one of the needles filled with clear fluid. She reached for my upper arm with her gloved hand, using her other hand to angle the needle toward my bicep.

I was barely conscious of the intern. Instead my wavering eyesight grew dimmer while I focused on attempting the transference. It was like looking at a picture, then unfocusing my eyes to find the three-dimensional object inside the two-dimensional drawing.

Everything dimmed. I saw nothing but pinwheels of faint light in front of my eyes. My stomach cramped. A roar like thunder stormed inside and outside of my body.

I was going to rip apart.

I spun into a dizzying black void with bright, whirling stars.

FOURTEEN

The transference was such a shock that I landed on my hands and knees. My clenched jaws reverberated from the impact.

I was out of my restraints and out of the examination room. I'd done it. I'd really done it.

Dizziness made my head spin and for a moment I couldn't move from my hands and knees. I'd never enjoyed going through a transference with my father, and I now knew I liked it even less on my own.

The effects of performing a transference for the first time by myself had my stomach churning. A sudden rush of bile rose in my throat. I vomited on the stone floor and groaned. The thought flickered through my mind that at least I didn't throw up much because Johnson had never provided me with a meal. Considering he thought I wasn't anything more than an "it," he probably would have given me dog chow, anyway.

I rubbed the back of my hand across my lips and wiped my hand on my pants before spitting out some of the acidic taste still in my mouth. Through my impaired sense of smell I thought I caught the smell of dust.

Through my hazy vision it looked much dirtier than I'd expected outside the examination room.

My sight remained as dim as when I'd first started the transference. My blue hair fell over my face as I shook my head while trying to clear my vision. Had to get up. Had to get up!

It seemed like much longer, but only a few moments had passed from the time I landed on my knees to this second. I had to hurry before the interns came at me with that spray. As quickly as time had passed, I hoped I had time to lock the interns in the examination room.

Careful not to step in my own vomit, I lunged to my feet to help Angel and the female Were. When I was standing, I froze.

I wasn't outside the examination room. I wasn't even in a place I'd been to before. My gut told me I was in the same building, but I had no idea where.

"Where am I?" In a slow turn I examined the room. It wasn't the transference that kept my vision dim. It was the room. The only light came from the partially open door, and through the doorway I saw a hallway with a single light bulb outside hanging from the ceiling.

Equipment surrounded me that had to be decades old, probably late 1950s, early 1960s. Looked to be around the time of the launch of the first men to the moon. I could picture men in headsets, wearing starched white short-sleeved shirts, pencil-thin black neckties, and thick black-framed eyeglasses. All sitting in front of the monitors and instrument panels crammed on top of desks lined along two walls.

Dust felt thick and powdery beneath my bare feet as I walked closer to a row of the antiquated monitors and panels that included dials, knobs, buttons, black telephones.

Letters had been stenciled in large dark-red letters on a few dusty black notebooks left on the surfaces in front of the electronics. The pages that peeked out of some of the notebooks were yellowed and fragile, and I avoided touching them. Didn't seem right to disturb them for some reason.

Over the stenciled letters on top of one bound notebook, I brushed away dust that clung to my fingers. "NORAD," I said. "This place was run by NORAD."

I was familiar with the acronym for the North American Aerospace Defense Command and had a good idea of the public's lack of knowledge of what the agency had done all those years ago. Norms' relatively small amount of knowledge, that was. I liked American history and I knew the agency had been considered vital during the Cold War decades before I came to the earth Otherworld.

"Bless it." I looked up at the stone ceiling. "We could be a mile belowground for all I know."

I settled back on my bare heels and settled my hand on the back of one of the chairs in front of the monitors and panels. Through the thick layer of dust, the chair's material felt as if it would crumble beneath my fingers. I rubbed my palm on my pants.

My mind churned over the possibilities of how the crazy modern-day scientists and their teams had ended up here, doing what they were doing.

Only two viable possibilities that I could see. That

was unless this NORAD facility was still active—which sure didn't look like that was the case. "As if NORAD would hire a fanatical religious scientist," I said as I stared around the room, "who believes it's his God-given duty to wipe out all paranorm beings with a manufactured biological weapon." I gave a hollow laugh.

Why this place was in operation now had to be that Johnson had stumbled over a decommissioned and abandoned secret NORAD underground facility in the Catskills.

That, or Johnson had somehow known about this particular location and now used it for his experiments.

I ran my fingers along a dusty desktop. "Maybe he was employed by NORAD way back when." Johnson looked like he was close to seventy, so it was possible that he had worked for the agency here when he was in his early twenties.

From some of what I'd read—all unofficial—there were abandoned facilities across the United States that the government tried to keep from public knowledge. Looked like this one had been kept a well-guarded secret until Johnson and his scientific team invaded it. A lot of paranorms knew far more about earth-government-guarded secrets than norms did, but we kept the knowledge to ourselves.

My strength was slowly returning and I almost felt back to normal. I let out a rush of breath. "As normal as I can without my elements," I mumbled. I still didn't sense any magic except for the waterfall, and wherever I was in this facility was not close to the fall.

My muscles loosened as I flexed them and rolled my

shoulders. I smiled. No more weakness from the after-effects of the transference or from the noise emitter. I could take on several of Johnson's techs—in a fair fight. Using the spray they had been downing us with wasn't exactly what I'd call fair.

I placed my hands on the soft leather covering my hips, wishing I had my daggers, buckler, and the Kahr K40 Johnson had taken from me. Could I possibly find them before I got to Angel and Kveta?

I continued to look around the room like it might give me some kind of answer to my problems: figuring out where I was, finding Angel and the Werewolf and releasing them, locating our weapons, searching for the pups, and getting us to an exit and safely out of this Goddess-blessed place—and all before the next full moon.

With everything I had, I prayed the pups were safe.

My fighting suit was ripped from the bullet to my knee, and my bare midriff, arms, and feet were streaked with blood and dust. Even though shifting had healed me, I'd still have blood on my face, too, from the abuse it had taken earlier. I grimaced, feeling sticky and covered in dirt.

I used the Elvin word for "clean," which also repaired my pants, and I felt a little more refreshed. I was ready to kick some scientist butt.

Could it possibly be as easy as in the movies where old equipment would spark to life and show me all the rooms in the facility on these monitors? Possibly even the outside exits?

Instead of rolling my eyes I shook my head, but still looked for a power switch or some kind of breaker on

the walls and everywhere else that I could think of.
Nope. Nothing that I could find that would magically
make everything work.

I pushed buttons beside the monitors, pulled switches
below them, holding out hope that I could spark something to life. Oh, and not launch a missile heretofore
forgotten. That ridiculous thought did make me roll my
eyes.

Buttons and switches felt gritty and useless beneath
my touch. I didn't waste much time on that equipment.
A girl had to try, though.

When I went to the door, I listened, the silence deep
and thoughtful, as if memories of the past were still
imprinted in the air. The door creaked when I opened
it, the sound echoing down the hallway. I winced at
the sound, but heard nothing that told me anyone had
heard.

The dimly lit hallway was dusty under my bare feet
like the room had been, telling me that this part of the
facility also wasn't in use. Where was I?

"The lights are on, but nobody's home," I murmured.

Some of the bulbs were burned out along the hallway. The dull and dusty light bulbs hung from tubes that
no doubt held electrical wires. I was probably lucky any
of them were lit at all. Next to the electrical tube ran a
larger pipe, probably for water.

I kept close to the walls, which were carved from
stone like every other hallway or room I'd been in. Here,
though, cracks in the walls jagged down to the floor, and
in some areas the stone floor, was cracked, too.

A fat gray rat startled me. I jumped back and cursed
in Drow under my breath.

The nasty thing scuttled in front of me before dodging into a wide crack in one wall. I shuddered. I'd faced far worse, but rats were disgusting virus-carrying creatures. Things like that would only be allowed to live in Underworld, never in Otherworld. Sometimes I did wonder if Otherworld was too perfect, but not when it came to rats.

Putting the vile thing out of my mind, I moved faster down the hallway, which went on and on. And on. When I finally heard voices they almost caught me off guard. The hallway had taken a wide curve, which was probably why I hadn't heard them sooner.

I pressed myself against the wall, listened, and studied the hallway ahead.

Male voices. Four who took turns speaking or talked over each other. The hallway was brighter from the direction of the voices. A slash of light about the size of a doorway cut across the hallway.

"Nothing on any of the monitors." The voice was Marton's.

"Purple skin, blue hair," one man said in a sarcastic nasal tone. "You have got to be kidding."

"No joke." It was Harrison who replied. "It even has fangs."

"It," I said, then made a hissing sound under my breath.

"Creepiest thing I ever saw." Terrence, whose voice I recognized immediately, was speaking now. "It looked totally human today, then changed into weird-ass colors and grew fangs."

I ground my teeth, then took a deep breath and shook out my arms, trying to relax my muscles to be limber and ready. Any moment now.

Marton said in a disgusted tone, "Can't believe the fucking interns let it go."

"Said it disappeared." Harrison sounded enthusiastic rather than disgusted. "The way we had it strapped in, there was no way it could have escaped without some kind of magic or something."

Nasal tech snorted. "Magic. Right."

"Whatever the hell happened," Marton said, "we've got to find it. Dr. Johnson will take the same gun he used on Lawson to kill all of us."

I would be delighted to do the job for Johnson. Now.

Every single time the men called me "it," I pictured myself breaking bones. All of their bones in each of their bodies.

The beat of my heart sounded loud in my mind, but it wasn't from fear. It was from the anticipation of taking these men by surprise and making sure they wouldn't be hurting anyone for a very long time. If ever again.

Without my elemental magic, my only weapon right now was my body. Good enough for me.

My bare feet were silent as I jogged down the hallway toward the light and toward the men, who were now discussing the best places to look for me and who they were going to send to each location.

I reached the doorway and stood just outside it. I peeked in and saw five men. The first four were arguing. The fifth was a huge redhead standing a few feet away from the other techs, his arms folded across his massive chest.

All of the men had their head masks off and none of them were armed with that spray. Guns, knives I could handle, plenty of which were sheathed in belts at each man's waist. Handling spray-wielding interns was another story.

"Okay, men." Marton, the man who looked like a big, blond Swede, gave one loud clap of his hands. "Let's get that freak."

They weren't going to get the chance.

Freak. The comment grated on my nerves, adding fuel to the fire burning inside. A lot of fuel.

The techs pulled on their facemasks, but with these odds, it didn't matter if I couldn't get to their faces.

Marton was the first out the door. From my position to the side of the door, I bent my leg to my chest and then thrust my bare heel down on his knee. The crack of bone echoed in the hallway as he screamed behind his mask.

He was so big none of the other men could see what had just happened, and I moved too fast to give them a chance.

I grabbed Marton's head and jerked it down at the same time I brought my knee up. His neck snapped from the power of my thrust. At full strength I have the power to kill in just about any way possible.

Before Marton's body slumped to the floor, I grabbed the hilt of his large knife and jerked it from the sheath on his belt. He fell too fast for me to snatch his handgun.

Harrison stood in the doorway looking stunned. "What the fuck?" he said as he shot his hand toward his holstered gun.

Those were Harrison's last words as I plunged Marton's knife into his heart. I jerked the bloody knife from Harrison's body right before his corpse collapsed onto Marton's.

No time to grab Harrison's gun or other weapons. Terrence stood a few feet inside the doorway, gripping a large handgun and training it on me. I dodged back around the side of the door just in time to hear the gun's report and see chips of stone fly directly across the hallway from where the bullet had hit the wall.

"Did you get the bitch?" Nasal Man shouted.

"Shut the fuck up." Terrence said in a low whisper that no doubt I wasn't supposed to hear. My enhanced hearing made it easy for me to catch every word. "You'll give away your position. There's only one of those beasts and we can take it."

Adrenaline poured through my body in an intense rush. That shot had been close, but it had also given me an extra edge to my power. In my Drow form and as a Night Tracker, I thrived on danger. Being shot at or physically attacked qualified as danger. I was a total adrenaline junkie.

"What do we do?" Nasal Man wheezed in his version of a whisper.

"Wait for her." This had to be the redhead speaking in a deep, throbbing tone that still managed to be low enough to barely hear. He sounded calm, confident, and I knew he was the one man to be reckoned with. "She will come to us."

"*It*, you mean," Nasal Man said in a nasty voice. "*It* will come to us."

The redhead didn't respond and the room went quiet. The redhead scored points for referring to me as she. Too bad I'd have to kill him.

While the men talked, I squatted beside the door, blood pounding through my veins. I wiped blood from the side of Marton's knife onto my pants and then carefully eased the knife near the floor. It was just enough through the doorway that I hoped it couldn't be seen and I could use the shiny surface like a mirror.

It was obvious the now-dead guy didn't know the first thing about knife fighting because having a knife shiny enough to reflect light could get a person killed. But for now, it could serve a purpose—providing it didn't reveal me in the same way.

I tilted the blade so that I could see into the room from where I crouched. Terrence was bent at his waist, easing his way closer to the door, his gun gripped in both of his hands, the barrel pointed toward the doorway.

The moment he got close enough to the doorway I lunged upward, forward-flipped, twisted, and landed in a crouch on the opposite side of the doorway. Like I'd hoped, my movement caught him completely off guard.

He started to swing the barrel of his gun toward me but I flung the knife straight for his forehead. It buried itself to the hilt in his brain.

Terrence collapsed onto his backside, sprawled into an unnatural position.

Again I dodged away from the doorway just in time. Several gunshots from inside the room spattered the stone across the hallway and nicked the doorframe.

"Fuck," Nasal Man said, and it wasn't in a whisper.

"Quiet." The redhead spoke in a low, very slow and deadly tone that made me shiver. "If you're not, you're dead. I'll be the one to kill you."

Nasal Man shut up.

The silence was eerie for a few moments. I couldn't reach any of the dead men's weapons without exposing myself, and I no longer had the knife to use as a mirror. Or a weapon.

I looked around the hallway. Nothing but stone walls and three dead men. My gaze traveled up the wall to the ceiling of the hallway. Above was the metal pipe that ran alongside the lights, along with the larger one that piped in water.

A very light scuff on the floor inside the room told me one of the men was close enough to swing around that door and shoot me.

I rose from my crouch and backed up, my steps quick and light. I rounded a corner—thankfully to a more empty hallway along with a few closed doors. The room with the two remaining living men was out of sight now.

With ease I hopped up, grasped the water pipe, and then balanced on it like a cat. I moved along it on my hands and knees back toward the room. I paused just a couple of feet from the room as Nasal Man came into view.

"It's gone," he said as he looked up and down the hallway. He might sound like an idiot, but by the way he handled his gun it was obvious he knew what he was doing. "Now what the fuck do we do?"

Redhead wasn't wearing his mask like the others. He remained silent as he stood inside the doorway. His gun was still sheathed along with his daggers. Confident bastard, wasn't he?

A chill ran down my spine. Could he sense me

somehow? One of those latent psychics Rodán said were on the earth Otherworld? I wasn't going to wait to find out.

I gripped the water pipe and swung down in a fast movement. I landed on Nasal Man's shoulders, grasped his head in my hands, twisted it, and snapped his neck.

Before he even dropped, I back-flipped off his shoulders and landed in a crouch.

Redhead reacted faster than I expected. He swung his leg out and caught me in the face with his boot.

The impact sent me sliding across the stone floor, so much pain shooting through my head and jaw that I was almost dizzy from it.

Adrenaline and training helped me get to my feet in a rush.

I expected Redhead to reach for one of his weapons but he walked toward me. Stalked was more like it. A big, hulking powerhouse of a man. It would be a shame to kill such a fine specimen.

My breathing was light even though my head hurt like crazy. I waited for him, my stance loose, easy.

"Tough bitch, aren't you?" Redhead actually sounded impressed. "Took down four trained men and didn't break a sweat."

"Who trained them?" I moved slightly, trying to find the best place to attack him. "Daffy Duck? Bugs Bunny, maybe?" The Looney Tunes cartoon references made me think of Adam, a distraction on my part, a stupid thing to have done.

Redhead feinted with his right, then lunge-punched

me with his left. He should never have caught me off guard, but he did. His fist hit my solar plexus.

If I had been an inexperienced fighter, the hit would have taken me down. It knocked some breath from me but I ignored it, spun, and caught him on the side with a solid kick.

The man was made of steel. He didn't even rock to the side.

Instead, he grasped my ankle and twisted it.

I moved in the same direction as his motion, flipping sideways so that he couldn't damage my ankle. I twisted out of his grip and landed on one knee.

He dove for me and I decided to take Redhead down, I was going to have to play dirty. I thrust myself forward at the same time he tried to reach for me.

I punched his testicles as hard as I could—and almost broke my hand. The man either had steel balls or was wearing a protective cup. Right then my money was on steel balls.

Pain shot through my fist but I didn't have time to think about that. He picked me up by my waist and swung my head toward the stone wall.

I grasped handfuls of his green suit, my back slamming into the wall instead of my head. An electrical current traveled like lightning through my spine, shooting pain through every extremity of my body.

He was still holding me when my back hit the wall. Thinking about the pain wasn't an option.

I rammed my palm up and jammed his nose so hard I crushed it.

"Fuck!" Tears flushed down Redhead's face, an

automatic bodily response to what I'd done. He couldn't have stopped it if he tried.

His eyes were filled with blood and tears as he released me. I landed lightly on my feet, reached forward, and jerked his handgun out of its holster.

Enough of this.

The second bullet to his brain dropped him.

FIFTEEN

Redhead's gun and a nice-sized jagged-edge dagger from his belt were perfect. I looked down at once-intelligent eyes that now stared into infinity. It really was a shame I'd had to kill him. But it was him or me, and I'd take me every time.

I stuck the gun in my pants, near my hip and low enough where it couldn't be seen above the waistband. I didn't have anywhere to put the dagger, so I carried it. Adrenaline continued to pump through me, and I felt sticky from Redhead's blood that had rushed from his nose onto my chest.

Noise from ahead echoed down the hallway and I stopped moving and pressed myself against a wall. I glanced up and frowned when I saw that the lights had changed and there wasn't an exposed water pipe. The ceiling covering the electrical wires and water pipe looked new and made of a prefabricated material. It made the hallway ceiling lower.

Voices accompanied the next sounds. Footsteps. I looked to either side of me. A door on my left. Nothing on my right. I chose the door.

Which was locked.

Voices coming closer. Female this time. Two, judging by the sound of their footsteps.

Using my strength, I twisted the knob, hard. The locking mechanism broke. The sound was so loud, how could it not be heard all over the station?

"What was that?" one of the females said.

"Maybe it's that blue-haired beast that the interns let escape," said the other. "Do you have your bottle of spray?"

"Of course."

A quick scan of the room told me no one was there. I started to close the door when I saw I'd left blood all over the doorknob from my palm. Blood had covered my palm when I'd jammed Redhead's nose up and crushed it. I said the Elvin word for clean, which made the smears vanish from the doorknob. It also cleansed the blood from me, and I closed the door as quietly as I could.

I gripped Redhead's dagger as I leaned my back against the door and waited until I heard the chatty techs or interns pass by.

When I felt it was safe, I took in the room. It was an office, a large study. An extremely nice one that looked like it belonged to a Harvard professor as opposed to someone in an abandoned NORAD facility below ground.

The room was, in truth, luxurious. A mammoth cherrywood desk commanded the right side of the room and the walls were painted deep burgundy. The desk was neat with almost no papers on its glass-covered surface. It did have a large, sleek, flat-screen computer monitor. It had a matching cherrywood extension to one side with a printer on it, and a stack of papers beside it.

A nameplate with *Joseph A. Johnson, Ph.D.* in script across it was front and center. To the left was a paperweight in the shape of a shield, with a paper and what looked like a couple of photos beneath it.

Cherrywood shelves lined with medical books and other bound reference materials covered the wall to my right, behind the desk.

The wall in front of me had hardbound volumes of fiction novels, mostly classics. Arranged on the shelves were different sizes and shapes of framed photos. They looked like family photos from where I stood.

I pushed away from the door and walked toward the shelf. The pictures included a man with the same eyes as the one called Dr. Johnson. From what I had been able to make out of his features behind his mask, I had no doubt it was him.

In the various photographs Johnson was standing with children and perhaps siblings, parents, and grand-parents. Some photos were old, faded, but a few could have been taken yesterday.

I looked away from the photos and ran my fingers along a few of the volumes. *The Adventures of Huckleberry Finn, All Quiet on the Western Front, Brave New World, Catch-22, Catcher in the Rye, Gone with the Wind, The Grapes of Wrath, Lord of the Flies* . . . All in alphabetical order.

Then I blinked in surprise. On the lowest shelf were an assortment of paranormal fiction books that included Philip Pullman's "His Dark Materials" trilogy and Stephenie Meyer's "Twilight" series.

The sight of all of those paranorm fiction books on Johnson's shelves was puzzling. A man who believed non-humans should be eradicated, reading books involving paranorms? A man who believed in God, keeping the books by Pullman, who killed God in the trilogy, the author also being a self-proclaimed atheist?

Maybe that had something to do with Johnson's hate of the paranormal.

To my left was a wall and large glass-fronted case containing shelves of what might be considered collector's items. For a white supremacist. The things inside it made my body hot with fury. I wanted to take the dagger and stab at it, shatter the glass and destroy everything inside.

An American Patriotic Christians, or APC, red hood perched on top of a red folded robe. Next to it was a plaque with a picture of Hitler and a Nazi swastika in black beside it. A shield with a cross and other markings, a symbol of Aryan Racial Purity Now, or ARPN—a white supremacist organization—was next to the plaque. I cursed in Drow at the doctor and those who had the same beliefs. My curses were far more potent than earthbound sayings.

On another shelf was a yellowed magazine with *Aryan Racial Purity Now* printed across it. Below the organization name, my gaze settled on the name of an article that was included inside the magazine.

In smaller letters below the article's title, "In the Service of God," was printed in italics *by Dr. Joseph A. Johnson*. The magazine was dated decades past, 1988.

A more recent copy of *Aryan Racial Purity Now*, the cover glossy with newness, was printed only a month ago. On the cover an article proclaimed the title "Ungodly" with a byline of Dr. Joseph A. Johnson.

I ground my teeth and clenched my fists at the memory of what Johnson had said to me in the stone room: *"God has given me this task, to destroy what does not belong in this world."*

Beside the magazine was a plain wooden cross in front of a black and white photograph of three burning crosses. The picture looked like it could have been taken back in the 1960s when APC had burned several African-Americans alive.

The anger surging through me magnified with everything I saw, including old and more recent framed photos of Johnson with known modern-day white supremacists. APC had been a suit-and-tie organization, where the men were considered professional businessmen from a variety of careers. APC had gone underground and was replaced by ARPN, which was almost entirely opposite, with few professional businessmen publicly supporting the organization.

In my studies of American history, I had found these practices beyond appalling. They were sickening, and it sometimes made me wonder why I liked living in the Earth Otherworld.

But in my heart I knew most of the earth Otherworld's people were not anything like Johnson and those he associated with. *They* were the minority.

On the fourth wall beside the door were all of Johnson's framed certificates proclaiming his doctoral degrees.

My body burned with anger as I walked to the spotless glass-topped desk. Near the eight-inch-tall, four-inch-wide paperweight in the shape of a shield was the richly designed nameplate with *Joseph A. Johnson, Ph.D.* in script across it.

Considering Johnson's intention of eradicating paranorms, as well as what he kept in his display cases, Joseph might be for Stalin and the A. could stand for Adolf. The thoughts of those men made my stomach churn with disgust. Anger.

Come to think of it, I hadn't seen a single human in the facility who would be considered a minority on earth. Everyone as white as white can be with very Anglo names.

Behind the desk were two lower shelves I hadn't seen from anywhere I'd been standing previously. I squatted beside the shelves and examined the materials on them. When I saw what they were, I wasn't about to touch them. It was like they would contaminate me just by contact.

Of the two bookshelves, one entire shelf was devoted to tomes on biochemical and biological warfare, neurogenetics, genetics, and genetic atlases. Books on social engineering and theories of intelligence seemed odd next to the other books. I muttered more Drow curse words that sliced the air.

I swallowed at the thought again of Johnson being able to manufacture a virus that would wipe out all paranorms.

The bottom shelf was filled with more books and bound newsletter collections, but these were all devoted to white supremacy. Sick.

Both concerned and disgusted, I looked away from the shelf and stood to face the desk. I studied the paperweight and saw that it was the Aryan Racial Purity Now shield in bronze with an engraved gold plate at its base that read:

DR. JOSEPH A. JOHNSON

FOR OUTSTANDING CONTRIBUTIONS

TO ARYAN RACIAL PURITY NOW

A shudder traveled down my spine and I almost backed away because of the negative energy surrounding the paperweight. But the shield pinned down a memo on yellow paper along with the edges of a couple of photographs. With such negative energy, no way was I going to touch the paperweight with my hands, but I wanted to see what was under it.

I took the dagger I was holding and pushed at the bronze shield. I'd only intended to move it off the paper and photos, but it tipped over and landed hard with a cracking sound. It splintered the glass on Johnson's desktop. So much for stealth.

The memo had slid away, revealing a photo with another picture under it. The corner of the memo was still tucked under the paperweight. I set the dagger on the desk. My fingers trembled as I ignored the memo and picked up the two photographs. They were recent and taken with a high-quality camera. So recent my stomach churned.

The top photo was of the Werewolf camp, as it had looked the day Olivia and I had arrived. The same six pups that had been playing nearby were in the picture, as were the two Werewolf males eating a haunch of raw venison and the other Weres we had seen.

The second was a photo of Olivia.

My blood ran cold.

Olivia. Why Olivia?

The reason why it was her hit me hard in my belly and my fingers trembled enough that the photos almost slipped from my grasp.

It was because she was the only individual in the camp who could clearly be considered a minority by her exotic appearance and her golden-brown skin. If they were human, all of the Werewolves in Beketov's camp would be considered Anglo because of where they had emigrated from. As it was, they were being experimented on.

Heart pounding, I dropped the photos on the desktop and snatched the yellow memo. The corner pinned beneath the paperweight ripped away and remained under the toppled bronze shield. I didn't care. All that mattered was the one line on the paper, written in a messy scrawl:

The Black will be disposed of immediately.

I crushed the paper in my fist and held my arm to my cramping stomach, almost bending over double. Dear Goddess, had they done anything to Olivia?

A sense of frantic urgency rushed through me like I might fly to her. I had to find Olivia. Make sure she was all right. Protect her. She might think she could protect herself in any situation, but I wasn't taking the chance of something happening to my friend.

The transference. If I could do it from the examination room, maybe I could do it from here. I closed my eyes and focused on moving my body and soul through the rock and dirt above the former NORAD facility.

I focused so intently that my head hurt, pain shooting through it as if a knife was jabbed into my skull. It wasn't the transference I was feeling, it was the power I was using to focus on my goal.

When I knew it was hopeless, I opened my eyes and my body sagged from the exertion. But fear for Olivia charged me almost immediately.

How had they managed to get pictures, and the Weres not know the cameras were there? The spray, of course.

I took a step to start running out of the room.

Just as I was turning, I saw again the neat stack of papers on the table's cherrywood extension, next to the printer.

The papers drew me. Called to me. And not in a good way.

Stomach still cramping, I hurried and snatched the pile of papers from where they rested. My fingers shook as I saw the first printout.

It was a basic drawing showing the outline of a Werewolf in wolf form cut into quarters. It wasn't an adult. It was a pup.

I thought my heart might explode. I put the top paper under the others and saw another page with the pup being dissected down to its bowels. The sick feeling inside me balled with so many things it hurt. Fury at everything Johnson was doing and what he stood for; the need to get to Olivia; getting Angel out of here along with the pregnant Were; and the dire necessity to find and save the three pups.

I shoved that paper behind the first and scanned a typed memo.

From: Joseph A. Johnson, Ph.D., M.D.
To: Beatrice Harkins, Head Intern

With the newly acquired information that additional paranormal beings exist, and the possible discovery of our location, we no longer have the luxury of time.

My team and I will leave for Manhattan immediately to test the final samples on the three smallest beasts as well as the three other subjects we selected.

While I am gone, I expect you and your team to handle the two beasts most recently acquired. You and your team are to thoroughly experiment on them as we have all of the other beasts we have gathered. I expect extensive documentation.

This task is to be completed by the time I return.

Attached to this memo is a list of additional experiments you are to perform on the subjects.

Joseph A. Johnson, Ph.D., M.D.

I hadn't thought the sickness in my belly could get any worse, but I had been wrong. I put the memo behind the others and scanned the next papers. The following page discussed the serums he and the other scientists had developed. Most of it was technical jargon, not clear to me, but I got the overall impression that they were close to finding the virus they'd been working to develop.

The last two pages showed experiments divided into

two categories. The first was a list of what was to be performed on a live pup. The second half was a list of things to be done to the dissected pup.

My body trembled. Too many emotions to identify anymore.

I made sure Redhead's gun was still secure in the waistband of my pants. A maelstrom of emotions in my core and my desire to get to the pregnant Were, Angel, Olivia, and to find the pups churned within me. Not to mention the fact that we had to stop Johnson.

Had to hurry. I bolted toward the door.

I didn't realize I'd left the dagger on the desk until it was too late.

SIXTEEN

I yanked open the door of the study—

And came face to face with one of the biggest humans I'd ever seen. He wore no mask, had no suit. Just wore jeans, boots, and T-shirt. Close to seven feet tall, every part of his body down to his forearms was so muscular he looked like he could crush stone with his bare hands.

His features were blocky, Neanderthal in appearance, a scraggly beard on his jaws. Black eyes pierced me with his intention to rip my head off.

And he was ready for me.

I wasn't ready for him.

Before I could drop and roll away from him, his big hands grasped me around the neck, above my Drow collar.

I gave a wheezing, impotent cry as he swung me by my neck and slammed me against the stone wall behind him.

My skull cracked. Pain exploded in my head and back. Blood immediately gushed from the wound and down my neck, hot and sticky, into my fighting suit.

Through the growing fog of being unable to breathe,

and the pain, I fought to think of a way out of this. Could I reach the gun still stuffed at the waistband of my pants? Normally a human would never have been able to harm me. But I'd been stupid, and the injuries too extensive.

Neanderthal jammed his boot on one of my knees and I screamed as bone splintered.

Thoughts of reaching for my weapons flew away as pain took its place.

He swung me to the opposite wall, this time smashing my face and side against stone. My cheekbone splintered. The gun dug into my hip and my fading thoughts were of the fact that the weapon would be useless in my slackening grip.

My vision was going black from lack of oxygen and pain. Then Neanderthal grabbed my hand and twisted, snapping small bones. I screamed again and again.

He started to swing me by my neck toward the other wall again.

"Stop." Harkins's cold voice came through her suit's microphone. It sounded like she was beside the man bent on killing me. "We need it alive."

Neanderthal's swing came to an abrupt halt. He dropped me on the floor. My already damaged head hit the stone.

As I fought to breathe and tried to ignore all of the pain, I almost wished I would black out.

I couldn't. I had to remain conscious. Who else was there to help us get out of here?

"Put it in one of the cages by the others." Harkins looked down at me and my mind spun as I looked up and tried to focus on her face. Hard to see through her mask.

"Any particular one, Harkins?" Neanderthal surprised me with a voice that sounded intelligent rather than like a big, stupid mass of muscle with a brain the size and consistency of a raindrop. "Do you want her shackled?"

I choked and wheezed as he spoke, and couldn't help a groan of pain.

"It, Sanderson." Harkins scowled. "Not a she." Then she gave me a satisfied smile. "I don't think it is going anywhere after your attention."

"Whatever you want." Sanderson leaned down, this time grabbing me by the waist. "But it murdered my friends and three other techs." He slung me over his shoulder. My face slammed against his muscular back and bones in my cheek ground together. My wrist hung down, limp and useless. My shattered knee hit his chest and there was no holding back another scream.

I closed my eyes as I almost lost consciousness. Everything seemed to spin, and pain in my cheek, head, knee, wrist, and every other injury threatened to rip me apart, too. I would have vomited if anything had been in my stomach, but after the transference I'd lost what little had been inside.

Harkins disappeared from what functioned of my peripheral vision. "Oh, it won't be alive much longer. We have our task and then we can dispose of it."

Sanderson started moving in the direction Harkins had disappeared in. "Give it to me," Sanderson said.

"It will be in pieces when we finish working on it." Harkins's voice came from ahead. "Dr. Johnson's orders."

One couldn't even be able to call this a mess I'd gotten myself into. No, it was a situation that I had no idea how to escape from, or if I physically would be able to.

Even if I had my elemental magic. I thought about the waterfall and knew at that moment I didn't have the strength to call to it. I didn't know how to use so much water with so much magic in it in this condition.

I think Sanderson ensured his steps were rough enough to cause me to bounce against his back like a rubber ball. Human curses seemed appropriate for the moment.

Like, *What the fuck am I going to do now*? And, *I'm going to beat the shit out of Sanderson before I kill him*.

As if that was going to happen for a while.

With the extent of my injuries, there was no way I'd be able to do a transference. I'd been lucky before at nearly full strength. Really lucky. And who knew where I'd end up?

A creak of metal sounded distant. My eyes were still shut tight and I realized we were at a cage when Sanderson flung me into one. Not set me into one. Flung. I screamed as I hit the back bars, then collapsed onto the floor of it. The cage was so small there was no way to land but curled up with my knees to my chest on my side. My shattered knee was beneath me, throbbing and shrieking with pain.

I didn't open my eyes. Thankfully I wasn't lying on my crushed cheekbone or broken wrist. The uninjured part of my face rested on my arm that also hadn't been injured.

My body started to feel numb and I was almost beyond pain. Unfortunately, not completely. Passing out would really have been nice right then. Still, I fought slipping out of consciousness and managed to remain awake.

Sanderson slammed the cage door shut and bars hit my bare feet. The sound jarred my eardrums. I would have ground my teeth together if my cheekbone wasn't shattered. The click of a lock was loud in the room. I heard low voices. My brain was too addled to make out words.

It wouldn't be long until I shifted back to my human form. I could sense dawn coming soon. I would heal a little, but unfortunately I wouldn't heal like I do when I shift to Drow. I don't know why that is. But when I'm severely injured, I have to wait another twelve hours to fully return to normal—when I'm Drow again.

What was I going to do?

"Nyx." Angel's concerned voice was somewhere around me and echoed in my head. I was too disoriented and dizzy to tell what direction she was talking from. "How badly are you injured?"

My words came out raspy from my windpipe almost being crushed by Sanderson. "I'll live." I almost couldn't speak with my crushed cheekbone.

"Until they experiment on you," came a terrified female voice that shook as she spoke. She had a heavy Slavic accent. "I heard them speak. They may start with you while you are injured." Her words were loud enough to make my head hurt and I winced.

"Kveta, please be calm for Nyx's sake." Angel's voice was soothing. "She has injuries to her head that may cause her pain if we talk too loud."

"My apologies." Kveta spoke in a whisper this time,

for which I was very thankful. "What have they done to you?"

The only thing I could do at that moment was respond with a groan.

Blood dripped down the side of my face from my head injury. It trickled into my eyes as I opened them. I blinked several times. I didn't even have the strength to use the small amount of magic needed to use *Avanna* to cleanse myself of blood, especially what slid across my eyelids and into my eyes. My blue hair was matted with blood, too, and a lock of it lay in a clump across my cheek.

Angel gripped the bars of the cage, the side of our cages that we shared. With the cuts across her face and her double black eyes, she looked like she'd been beaten even more than the last time I saw her. But she was lucid, her eyes clear.

She reached through the bars and pushed my hair from my face in a careful motion, like I was fragile. Then she used her fingertips to wipe blood from my eyes and forehead before cleaning her hand on her bloodied jeans.

I could see better now. We were in cages on the floor. I frowned when I looked at the cage bars. "Why didn't you shift?" I squeaked out the words and I knew they were too low for anyone else to hear. I could barely hear them. "They're wide enough that this shouldn't hold you."

"We needed information." Angel glanced to the side, toward the techs and interns. "I've been waiting for the right time." She looked back at me. "I needed to know where you were and what plans they had for Kveta and where the pups are."

She continued with a note of frustration. "This place is always guarded. I could have taken out the techs and interns anytime I wanted, but I didn't know where to begin to search for you. And I couldn't leave Kveta."

"Smart," I said. "So they don't know your animal form?"

"No."

Angel looked thoughtful. "Will you heal when you shift back?"

I couldn't shake my head even though I almost tried automatically. "Not much when I become human." I sighed. "A little. Maybe enough to clear my mind or to be able to move my head. I think the wound on my skull might repair itself when I go human, but not my cheek, wrist, or knee."

"Fuck." The curse word didn't seem so strange coming from Angel right now, considering our situation.

A situation that felt almost hopeless. But I had always believed nothing was ever hopeless, and I was going to hold onto that thought with everything I had.

Nothing is ever hopeless.

"You have no choice now." I didn't know if I'd get full use of my voice until I shifted back to Drow. "You have to take your Doppler form and find help. I'm pretty much useless for a while."

Angel frowned and looked out of her cage again, in the direction of the voices. "I can take them."

"I have something that might help." I would have laughed if it was possible. "They didn't check me for weapons. I've got a handgun."

"Sweet." Angel's eyes met mine. The diamond-brightness that had been in them before we were captured had dulled some, but her intelligence and determination was still there. "Close enough for me to reach?"

"It's going to be a stretch." The thought of moving at all made me want to whimper. "The gun's at my hip." It still hurt where it had dug in when Sanderson had slammed that side of me against the wall.

After checking to see if any of the interns or techs were looking, Angel reached through the bars. Her fingers were two inches from being able to draw the weapon from my pants.

"Damn." She settled back and grasped the bars.

"Hold on." I bit my lip to hold back any screams as I shifted my body forward, using my hips and thigh. As the screams threatened to rip from my mouth, I thought I really was going to lose consciousness.

I forced myself forward enough that Angel could easily draw the gun from my pants after she checked to make sure we weren't being watched.

She brought the gun through the bars, careful that she didn't hit the gun against the metal. When she had it she sat cross-legged with the gun hidden between her thighs. She studied the interns and the techs, cool calculation in her eyes.

Angel raised the gun, holding it in a two-fisted grip as she aimed it at an intern. "Let's see if we've got a full cartridge."

The shots were louder than I expected. But the screams weren't.

I ignored all pain in my body as I craned my neck to watch. With a deliberate intensity, Angel took each tech and intern down with a single shot to their heads.

She eliminated the techs first, with the exception of one tech who flung himself behind a piece of medical equipment. Angel shot at the piece of equipment and I heard a scream of pain.

I was amazed by the complete calm on her features as she took out the three interns before they even had a chance to take a few steps.

The remaining tech peered from around the piece of medical equipment, pointing a gun at Angel. Angel didn't make a sound as a bullet buried itself in her shoulder. She repaid the tech by putting a bullet in his head.

"I'll shift and get out of the cage and go for help." Angel set the gun down, blood coating her shoulder. The wound would heal when she transformed, so I wasn't worried.

"Angel." My voice was a croak as I panicked. My mind had been so befuddled from being broken and slammed against the walls. I told her about the pups, the serums. "And Olivia. They plan to kill her. This nutjob is a white supremacist and because Olivia's not—"

"They want to do away with her." Fury shifted Angel's formerly calm features. "No way is that going to happen."

"You'd better hurry, before backup comes," I said. "Someone is bound to have heard the shots."

"I'm out of here." She looked at the weapon. "I'll shift back and take the gun with me so they don't think it was you. Then I'll ditch it before my next transformation."

I frowned. "Shifting from one form to the other so fast will weaken you."

"You'd better fake being out of it or they'll think you're responsible." She ignored me as she balled her hand into a fist and slipped her arm through the bars. "Better yet, you're better off unconscious."

I opened my mouth and widened my eyes right before she punched me.

SEVENTEEN

When I woke the pain was so great I almost slipped back into darkness. I was strapped to a gurney in the examination room. Again. It was quiet and I sensed I was alone.

Without looking I knew I had shifted to human form while I had been unconscious—I feel different as a human and unfortunately pain is more acute.

Thank goodness for shifting while being out of it. I don't know how I could have handled the additional pain of the transformation with the extent of my injuries.

Not to mention the interns strapping me to a gurney in this condition. It would have been excruciating. Suddenly I was more than grateful to Angel for knocking me out. Even though I wanted to be on the front lines, I knew I'd have hindered her more than helped her in my condition.

As I lay there, I identified each injury from top to bottom. My head felt a little better, as I'd thought it would as a result of the transformation. My neck still hurt, but the pain had lessened from where I'd nearly been strangled. I do heal faster than norms, but not from major injuries.

Where pain nearly crippled me was in my cheek, wrist, and knee. The bones had not mended. If anything, the areas hurt worse, as if the shift had jammed the bones together. I'm smaller as a human than as Drow. Not a lot, but enough to make a difference in how I feel. I sure hoped I'd slept a good, long time so that evening wasn't that far away. Right now I couldn't tell.

I was fortunate that I could turn my head in the direction of the area outside the examination room without rolling onto my cheek. I saw suited techs cleaning blood splattered on the floor and walls. Body bags housing corpses had been stacked to one side of the room. I couldn't have been out too long if they were still cleaning up blood.

Had Angel made it out okay?

My heart leapt. What about the pups and the pregnant Were? I squinted at the cages and relief flooded me as I saw Kveta in her cage, her belly swollen with her children.

The thought of anything happening to her and her babies shot sharp pains through my gut.

I took a deep breath, then another. What now?

At least my mind was clear so that I could search my thoughts for ideas on how to get us out of here. I would fight regardless of my injuries, but I had to be careful how I did it. I could handle a gun—if there just happened to be one lying around.

The only element available was the underground waterfall, which was filled with magic so powerful it sang to me. If I flooded the facility with just a few feet of water, that would put an immediate stop to the experiments and buy us some time.

Yes, that would work. Did I have enough strength? Could I control it or would I be unable to, like when the burst of electricity still in my body had caused the landslide?

Perhaps . . . if I was careful. I wasn't strong enough to do too much. I started to call to my water element with my mind. To my surprise I felt it respond at once, ready to do what I wanted it to.

Then I went still and let the element slide away.

Kveta. I looked in her direction. She was cramped in a bottom cage and could drown.

Pain shot through my cheekbone and head the moment I clenched my teeth with frustration and black spots flickered in my eyesight. Immediately I forced myself to relax. What could I do now?

Hope that Angel had been able to find her way out of the facility and was getting help.

"Little bitch." A man's voice was loud as he came into the area outside the examination room. "But I got it."

Sanderson. The big Neanderthal of a man lifted something by its tail.

A squirrel.

Angel.

She was fighting with everything she had, sharp teeth and nails, but Sanderson swung her back and forth, keeping her off balance. He wore a thick work glove. Strangely, he still didn't wear a suit. I wondered if Johnson would shoot him.

"It won't be doing anything." Sanderson opened up a tiny cage only big enough for a small animal.

No chance for such a petite creature as Angel in squirrel form to escape, considering the additional wire mesh around the close-fitting bars. Sanderson flung Angel into the tiny cage and used a padlock to secure the door. Angel looked as fierce and angry as I imagined a squirrel could look.

Sanderson took off the thick glove and pocketed it. "It'll just be waiting for someone to dissect it—alive."

Fury rushed through me. Anger at this entire situation and everything that had happened and everything that might happen.

The men were all speaking loud enough that I heard them clearly through the glass examination wall.

"I think we should just beat it, chop it into little pieces, and be done with it." A small man whose tone was sharp-sounding from his suit's microphone went up to the cage and poked his finger through the wire.

In a movement almost too fast to see, Angel darted forward and bit his finger.

The man screamed and blood poured from the missing tip of his finger.

Angel lifted the piece of finger with one tiny paw and I could almost see a human expression on her little squirrel face as she dropped the small hunk of flesh down through the mesh floor and into an empty cage below.

"I'll kill it!" the man screamed. While holding his bloody finger to his chest, he lunged for Angel's cage. "I'll kill it!"

Tiny squirrel Angel put her little paws on her hips and I knew she was smirking.

Two big techs grabbed the screaming man and pulled him away from the cage.

"Johnson will kill *you*, Barker," one of the men said.

"Might not be a bad idea to let him," the other tech holding Barker said. "I won't be too choked up about Johnson getting rid of this piece of shit."

Said piece of shit went still but continued to whimper as he cradled his arm to his chest.

All of their voices came out almost eerie from their microphones in their suits.

"Get out of here and get to the infirmary," the first tech said. "The thing might have infected you because you passed through the barrier and you were bitten. Remember how Johnson took care of Lawson?"

"I'll—I'll be okay. I'll go straight go to the infirmary." Barker scuttled down the hallway, stumbling as he ran.

Sanderson, the hulking mass of a man, headed in the same direction.

More techs showed up. By the blue armbands, there were four. Five interns and the techs turned their attention from Angel and looked through the glass of the examination room to stare at me.

"It looks so human now," I heard someone say as I glanced at Angel. I didn't try to pick out whose voice belonged to whom. "It was purple with blue hair."

The squirrel looked around her cage in a calculating way. Every direction including above and below. She moved the few inches she could and started exploring each side of the cage.   .

"Unbelievable," another tech or intern said. "The fangs were hideous."

I didn't let the comment bother me as I continued to watch Angel. She tugged at the wire mesh, testing it, then used her tiny paws to pull at the bars that were far slimmer than the bars of the larger cages. For a human, her bars might be easy to bend, but for a tiny animal, likely impossible.

"I said it before," a voice spoke up. "It's nothing but a freak."

Angel stood in the middle of the cage again, hands on hips, now studying the backs of the techs and interns who were staring at me.

"It looks so innocent now." The words of the female surprised me even as I watched Angel. "And pretty."

A flash of what Angel might be considering went through my mind as a brief vision. She was going to shift inside the cage and tear it apart with her much larger body.

"Give me a goddamned break." Harkins's voice was so familiar I didn't have to even think about who was speaking. "It's a fucking *thing*. Just like the dogs."

What would it do to Angel to try that? She could seriously injure herself, maybe fall off the other cages. She'd already shifted three times that I knew of. Twice before we were captured and the one time here. She had to be exhausted.

"And that other creature," a man said. "Turning into a squirrel? How freak-assed is that?"

Everyone looked at Angel, who went still but looked back at all with a contemptuous squirrel expression. I was getting really good at reading squirrel.

"Ought to fry it up." One man laughed as they all turned their gazes back on me and I forced myself to look away from Angel. Whatever she had planned, I didn't want to tip them off. "After you put some holes in this one."

"We're going to do better than holes." Harkins's laugh was snide. Mean.

The thumping of my heart picked up as she went through the procedure to open the sanitation room. She started putting on a red suit while other interns with red armbands followed her and did the same. Red. Like blood.

Adrenaline pumping through my body made me feel like I might combust. With no outlet, no way to use that adrenaline, I felt like I'd probably go crazy. The only benefit was that my injuries didn't hurt as much—my body was too charged to care.

A sound like a small explosion.

From outside the examination room.

I jerked my head in the direction of the sound.

Angel crouched on the floor below her shattered cage.

Blood poured from cuts on her face and forearms. Her T-shirt was ripped.

Angel rolled forward, straight for a tech, just as a shot rang out.

Stone chips exploded from the spot Angel had been in.

She slammed her fist against the tech's groin. He screamed and dropped his handgun.

Angel caught the gun. She was on her knees. Aimed and shot a tech.

She stretched out her body and rolled. Chips of rock exploded from the stone floor just behind every one of her movements.

No place to hide.

On her back, her knees bent and shoulders raised, Angel shot another tech.

A shot was fired from one of the men.

The bullet buried itself in Angel's neck.

Kveta screamed from her cage. "Angel!"

Shock at seeing Angel shot almost made me stop breathing.

But she kept going. She pulled off another shot and a third tech dropped.

The tech she'd taken down by the balls now had another weapon.

He turned the gun on Angel, who had blood flowing from the wound on her neck.

She put a bullet into him and dropped him for good.

Angel grabbed a second gun from the floor and stuffed it in the front of her jeans.

She lunged to her feet and pointed one weapon at the interns, who had locked themselves in the airlock.

"Stop!" a woman shouted beside me, and I started. I'd been so focused on watching Angel that I hadn't realized the woman had come up on me from my side. A wicked-looking syringe with a long needle was in one of her hands. She gripped the syringe like a dagger and held it a foot over my heart.

Angel came to a stop. Then raised one gun. The first shot shattered the examination room window. The second buried itself in the intern's heart.

The intern dropped, the clatter of the syringe somewhere close to her.

Angel faced the remaining interns.

Like an avenging angel, she showed no mercy. "Join your hateful Gods."

The airlock's glass window exploded with one bullet. Four more shots, and all that remained was a heap of red suits and crumpled bodies.

Angel tossed aside the weapon she'd been using and then grabbed one from a dead tech's hand. Then she found two knives on the second and third bodies she checked. She ripped the gun sheaths from the belts like paper. All the while she kept her eyes on the hallway behind the area we were all in.

Keeping low, she stuffed both sheathed daggers into her back pocket and went for Kveta.

Relief yet a continued sense of fear for all of us went through me. Strapped to the gurney, I was absolutely helpless and useless.

"Please hurry," Kveta said, her voice filled with panic. She was wearing a simple dress that was dirty and stained over her swollen belly.

While glancing over her shoulder at each hallway, Angel unsheathed one of the daggers and in two seconds had picked Kveta's cage's lock.

Angel helped the female Were from the cage. "Can you shift?" Angel asked. "You can move faster."

"Of course." Kveta began to transform.

When Kveta started shifting, Angel was already rushing through the shattered examination room window, straight for me. She took the same dagger she'd used to pick the lock to slice away the straps that had secured me to the gurney.

I felt relief compounded with fear that one of Johnson's techs or interns might come too fast for me to get off that gurney.

Even after I had seen what she'd done to that cage,

Angel's strength surprised me while she helped me off the gurney. If Drow had tear ducts, I would have been crying rivers from the pain shooting through me like jagged knives.

I balanced on one foot and used my good arm to brace myself on the gurney.

She stuffed the extra gun into the front of the waistband of my pants, in the right position that my good arm could reach across and draw it if I needed it. Then she put the second, now re-sheathed, dagger next to the gun.

I looked at her bloody neck. "Your neck—you need to shift."

"Surface wound." Angel slid her arm under mine on my side with the injured wrist so that my good arm would be free to grab either weapon.

When we were ready, I drew my gun, and she gripped hers. My broken wrist wasn't happy about being moved over her shoulder, but that was nothing compared to the screaming pain in my knee as I tried to keep it from moving and hop along with her in awkward steps.

Her strength fed my own, though, and I found I could move faster as we went. Stepping through the broken window was the biggest challenge so far. I almost fell and brought Angel down with me, but she managed to get us both through.

Kveta was waiting, sitting on her haunches.

My senses came alive the moment we were balanced again.

Kveta's head swiveled in the direction of the right hallway. She braced herself on all fours, her hackles raised, teeth bared. A low rumble came from her throat.

"More than one—almost here." I could feel life forces coming toward us in a rush. "Four, I think."

Angel and I both raised our weapons.

Kveta stayed by our sides and I didn't think she would move no matter what we said.

Angel's voice was low, hard as stone. "Whatever comes out of that hallway, no mercy."

I nodded even though a strange feeling tugged at my senses. "Something's wrong, Angel."

"No mercy," she repeated.

Her gun was steady as she kept it aimed.

Mine was, too.

Three men and one woman rushed out of the hallway.

EIGHTEEN

Olivia, Ice, Joshua, and Adam.

Adam? The fact that Adam was here made me wonder if I'd started hallucinating.

I sagged in relief against Angel and she took my weight with no problem. Fortunately, she hadn't shot any of them.

Ice and Joshua kept their backs to us, their guns covering each hallway entrance.

Adam and Olivia started toward us and Kveta growled.

"They're our friends," I hurried to say and Kveta relaxed her stance.

Thank the Goddess neither Olivia or Adam tried to hug or touch me when they reached me and Angel. Not that Olivia was the hugging type.

"Jesus," Olivia said as she looked at us.

"Christ," Adam said at the same time.

I laughed. A weak laugh, but one just the same.

Olivia had probably thrown on the first thing she grabbed, but I saw her T-shirt and I gave a delirious giggle.

3 3 3. Only half evil.

Adam didn't seem to find anything amusing. "Where are you injured?"

Angel still supported me. "Wrist, knee, cheekbone, all crushed," I said. "Everything else is bearable."

Adam looked furious, too angry to watch his language around me like usual. "Who did it to you? I want to beat the shit out of whoever it was—before I kill the bastard."

"I'll take care of him." I scowled. "He's mine. After I shift and I'm healed, I'm coming back."

"Like hell." Adam and I probably wore matching storm-dark scowls. "You're staying in the camp."

"Don't even go there," I said.

He started to say something, but Olivia said to Angel, "How bad is your neck?"

"Surface wound," Angel repeated.

"You look like shit." Olivia cut her gaze from Angel to me. "Both of you."

"Nyx took the worst of it," Angel said.

Angel looked at Adam. "It's going to be painful for her, but she needs to be carried." I started to shake my head. Angel narrowed her eyes. "You'll slow us down."

Despite the fact that I hated to be carried like some swooning maiden, I had to admit Angel had a point.

I noticed Olivia was favoring one arm.

"What happened?" I said in a rush. "Did anyone hurt you?"

Olivia shrugged. "Some asshole shot me in the arm while I was in camp." She patted her side. "Took care of him, though." She frowned. "He died before we could find out anything from him," she said with a scowl. "He was set up like a lone sniper without a spotter."

I kept my mouth shut. She didn't need to know she'd been targeted because she wasn't white.

"Where are the pups?" Olivia asked.

"In Manhattan," I said. "I'll explain when we return to the surface."

"Hurry up," Ice said. "We need to get the fuck out of here."

I bit the inside of my cheek to keep my cries of pain to myself as Adam tried as hard as possible to pick me up without hurting me. I leaned against him, my good cheek pressed against his muscled chest, my broken wrist cradled to my belly, the gun resting in my lap, my good hand still gripping it tight.

Joshua came up and to my surprise handed Angel her whip. To my huge relief, he also carried my weapons belt over his shoulder. "Found them in one of the rooms we checked."

I wanted to reach for my weapons, but my body hurt too much and Joshua had already turned away, my belt still slung over his shoulder.

When we started down the hallway, Ice took the front with Angel following, then Kveta in wolf form. Angel held her weapon down, but ready, and appeared as if she wasn't the least bit injured. Joshua covered us from the rear. Olivia walked directly behind Adam and me, backing up Joshua.

"How did you find us?" I asked.

"Later, Nyx," Ice hissed my name in obvious irritation. "Shut up."

My own irritation at his tone and order made me want to hiss back, but he was right. I also realized I was on the edge of turning delirious from the pain and shock that I'd fought off ever since Sanderson had beaten me.

The sound of the waterfall grew louder and I sensed its magic calling to me the closer we got to it.

After walking so long my eyes wanted to cross, we went through a doorway and the rush of the waterfall was loud and joyful in my ears.

"The room looks like the waterfall was once used to generate electricity," Adam said just loud enough for me to hear over the water's roar. "Whatever the reason, it's not functional any longer."

"How do we get out of here?" Thoughts sprang into my mind, pleasant thoughts, as I imaged us all aboveground again.

"There's a rock staircase behind the waterfall." Adam gave a nod toward the fall. "Looks like it hasn't been used in decades."

"Stop," I said as the idea flared sharp and brilliant in my mind. "I need to talk to Olivia and Joshua."

Adam looked puzzled, but did so.

"Joshua, Olivia," I said as Adam turned enough that I could see them. "Block that door open as securely as you can. I have a plan. Block it so that nothing should be able to close it without some work."

Olivia shrugged at Joshua. "When she's got that look in her eyes, she's up to something. No stopping her."

Adam called out ahead for the others to wait, then we both covered the pair who used the door's built-in hydraulic locking mechanism to lock it in the open position. Then they rolled a couple of barrels that might have been drums filled with crude oil.

"I hear something," Joshua said as he and Olivia jogged up to us just as they finished. Kveta had raised her hackles. "Get out of here," he shouted.

Joshua called ahead to the others as we ran. I bit my lip as pain bounced through me while Adam picked up his pace.

"Hope whatever you have planned works," Olivia said behind me.

"It will—if we can get behind that waterfall," I said.

Kveta, Angel, and Ice had disappeared behind the waterfall when shots started zinging past the rest of us.

Adam ran faster. I bit my lip harder.

I craned my neck and looked behind Adam. Three men were chasing us. Joshua vanished, turning into a shadow when one of the men shot at him. I let out a breath as Joshua reappeared.

Adam jogged up a short flight of steps made from rock beside the waterfall, then we dodged behind it. The smell of pure water, old stone, and moss was strong enough to reach through my impaired sense of smell.

The elemental magic in the clean, pure water was powerful. This was water not touched by pollution or man. It had stayed underground from the time of its birth.

Joshua and Olivia were right behind us. I could hear shouts even over the sound of the waterfall. The men were gaining on us.

"Hurry!" I shouted to everyone. Then to Adam I said, "Stop on the other side of the waterfall."

I started drawing the elemental water magic to me before we reached our destination. Power filled me.

More than usual because I'd been unable to use any of the elements for so long.

Magic engulfed me, as if I was in the waterfall itself.

We reached a flat surface beneath a stone staircase that seemed to go up forever.

"Get out of here," I shouted to Olivia and Joshua as I raised my good arm.

They darted past Adam and me.

On the other side of the waterfall two men raised their guns.

I brought my arm to me and made a shoving motion, as if I was pushing the men back. In that motion I released the elemental magic that had gathered in my body.

The waterfall changed direction.

It blasted the men and they vanished.

Water rolled away from the falls, the crash and roar filling the entire room. It shot through the open door.

The water from the falls continued its rampage throughout the facility. I closed my eyes and pictured doors ripped from frames, rooms flooded. Especially the examination room and Johnson's study.

Stone doors crumbled under my command and the stone room I had been confined in was in ruins within minutes.

When I felt that everything possible had been destroyed, I ordered the water to move the barrels and slam the door to the electrical room shut. The room filled high with water, the pressure so great there was no way that door was going to open.

Slowly I released the waterfall and it returned to tumbling down into whatever abyss it belonged in.

"Thank you," I whispered to the water elemental. I felt something like water sliding over my skin even though I remained dry. Like a caress.

The power I'd used took so much out of me that I sagged in Adam's arms. "Take me to camp."

He kissed the top of my head and started climbing the stairs, into the sunlight.

I was beyond exhaustion. A limp bloom and stem in a flowerpot that had survived days without water.

When we reached the surface, Beketov was waiting. The expression of pain on the Were's face made my heart hurt when I told him what little I knew about his pup and the other two being taken away.

Adam carried me to a tent, pulled aside the flap, and dodged into it. A double sleeping bag was spread out on an air mattress. I couldn't wait for it.

"To bed." He settled me onto the mattress and I didn't even wince. I was too tired to feel pain. One benefit of complete exhaustion.

After he had me settled on one side of the bed, his movements were slow and careful as he tried to keep from rocking the mattress while he lay on his side beside me.

I gave him a sleepy smile. "Thank you for rescuing us."

His features were so filled with concern. "You will heal when you shift?"

I would have nodded if it wouldn't have hurt. "I'll be back to normal as soon as I'm Drow again." I gave a little smile. "I guess if you call being Drow normal."

Adam brushed his lips over my forehead, a touch so light it was as if the water were caressing me again. "Go to sleep, Nyx."

My smile was still on my lips as I drifted off.

A long warm body was pressed up to me when I woke. Of course it was Adam who held me, his arm around my waist. His bare chest felt hard, muscular against my back.

I fell asleep with a smile and I woke with a smile.

When I blinked my eyes open, I ran the tip of my tongue over my small fangs. My cobalt-blue hair that had fallen over my shoulder was tangled, lying over the amethyst marble of the skin of my bare upper arm.

I had shifted back to Drow in my sleep and my injuries were healed. I felt nothing but a pleasant sense of security. I did remember going in and out of sleep while I shifted and when I was done insisted that Adam hold me even though he was concerned he would hurt me. I think I threatened him if he didn't. Something about him walking bowlegged and holding his groin if he didn't hold me.

As I snuggled deeper into Adam's secure, warm embrace, I realized I was sticky with dirt and blood and my hair was completely matted, snarled. I probably didn't smell that great, either. With my curtailed sense of smell, I didn't know that for sure.

I murmured, *"Avanna,"* and the moment I finished saying the word, I felt refreshed, clean, as if I had just taken a long, hot shower. Being half Elvin has a lot of perks.

My gaze flickered around my surroundings. I hadn't

grasped much more than him when I slipped in and out of sleep. It was dark outside, but inside the tent a light burned in one corner. It must have been battery-operated, but I wasn't sure how it stayed where it was.

The tent was dull orange in the dim light, a tent just big enough for two. My gear was piled on one side of the tent and my weapons belt was on top. To see it sent so much relief through me again. I didn't see the Kahr—I'd have to buy a new handgun, but that was a small price.

Despite my difficulties smelling much of anything, I swore I was breathing in and capturing Adam's coffee, leather, and masculine scent. I might have imagined it, but it felt real enough.

I turned in his arms to face him. His eyes were open and he was studying me with concern.

"You're sure you're okay?" Adam loosened his hold on my waist but I pressed myself more fully along his length.

"I feel perfect." My words were a bit muffled against his bare chest. "I feel fabulous. I'm with you."

He stroked my hair and I didn't worry that he might consider me odd with my blue hair and amethyst skin. He had so clearly accepted me unconditionally for who I am the first time he saw me change. Before I'd even had a chance to tell him, to explain to him ahead of time. That unconditional acceptance felt so amazing that the love I felt for him, love I kept secured tight within my heart, magnified.

"It feels like it's been so long since the morning in the apartment." I slid my hand down the hard planes of his chest and abs and was very happy to find that he had an erection. I cupped it, only his cotton boxers separating his flesh from my palm. "So long since I felt you between my thighs."

Adam made a low rumbling sound in his chest, sparks seeming to flicker in his warm brown eyes. "Nyx, if you keep that up, you'd better be completely healed."

I grinned as I raked my nails up the length of his erection and he groaned. "Never felt better than I do right now." My voice was sensual, promising.

He looked so serious as he ran his fingers through my hair, the strands clean and untangled now. "I was so afraid for you. That I'd—that we'd—lost you."

I moved my hand from his groin, slipped my fingers behind his neck, and brought him closer to me for a long, slow kiss. I might not be able to draw in his scent like I usually could, but I could taste him, and it was magnificent.

"Not that I'd want anything else in the world right now," I said against his lips, "but what are you doing here? I told you to stay in the city."

Adam's mouth curved up into a wicked smile. "You're not the only one who doesn't listen to advice."

I gave his shoulder a playful slap. "No way could you have found this camp on your own."

"Olivia contacted me when you disappeared." He didn't look so teasing now. "She promised that if anything happened to you that she'd get a hold of me."

"No cell phone service this deep in the forest," I said.

"I think you know better than anyone," Adam said, "that nothing can stop Olivia. She convinced the Weres to go to a high point in the mountains where they could get enough of a signal to reach me."

I grinned. "That's Olivia."

"Like you said, Weres don't seem to like humans." Adam looked a little amused rather than bothered. "Three of them, none of them I'd consider friendly, met me down at the end of the line. The end for anyone who isn't crazy enough to take a vehicle on what the Weres consider a trail."

"Like Olivia," I muttered. "She's nuts." Then I smiled. "But she got you here."

He nodded. "I'm keeping you right where I can see you, too."

"Yeah, right." I made a scoffing sound. "As if you could pin me down."

Adam's hand drifted lower and I gasped as he slid his hand between my thighs and pressed his fingers against the leather covering my center. "I know exactly how to pin you down."

"Sometimes." I shivered with pleasure, my eyelids growing heavy from desire. "I'll give you that."

He pushed harder, forcing the leather of my fighting suit against the most sensitive spot on my body. I groaned. I couldn't help it.

"I want to know . . ." My voice actually trembled. It took effort to get the words out. "How did you find Angel, the Were mother, and me?"

"Ice," he said.

I raised my eyelids that had started to feel weighted down with need. "How?"

"Ice shifted into a white falcon." Adam's expression went serious and he moved his hand to the inside of my thigh and settled it there. "Never seen anything like it, Nyx. He searched and searched too many hours to count. Ice didn't stop to rest, only to drink water."

Adam continued, "That's how he found an entrance to that place. He came down to drink from a small pool of water. He caught a glimpse of those stone stairs and heard the waterfall. He went far enough to find the electricity generator, then came back to camp."

"Unbelievable," I whispered. Again I wondered—how had I discounted Ice so much?

"When Ice got back," Adam said, his expression intent, "he only came to the Trackers and me. Told us we needed to get our asses over there to check out something that he'd found." Adam shook his head, tousling his brown hair against his pillow in adorable waves. "You've never seen a group of people—or beings—move so fast."

"Then you searched the facility," I said.

"Not one of us gave up hope that you were there." He gave a short nod. "We searched every room, every hallway."

"Until you found us," I said.

He gave me a look that made me feel precious and cared for. Like I was the most important person to him in the world. "Until we found you."

NINETEEN

Adam's kisses were like traveling to an Otherworld, someplace I only went to with him. A place where we were the only two people who existed.

I lost myself in those kisses. Sweet, precious. His taste filled me, his presence surrounded me, his very being possessed me. I was more alive with him, my life force stronger, more powerful.

Horrors and heaviness from every terror I had ever experienced slipped away and nothing touched me but a glorious feeling of light and joy. I grasped it and held it tight to my heart.

Adam became my world with those kisses.

His mouth was firm against mine and he traced my lips and my teeth with his tongue. The tip lingered on each of my small fangs and the erotic feeling that shot through my body startled me. But only for a moment.

I explored him, too. I kissed him and kissed him and kissed him.

Our hands moved, touching each other's bodies, lingering in places that made us both moan.

When he squeezed one of my breasts I tipped my head back and moaned. Adam gave a soft laugh as he moved his hand to my mouth. "We're surrounded by a lot of . . . people."

"And I care because . . . ?" I teased him with my smile.

He pushed himself to a sitting position. I tried to keep my laugh low when I saw his boxers. Looney Tunes Tasmanian Devil. When I looked at his wicked grin as he extended his hand to me, I said, "You look just as devilish as Taz right now."

That wicked look was still on his face as he said, "Let's just say my thoughts are anything but innocent."

I took his hand and sat upright before he started pulling on his jeans from a sitting position.

"Hold on." I shook my head. "No way. You're not going anywhere."

He left the top button of his jeans undone. Dear Goddess, that looked sexy.

"*We're* going somewhere." He got to his knees and helped me to mine.

Adam unzipped the tent flap and pushed it open. A cool breeze rushed in and I was sure I could smell sweet mountain air, pine and birch trees, and rich loam. Maybe my sense of smell *was* returning.

Stars sparkled crisp and clear in the rain-washed sky. No clouds, no rain, but the ground was wet beneath my bare feet. I still wore my Elvin-magic-cleansed fighting leathers and Adam wore Levi's and boxers.

As the waxing moon touched Adam's body, the beauty of it stole my breath away. He had such a fine build. Not too big, just perfect.

My mouth watered. I imagined myself tasting his

skin, letting the salt and male flavor fill me. Licking paths down the hard contours of his tanned body that was tight, corded with lean muscle. Running my hands over his strong shoulders and biceps. Feeling the wiry but smooth hairs on his forearms. Touching the flat plane of his abs leading to his waist where his jeans were slung low, riding just below his hipbones.

While we walked, his big hand engulfing mine, I allowed myself a glance over my shoulder to enjoy the way his buttocks flexed beneath the snug cotton of his light blue Levi's. His thighs were strong, his legs long. I even liked the size and shape of his bare feet.

Most of all I couldn't wait to have him between my thighs. Needed him there.

The camp was mostly silent, but Werewolf sentries in pairs surrounded it. They let us by without argument, which surprised me a little. The facility where their pack members had been taken to was destroyed, but they weren't letting their guard down.

The crazy white supremacist scientist was still out there, one who believed that all paranormal beings were abominations and should be exterminated.

A shiver of revulsion passed through me at the thought of the man and I immediately jerked my mind elsewhere. I wasn't going to think about that right now. All I was going to think about was Adam.

After we passed the sentries, Adam looked down at me and his teeth were white against his tanned skin when he smiled. He squeezed my hand and I fell into the world again where it was only Adam and me.

We traveled in a direction I hadn't taken before, but

he seemed to know his way. He had probably searched for me here, but I didn't ask. Didn't want to know.

It wasn't long before I heard water running in the distance. Not just a stream or river, but a waterfall. We didn't talk. It seemed right to simply listen to the night sounds of wind shaking tree leaves and whispering through pine. Insects that braved the cooler temperatures clicked or chirruped. Scampering rodents, such as woodchucks, squirrels, mice, and raccoons, made the barest of noises as they made their way through the darkness. We came closer and closer to the sound of rushing water.

I love that sound. Love the pounding, the pulse, the beat.

It was a small waterfall, but beautiful, droplets sparkling in the moon and starlight. Water tumbled into a small pool before speeding away in a small river of silver.

Mist from the waterfall dampened my skin when we reached the edge of the pool and Adam stopped us. He brought me around to face him and placed his forehead against mine. "That you're here," he said, his tone low and rough. "I almost can't believe we found you. I was so afraid—"

I placed my fingers against his mouth. "I'm here. You're here. That's what matters."

My fingertips slid across his lips and into the rich sable of his hair as I drew back and looked into his gaze. I wished I could see the alderwood shade of his eyes, but the moonlight wasn't bright enough. I moved my hand into the short, thick strands, cupped the back of his head, and brought him to me for another kiss.

No hesitation. In the tent our kisses had a natural magic that had made me feel like nothing had ever felt before. Now there was urgency with that magic. An urgency to possess, to make real what we had grasped tendrils of. To make it stronger, even more precious than it already was.

Our lips were moist and I felt cool air against them as he drew away. He brought his hands to my face and held them still, looking into my eyes.

"Almost losing you made so many things clear." He moved one of his hands to push hair away from that side of my face. "I can't let anything happen to you."

"I'm a Night Tracker, Adam." I took his hands from my face and clasped them in my own. "You're an NYPD detective. Danger is a part of our lives."

He shook his head, but I don't think he was denying the truth in what I'd said. "I need you too much to let anything ever happen to you. You're—you're important in ways to me that I don't understand."

"Hey." I reached up on my toes and brushed my lips over his before settling flat on my feet. "We are who we are. We do what we do. I'll be careful. You'll be careful. We'll still be here for each other, okay?"

He nodded, but the worry lines around his eyes said he didn't like that I lived so dangerously every day of my life.

"No worries for now." I released one of his hands but held the other as I drew him to a rocky outcropping, then let him go.

I started with my leather top, slowly pulling it up and over my head before setting it aside on the rocks.

Adam's throat worked as his eyes traced the column of my neck to my firm breasts. The waterfall's mist drifted across my chest and my nipples tightened, then ached as his gaze rested on them.

Adam took one step toward me, but I held my hand up, telling him to stay where he was with that gesture. His bare chest and biceps tightened as he clenched his fists, his expression fierce, hard, raw.

With deliberate slowness, in a provocative movement I spread my fingers over my firm breasts and then slowly moved my hands down my flat belly to my leather pants. I had to hold back a smile as I watched his jaw tighten and his body lean slightly like he wouldn't be able to hold back coming to me and taking me to the ground.

My fingers drifted along the edge of my waistband before I hooked my thumbs in the soft leather and started easing it down over my hips.

Drow are inherently sexual beings and every movement I made was slow, enticing, sensual.

I wasn't sure Adam was going to survive my wickedness considering the hard strain of his erection against his jeans.

Beneath my fighting leathers I didn't wear my silky Victoria's panties. Instead I was completely bare, and he couldn't move his eyes from my hipbones, then the V at the juncture of my thighs.

My long, firm legs held his gaze as I stepped out of the soft leather. I didn't move my eyes from his as I bent to pick up my pants, folded them, then set them aside on the same rock as my top.

The moment I crooked my finger toward me, in a

teasing "come and get me" motion, he had me in his arms before I could catch my breath.

He kissed me hard this time. Not like the slow, mind-spinning, magical kisses we'd shared earlier. Now he kissed me like a man who had to possess me. This was a different Adam than I'd ever seen, a side of him that brought out my own primal nature.

Dark Elves are a male-dominated society, a version of a BDSM lifestyle that I rejected growing up. My human mother raised me to never bow to any man.

It shocked me to my core when a thought flashed through my mind—of Adam taking control someday, dominating me, making me his.

No, I told myself.

Why not? my own voice said back to me.

Not now. Not here. No thoughts so crazy, so insane belonged in this moment.

I closed my eyes as Adam moved his lips from mine and kissed the side of my jaw before moving his mouth to the hollow at the base of my throat.

My breath caught, then I gasped as he held my breasts in his hands. A rumble came from his chest as his warm mouth found my nipple and he sucked. I couldn't stop moaning as he licked and sucked and teased my nipple, and I cried out when he bit it harder than I would have imagined he would. It hurt, then the pain faded to pleasure as he gave another tantalizing lick before moving his mouth to my other nipple.

The moment Adam touched me I had forgotten the night breezes, the cool mist of the small waterfall and its rumbling tumble and its thrusting, deep penetration into the pond.

Sensations in my body magnified as I absorbed what I heard and it mingled with what my body felt. Moonlight silvered the strands of Adam's sable hair as I bunched my fingers in its softness while he sucked my other nipple.

I was barely aware of any moans or whimpers I might have made. I know I did, but the sounds were lost in the throb and pound of the waterfall and the whisper of the breeze wandering through tree leaves and pine needles.

When Adam released my nipple I had trouble breathing without gasping. My heart pounded and I clenched my hands tighter in his hair as he moved down, licking circles on my belly. Payback. This was payback for my teasing him, and he was doing a really good job of it.

He grasped my hips with his large hands and nuzzled my hairless mound. My stomach clenched. I heard his long, drawn-out inhale as he took in my scent and his rumble of satisfaction. Then I didn't think I could breathe at all anymore when he ran his tongue along the smooth slit hiding my folds.

Adam moved his hands from my hips and parted my slit with his fingers and I quivered. He licked my folds in a long broad stroke. I think I screamed. I don't know, don't remember. All I knew was that one tantalizing lick almost sent me straight into orgasm.

He teased me more with his tongue, darting in and out and murmuring sounds of approval and telling me how much he loved my taste. A lull in my hearing, like the calm at the center of a storm, kept me from knowing exactly what he said. Sounds were almost nonexistent as power built within me. Turned, twisted, raged.

The short strands of his hair almost slipped from my grasp as my climax hit me full force, like a class-five hurricane.

I did scream then. So loud the sound probably carried back to the Were camp. I didn't care if they would send every member of the pack and my own team to see what happened to me. I'd just had the most amazing orgasm of my life.

Spinning, churning, an almost destructive force threatening to rip me apart. So explosive that all the pleasure turned into pain, then spun into pleasure again.

Pleasure turning into pain turning into pleasure. That was something that Dark Elves thrived on during sex and I didn't want to be anything like the Drow when it came to sex.

This was Adam, though, and anything I shared with him would be precious. Always.

He stood, sweeping his hands from my hips, along my waist to my shoulders and held my trembling arms in his firm grip. He murmured something that I could almost hear through the windstorm in my ears before he kissed me again. Long and sweet, and different with the flavor of me on his lips and tongue.

Adam put his forehead to mine. "You fill me, Nyx, in ways I've never believed possible."

"I feel every bit the same." Was my voice a little shaky from the orgasm that still reverberated throughout my body? "I just . . . Goddess, I don't even know how to explain the depth of what you do to me."

Except that I loved him. But I wasn't ready to tell him that.

"Enough talking." I took him by the hand and led

him toward the pool. "Think you can handle a little cold water?"

He paused, shook his head and laughed. "Not if you want me to not, er, have a problem . . ."

"I can fix that." It felt so good to be able to grasp and use my elemental magic.

Fresh air has enough static, a static inherently magic, that I can use to draw fire to me, to start a fire, or to create warmth.

My body hummed and heat radiated from me to envelop Adam.

"Nice trick." Adam's sensual smile heated me more than the elemental magic burning throughout me.

"That isn't anything." I pointed my finger at the basin at the foot of the small waterfall.

The icy water frothing at the foot of the falls started to steam, tendrils of white twisting up in a sensual dance on the water's surface. The water took on an almost glowing, warm blue hue the color of sapphires.

I looked up at Adam and he raised his eyebrows but smiled, and I held his hand as we walked to the pool. Grass, leaves, loam, and moss were now warm and soft beneath my feet. Just warm enough to send more pleasure through my body.

We stopped beside the pool, my body tingling in a way that continued to radiate the aftereffects of the climax through my every limb. Maybe through every cell. I reached up and brushed my lips over his before I started to make a trail with my tongue down his jaw to his collarbone, where I paused and kissed it.

When I reached one of his flat nipples, Adam gave a groan and stroked my hair. I licked his nipple in slow, sensual strokes. I bit it and let my small fangs slide into his skin. The fact that I'd bitten him hard enough to draw droplets of blood shocked me. But Adam gave a hiss of pleasure that excited me in ways I never expected.

I licked away the small trickles of blood before biting his nipple with my front teeth. I loved the rich sounds he made as I touched him, tasted him.

His other nipple needed the same attention. It surprised me how much I enjoyed piercing his flesh and hearing his groans that sounded more like pleasure than pain. He murmured my name and I think he told me to not stop, but his voice was so deep and throaty I couldn't tell for sure.

I didn't intend to stop anyway. After a few more enticing swipes of my tongue over his nipple, I moved my lips lower, over his stomach to where a light V of hair led me to his Levi's. How convenient that he hadn't buttoned the top of his jeans. I grasped the zipper between my teeth and dragged it all the way down.

His different Looney Tunes boxers made me smile like they did each time we'd been together. Taz's wicked expression couldn't have matched the wicked look in my eyes as I tugged at his jeans and boxers at the same time, down his strong legs. He stepped out of them and he was mine.

I caressed his erection with my fingertips, his cock so hard and swollen that it made my thighs ache to have him inside of me. But I wanted to taste him, too.

The pearl of semen at the tip of his erection drew my attention. I wrapped my fingers around his length and I licked the small drop away in a long sweeping stroke.

Mmmmm. He tasted wonderful. Warm, a little salty, and uniquely Adam.

As I swirled my tongue over the head of his erection, he stroked my hair. I looked up at him and met his gaze. While our eyes held each other's, I slipped my mouth over his erection, taking him deep, to the back of my throat. The expression on his face was one of need, desire, and pleasure. I brought one hand up and grasped his balls while my other hand moved up and down him with the rhythm of my mouth.

I squeezed his balls harder than I intended but Adam's groan told me he liked it. He liked the pain.

A thought flashed through my mind—if Adam liked to be dominated as well as dominate—switch—then maybe I'd enjoy it. Being half Drow, it came to me that there was a part of me that I'd never acknowledged before that yearned to be controlled.

I almost stopped my movements but I continued to lick and suck. The human half of me rebelled—I'd always rejected the BDSM lifestyle of the Dark Elves. But right now the human half found the thought of dominating Adam exciting. What would he do if I tied him so that he had no way of moving while I teased him, ran my lips over his body, made him my play toy for the night?

And what if he made me his?

I didn't close my mind to the thoughts. Instead I let them simmer in my mind while I gave Adam the kind of pleasure I'd been wanting to for so long. I scraped my teeth along his erection and he held my head between his hands as if he wanted to control how much pleasure I gave him.

With my eyes still focused on his, I smiled around his erection before bringing him deeper into my mouth, sucking him harder. And then I drew again on my fire elemental magic, so very lightly by pulling static from the air. I used that power to send a faint electrical sensation over his skin that caused him to gasp.

He moved his cock inside my mouth, wanting what I was giving to him more and more. I could see it in his eyes. I sent fissions of the electrical sensation around his balls and sliding along that sensitive place between his anus and his erection.

Adam sounded like he was gritting his teeth together, trying to hold back making a sound when he climaxed. He failed and something between a growl and a loud groan came from him. The warmth of his semen jetted from him as he pumped his hips hard against my face. His semen filled my mouth and I swallowed, taking it all into me until there was nothing left but for me to lick his spent cock and let him slide out of my mouth.

He braced his hands on my shoulders, his head bent, his chest rising and falling, his breathing harsh.

I rose to my feet and he embraced me as I laid my head on his shoulder. I liked the way his chest rose and fell beneath my ear, the feel of perspiration on his skin as his body touched mine. Remnants of his semen were warm and delicious in my mouth.

"Come." I took him by the hand and led him to the small pool and stepped into it.

"The water's warm." Adam sounded surprised even though I had heated the air earlier.

When we were up to his hips and my waist, I pushed him back on a flat rock. "I need you inside me."

He smiled. "You might have to give me a moment."

"Uh-uh." I closed my eyes just a moment and willed the water to circle his cock, to stroke it, to make it feel like it had never felt before. I opened my eyes and looked into Adam's gaze.

"Nyx." Adam looked nearly in agony from the amount of pleasure I was giving him with my element. "How the hell are you doing that?"

"I have lots of talents." I moved onto his lap and bade the water element to stop so that I could take over.

"No kidding." Adam reached for my hips. "I more than need you now."

I grinned until I slid onto his erection and gasped at how much he filled me. He was so thick and heavy from stimulation that he must nearly have been bursting.

With his hands on my hips and my palms on his shoulders, I began to ride him. "You feel so good." The words came out in gasps.

He thrust inside me, hard and deep. The warm water lapped at our bodies and I used my water element again, this time to enhance our excitement.

My orgasm rushed through me, pounding through me like the waterfall pounding into the pool. My body shook, mind filled with glittering images like water droplets sparkling in a clear sky.

I was so far gone I barely heard his groan or felt him pulsing inside me.

When I collapsed against him I felt like he might not have been able to support us both if he wasn't sitting.

He stroked my hair. "You're amazing, Nyx. Always so incredibly amazing."

I smiled, but then it faltered as I looked at the waxing moon.

We were almost out of time.

Tomorrow night was the full moon.

Dawn broke and I arched my back like a cat beside the pool before moving with feline grace. The rich loam was soft beneath my bare feet and the waterfall's mist was a whisper on my naked flesh. Finally I was able to change to my human form the way I was used to doing.

Adam sat on a rock, his boxers and Levi's on, his sable hair tousled, his arms crossed over his chest. He watched with fascination as I moved slowly, sinuously, enjoying my transformation as my muscles returned to my human size and shape. Toned, but not so defined as they were when I was Drow. My tiny fangs retracted into my gums and I knew my features became softer-looking.

The amethyst shade of my body faded into pale, fair skin. When I leaned forward to stretch over my leg, my blue locks covered my face, then shimmered into a long skein of straight black hair.

The change was wonderful, made me feel complete, whole. No pain, just pleasure. Even more pleasure to have Adam watching me.

When I finished, he came to me and took me in his arms. "No matter whether it's day or night," he said, "you are the most beautiful woman I have ever known."

So much joy filled my heart that I almost told him I loved him.

Shouts came from the direction of the camp.

We looked in that direction, then looked at each other.

A white jaguar broke the treeline and growled when it came to a graceful stop in front of us. It was too late to put on my clothing as Ice shifted so quickly.

Ice looked directly at me and ignored Adam. "Joshua found a survivor from the hellhole below. An intern who knows where Johnson and the pups are."

TWENTY

My heart thudded, my blood rushing hot and fast through my body. I hurried to grab my black leathers and started tugging them on. "The exact location in Manhattan?"

"According to the bitch that Joshua captured, Johnson is certain he's found the virus he's been searching for to eliminate paranorms," Ice growled, sounding like a jaguar even in his human form. "He's planning to experiment and possibly release it today."

My clothes were on by the time Ice finished his last sentence. "Tell me everything."

"In camp." Ice's words came out distorted—he was already shifting back into a jaguar as he spoke. He turned and sped through the forest, his body lean, graceful, beautiful.

Adam and I followed at a run. I kept pace with Adam, not letting my feet fly over the ground like I wanted to in order to get to the camp as fast as possible. He needed to be there to hear everything at the same time I did.

We reached camp within minutes and came up to a furious Beketov and a group of Weres—one female and three males in addition to the alpha. Olivia, Joshua, Angel, and Ice were all armed as well and it was clear everyone was ready to leave to go after Johnson.

In the midst of the Trackers and Weres was a woman, her back to me, her hands bound behind her. Tangled, wet, and dirty dark hair fell around her shoulders and she was wearing one of those green suits with a red armband. The suit was ripped and torn, but the rips looked fresh, not coated by dried mud like other parts of her suit. Streaks of blood lined the rents in the clothing. I glanced at Angel and the barbed whip on her belt.

The woman pivoted and faced me, hate in her eyes. Shock and anger rolled through me when I saw the bruised, battered, and scratched face and recognized who it was. "Harkins."

"Dr. Johnson will eliminate you all." Harkins glared at me, but she was speaking to everyone there. "Abominations." She hissed the *s*. "Sick, vile creatures."

Wrong thing to say.

Angel slugged Harkins. The intern dropped to the damp ground.

Joshua looked on with approval. "Nice."

Ice smirked. "Didn't know Perky had it in her."

Angel rounded on Ice and I rushed to move between them. "You have no idea what that girl can do," I said.

She stepped around me. "Don't push me if you don't want to end up choking on your own penis."

Every male standing around us turned a shade of green, including Ice and Beketov.

Olivia and a male Were jerked Harkins to her feet by the intern's upper arms. I glanced at Olivia's light brown T-shirt with dark brown stenciled words, and wondered how many of her shirts she packed in order to pick out one that often fit the occasion.

Warning: Does not play well with others.

Heh.

"We waited as you asked." Beketov fixed his gaze on Angel and Olivia, his muscles bunching as if ready to tear into something. "Your partners are here now. Tell us what you learned from your interrogation."

I appreciated that they had waited for all of us to arrive. I met Olivia's eyes, then Angel's. "What did you find out?"

Olivia spoke and I glanced back to her and Harkins. "The doctor took a team of four scientists." Olivia's arm had a fresh bandage, and it was white against her dark skin. She didn't flinch or wince from pain as she gripped Harkins's upper arm. "Johnson took the pups with him."

"He's been at the Guardian Scientific Research Center." Angel gestured toward Harkins. "According to the bitch, Johnson needed equipment that is more sophisticated than what he had at the facility."

Olivia's flawless bronze skin had a dark flush on her cheeks. "As of yesterday afternoon, before we eliminated his facility, Johnson had told Harkins he thinks he's found the one. The one virus that will exterminate paranorms."

My partner's fingers dug into Harkins's arm. I wasn't sure if Olivia did it intentionally, or if it was from the anger in her words as she continued. "He intends to mass-produce it and release it into the air in Manhattan before bringing it back here and killing all of the Weres here, too."

"First he's going to test it on the three pups." Angel smacked her barbed whip against her thigh over and over, as if ready to use it. The barbs didn't seem to bother her through her leather fighting suit. "He intends to make sure it's contagious to paranorms only and that it won't kill humans."

I glanced from Angel to Harkins, whose venomous expression made me want to punch her as hard as Angel had. "How is he going to do that? Make sure norms don't die from the virus?"

Ice's features shifted to one of unbelievable anger and he almost looked like a jaguar as he bared his teeth and spoke in a snarl. "The fuckhead captured three norm children from another camp and plans on using them to make sure the virus doesn't affect humans."

His fierceness over children being abducted, hurt, abused still surprised me, and a tinge of chagrin went through me at misjudging him. I hadn't thought he cared about anyone but himself and the glory of a Tracker kill.

"Goddammit," Adam said, the muscles of his bare chest bunching with tension. "Pups and human children. Sick bastard. Not to mention his plans for all paranorms."

"From what we *convinced* Harkins to tell us," Angel said, with frost in her blue eyes as she looked at Harkins, "Johnson is punctual. He stops work at exactly six in the afternoon and he'll get to the center at eight in the morning. That's been his work schedule in the abandoned NORAD facility and he never varies."

I wondered just exactly what had been done to Harkins to convince her to talk so much, then I decided I didn't care.

Adam said, "It's still early enough that by leaving now we can get there close to eight."

Angel nodded. "And stop him from doing any experiments on the children and pups."

Beketov turned away and started toward the trail we'd taken from the Jeep. "We waste precious time."

"Adam and I will catch up." I ran for the orange tent we'd slept in, crouched, and crawled inside with Adam following.

My weapons belt was on top of my boots and the belt felt comforting when I fastened my buckler and the sheathed daggers settled at my hips. I tugged on my boots, then almost smacked into Adam, who'd pulled on a T-shirt and had his shoulder holster on with his weapons secure in it.

"Just a sec." Adam grabbed a pair of thick socks that were on top of his hiking boots. He tugged socks and boots on fast enough to be worthy of a paranormal warrior, then shrugged into his worn, brown leather bomber jacket.

Everyone in the party was gone from the camp with the exception of Olivia, who was waiting for us. She held Harkins by her upper arm and had her Sig pressed against the woman's temple.

"Bunch of damned paranorms." Olivia holstered her handgun. "They shifted and they're history. Probably almost to the main trail. One of the Weres didn't go wolfie and is carrying everyone's weapons."

Adam took Harkins by her other arm and he and

Olivia had to drag her and force her to walk as we started out of camp.

"I don't get how they keep their clothing on when they shift," Adam said.

"It's called magic." I shook my head at him. "All paranorms have some kind of power, and that's one thing any kind of Shifter or Doppler can do."

"Shut up and move faster." Using the hand of her uninjured arm, Olivia yanked Harkins along, Harkins still with her wrists cuffed behind her back. No pain registered on Olivia's face, as if she hadn't been shot just yesterday.

The intern was muttering, "Vile, filthy spawns of Satan."

I almost punched Harkins this time, but instead started jogging ahead of Adam and Olivia.

I'd thought Olivia had driven like a maniac before. This time, as she drove Adam's SUV in the pouring rain, it was like she'd gone completely insane. As if followed by a wake of devils trying to catch up with us, chasing us away from Devil's Tombstone, once we got in Adam's SUV.

Adam sat in the back seat, guarding Harkins but looking like he was regretting letting Olivia drive. I was in the front passenger seat, holding onto the "Oh shit" handle with a grip that almost cracked it.

We'd taken Adam's vehicle because his SUV had the flashing red and blue law-enforcement headlights as well as a siren and a radio. We needed to get to Manhattan safely and without being pulled over.

Windshield wipers were on hyper mode as they went

back and forth to push the rain from our view. My skin chilled as my mind turned toward thoughts of the possibility of Beketov and the other Weres being in New York City tonight during the full moon.

Thank the Goddess it hadn't been long past dawn when we set out. We had to find the pups as fast as we could. Beketov and his pack had to get back to their camp so that they had time to break everything down and hike deeper into the Catskills so that humans would be safe from the Werewolves during the full moon.

Beketov had refused to move his people yet. Until he recovered the last three missing Weres, the pups, in whatever condition they were in, he didn't plan to take his pack anywhere. With his son missing, he wasn't being rational, as far as I was concerned.

When we reached the city, the SUV's emergency lights got us through rush-hour traffic jams, although not as fast as any of us would have liked. Olivia still drove like devils had lit her butt on fire as she whipped the SUV around vehicles on the packed streets, veering onto sidewalks, and dodging pedestrians.

I picked up one of Adam's police placards from the floorboard and tossed it on the dash so that we could park anywhere but in front of a hydrant without being towed.

We finally reached the Guardian Scientific Research Center in Manhattan. The bright blue digital numbers on the dashboard told us it was almost a quarter past eight.

Olivia whipped into a no-parking zone and the SUV's tires scraped the sidewalk. She came to a hard stop behind the Weres' SUV and I jerked forward, the seatbelt digging into my shoulder before I flopped back again.

Surprisingly, or maybe not so surprisingly, the five Weres were just strapping on their weapons when we arrived, and not already in the building. The way Olivia had driven, it shouldn't have been a wonder we'd caught up.

The Were SUV was parked just as illegally in front of us. I snatched the second police placard from the floorboard before opening my door, getting out, and heading to the Weres.

In front of the research center, the street was crowded with people going to work. Some pedestrians looked at the males and their rifles, but most just remained focused on their destinations. One thing about New Yorkers— they didn't usually make eye contact with anyone they didn't know.

Adam had to drag Harkins from his SUV because she refused to move willingly. With her hands cuffed behind her back, she stumbled on the asphalt and landed hard on her knees. Olivia grabbed Harkins's upper arm again and, along with Adam, yanked the intern to her feet.

Olivia drew her Sig and pressed it against Harkins's spine. By positioning her body close and just behind the intern, Olivia kept the handgun hidden from view.

I gave the Weres the extra placard to put on their dash to keep their SUV from being towed. Not that the Weres probably even gave a damn. They just wanted their pups.

And revenge.

It was in Beketov's gaze. I saw Johnson's death in those tawny eyes and I knew it was in my expression, too. Johnson would not live through this.

Security tried to stop us, but Adam flashed his badge and told them it was a highly sensitive matter. His words were already fading as I hurried after the Weres. I heard Adam add that it would mean the security guards' jobs if a single word leaked out.

When I glanced over my shoulder, I wasn't sure Adam had convinced the two guards. The way they were looking at the Czech SA Vz. 58 assault rifles the five Weres were carrying wasn't good.

Ice and Joshua must have been reading my mind. Next thing I knew they were on the guards and had them bound and stuffed under the security desk. They'd used strips of the guards' own shirts to tie and gag them and had done it amazingly fast. I had a feeling a little magic might have been involved to make sure the guards wouldn't get away.

We didn't risk the chance of taking an elevator and having anything happen—like getting stuck or even gassed. Who knew if word had gotten to Johnson and he was expecting us.

The Weres' boots, along with Adam's and Olivia's, clunked on the marble floor of the center's lobby, the sounds echoing in the enormous area. Obviously Weres had a problem with making noise when not in wolf form.

They were even louder as they pounded up the stairs to the fifth floor.

Harkins stumbled a lot as Olivia and Adam dragged her up with us. Her face was red with exertion and she constantly mumbled things like, "It's too late," and "All of Satan's spawn will soon be exterminated," and "You abominations are already dead."

I wanted to club the back of her head with the hilt of one of my daggers.

The Weres were quieter when we reached the door from the fifth-floor stairwell but Beketov growled when they discovered it was locked.

Beketov was about to try to bust the door in with a kick when Joshua grabbed the alpha Were's arm. "Hold on, mate."

With a growl Beketov jerked his arm to get out of Joshua's grasp. But nothing was holding him as the Shadow Shifter faded. Angel caught Joshua's flail before it clattered to the concrete stairs. It was so heavy it probably would have taken a chunk out of the stairs, but Angel handled it like it was as light as a yo-yo.

A large shadow moved away from Beketov, then passed through the space beneath the door. Not even a moment later and a loud click bounced off the stairwell's walls and the door creaked open.

I winced at the sounds, hoping Johnson and his team of junior scientists hadn't heard. It was possible he'd brought techs for protection, too.

It occurred to me that Harkins might yell to warn the scientist despite the gun at her back. When I cut my gaze behind me, I saw Olivia stuffing a roll of white surgical tape into her front pocket and Harkins looking furious with tape from the roll covering her mouth.

"Good look on you," I said to Harkins before I turned and followed everyone out of the stairwell.

To my surprise, Beketov's team moved with military precision, as if all of them had been in a branch of the armed forces.

Angel handed Joshua his flail as she passed him and he gave her a short nod that she didn't see because she was so focused on our mission.

The hallway we crept into was long and sterile. I shuddered from its eerie familiarity. It looked too much like the hallways at the NORAD facility Johnson had converted into his own personal research center to use for perverted means.

Everything was silent as we moved into the hallway. The Weres held their rifles high, ready to take the first shot they had. Each of them had a handgun sheathed at his or her waist.

Adam and Olivia had their handguns drawn, holding them in two-fisted grips. Angel, Ice, Joshua, and I held our own weapons. My Kahr was gone, but I gripped one of my daggers, Angel grasped her whip, and Ice was prepared with his throwing knives. Joshua had a tight hold on the handle of his flail, the spiked ball at the end of the three-foot chain swinging back and forth in an almost hypnotizing way.

We had just entered the hallway when Adam signaled to the others and pointed to cameras positioned in several places down the hallway. All of us pressed ourselves against the wall, everyone looking grim. The five cameras that I could see extended about four inches from the ceiling and were aimed in enough directions to keep us from moving by without being spotted.

My heart pounded a little harder. How careless of me not to think of cameras, especially after being locked in that room.

"Catch," Ice murmured as he moved by me and I

barely snatched his weapons belt as he shifted into a white falcon.

He was the fastest Shifter I'd ever seen. He skimmed the ceiling of the hallway and I was pretty sure he was above the cameras' range of sight.

Ice landed on one extended camera, peeked over its edge, and started hammering at the lens with his beak. Impressed, I watched him punch holes in the lens until it shattered. Then he moved on to the other four cameras that we could see and took care of them, too.

He flew lower when he returned and he shifted into his human form again without having to land on the floor first. One moment he was in the air, the next he was standing beside me, tall and lean.

"Excellent," I said as he took his belt from me.

Ice shrugged and Beketov's team of five, along with my team of six that now included Adam, started working our way down the hallway.

We neared a set of double doors. Windows were in the top half. The doors no doubt led into the lab.

A mixture of feelings that had been balled inside me began to unravel.

Fury at what was being done by the scientists, hate for Johnson, fear for the pups and human children, and even terror for all paranorms who could be exterminated if we were too late to stop Johnson. The feelings were almost overwhelming, almost dizzying.

We reached the double doors and kept low as half of our number crouched so that they wouldn't be seen as they moved to the other side of the doors.

Beketov gave the signal to go through the doors, to break them down if we had to.

Shots echoed in loud bursts in the hallway.

My ears rang.

One of the Weres shouted. Collapsed onto the tile. Blood poured from the center of his chest.

Ice dropped as well.

A red stain expanded on his white T-shirt.

Over his heart.

TWENTY-ONE

"Ice!" I cried out when he hit the floor.

He lay motionless.

Goddess, no. He couldn't be dead.

Adrenaline pumped through me as shots zinged in the air, dented the door, chipped paint off the walls.

Harkins made muffled sounds of terror behind the white tape as Adam and Olivia jerked her down to the floor.

Angel dropped her whip. She shifted into a much smaller target, her squirrel form, and scampered along the hallway. Her small blue eyes searched the hallway, looking for locations where the attacks could be coming from.

Despite the rain of bullets, Beketov tried to open the door to the laboratory.

Locked.

He growled. He slammed his shoulder against the door again and again. It didn't budge, but he created a good-sized dent in the metal, the dent growing with every hit of his shoulder. He didn't seem to feel the bullet that caught him in his hip. He didn't stop trying to break down the door.

I almost tripped over the flail that lay abandoned on the floor near the doors. A shadow passed under the double doors to the laboratory.

"Where is the gunfire coming from?" Olivia said over the noise.

Angel reappeared close to me. "Above," she shouted so that everyone could hear. "Let them have it!"

I shot my gaze up and saw rifle barrels pointed through the suspended ceiling tiles that were low enough for duct work—and hiding scientists or techs.

Everyone on our two teams who had handguns or rifles raised their weapons and let loose a storm of bullets up and down the hallway ceiling.

Beketov continued to slam his shoulder into the door.

Blood began to drip from tiny holes at various points in the ceiling tiles as the Weres' bullets hit home.

Enemy fire stopped.

The laboratory doors opened just as Beketov slammed his shoulder into it again, and he stumbled forward into an open area. No sign of Joshua, who must have been the reason for the doors suddenly opening.

We scrambled into the laboratory with caution but it didn't matter.

Beketov had gone completely still the moment after he charged into the room. My eyes followed the path he was staring down and I went cold and still, too.

The scientists. Johnson and two others had all three pups with two other green-suited scientists beside them, yellow armbands encircling the arms of their suits. The five stood in front of a laboratory table with a sink, a large microscope, and empty glass beakers on it.

The scientists holding the pups each held a syringe

filled with green fluid—the needles ready to jam into the Werewolf pups' necks. The pups were held tight to the scientists so that they had solid grips on the little Weres.

The pups' eyes were wide and filled with fear. They didn't move at all. It was the first time I'd seen the pups, and fear for them was hard, like a ball in my chest.

Behind Johnson stood five more men. Techs, by the blue armbands on their suits. With the scientists and techs, there were ten of them. Without Ice and one of Beketov's males, there were nine of us. When I realized Joshua wasn't standing near us, I almost started with surprise. I changed my count to eight.

Where was Joshua? A slight feeling of hope dared enter my bloodstream when I saw the Shadow Shifter was nowhere in sight. We had an inside man. Would he find some way to get to Johnson and save the pups without the little Weres getting hurt or jabbed with whatever was in those needles?

I thought of Ice's body in the hallway and prayed he wasn't dead. He had lain there so motionless that I didn't know if I dared to have hope.

One man was huge—and had his handgun trained on me.

The same man who had beaten me so badly. Sanderson.

Good. I was going to take care of that bastard myself.

Whatever way we managed to figure this out.

To get my bearings, my gaze quickly swept the room that was filled with gleaming white and silver equipment so high-tech that I couldn't even guess at what most of it was.

The hammering of my heart increased when I saw

the rows of small silver cages to the left. Three human children with tear-stained faces pressed themselves to the back of their cages, obviously terrified.

When I swung my gaze to Johnson, he smiled. A cool, self-assured smile of a man certain he had nothing to fear and everything to gain.

Johnson didn't look like the insane man I was certain he was. No, he had an expression that appeared to be like any scientist devoted to his work while experimenting to find a cure—or in this case, a biological weapon.

"Guns, knives, and anything else dangerous, toss into a pile in the center of the floor." Johnson nodded to a space about six feet from us. Johnson, the other scientists, and Sanderson were another to six to seven feet beyond that. He looked at Angel again. "That includes the whip."

Both Beketov's team and my own started to disarm ourselves. No one was willing to take a chance with the pups' lives by not obeying him.

Standing next to me were Olivia, Adam, and Angel. Olivia and Adam had Harkins in a tight grip between them.

Johnson noticed Harkins for the first time. At first a startled expression crossed his features as he took in the rips and tears and blood on her suit, her face that was not covered. Accusation and anger flashed in his gaze.

His voice was loud through the microphone. "You have been in the possession of these beasts. You brought them to me. And you are now contaminated."

Harkins's eyes widened and she shook her head. A movement that was a plea, not denial. She made sounds behind the tape covering her mouth, trying to say something.

"Sanderson." Johnson gave a slight nod in Harkins's direction. "She must suffer no misery or spread any contaminants."

The intern only had a moment for a brief attempt at a scream behind her taped mouth. Olivia and Adam started to push Harkins onto the floor to get her out of the line of fire.

The barrel of Sanderson's gun followed the movement with deadly precision. The sound of the gun discharging rang in the air. He shot her once. Twice. Both bullets went into Harkins's head. The wall behind her splattered with red that trickled down its surface.

Johnson's cruel disregard of a loyal employee's life shouldn't have surprised me after what he had done to Lawson. Yet my stomach churned as Harkins sagged between Olivia and Adam, the intern's eyes wide and glassy in another silent scream.

Johnson motioned to the floor. "Release her."

Olivia and Adam both looked grim as they let Harkins's body slump onto the floor.

Johnson brought the needle closer to the neck of the pup he gripped tight to his body while the group started tossing weapons. The rifles, handguns, daggers, and whatever else the Weres and my team were wearing made clattering noises as they hit one another. A pile grew. And grew.

"I have discovered the *one*." Johnson acted like he hadn't just had his lead intern murdered. "The virus that will destroy all perversions attempting to invade God's world."

It clicked with me then that the pup Johnson held had fur the same bronze shade as Beketov's hair. Like the alpha Were, the pup also had large tawny gold eyes.

Without a doubt in my mind, I knew the pup was Beketov's son.

I glanced at Beketov from the corner of my eye. He didn't move. Didn't blink. Showed no expression that might give anything away. Not even fury. Blood stained his jeans where he'd taken a bullet in his hip. No sign of pain was in his stance. He stood solidly and did not favor that side of him.

"Go on." Johnson looked at each one of us. "Drop the weapons. My patience lasts only so long."

Johnson looked genuinely pleased to see Angel and me. "You remember how short I am on patience, don't you? It must have been unpleasant to have bullets tear into your flesh when answers were not provided as fast as I requested."

We said nothing, just stared at him while disarming.

"It is an immense pleasure to have you both join me again." He smiled. "We can finish what we started."

I leaned down to set my unsheathed daggers on the floor before pushing them to the edge of the growing pile. I straightened again. "This meeting will give me a chance to make sure you are put out of our misery."

A scowl blossomed on Johnson's features, his face suddenly going from pleased and rational to dark, furious, and definitely irrational. Insane even. "You abominations, you beasts, you evil creatures. *You* will be out of all of mankind's misery soon."

I wanted to scream that I was so tired of hearing those same words coming from him and from the techs and interns. Over and over and over. I wanted to fold his face in on itself into a tiny piece of paper, hack it into pieces the size of confetti—and burn every piece with my fire element.

Adam had placed his handgun on the floor a foot away from him before kicking it to the other weapons as Olivia did the same. They both added their sheathed knives by tossing them onto the pile, each landing with a thunk. Adam added his police baton when Johnson ordered him to.

I didn't remove my buckler and thank the Goddess that Johnson said nothing about it. Storm looked like a large belt buckle, not the dangerous weapon it was.

A lot of firepower, daggers, and other weapons were in that pile . . . but paranorms don't necessarily need weapons. We have our own ways of dealing with situations. I was counting on that.

Something had to happen to set things in motion.

But what?

Johnson's face relaxed. "I want the phones, too."

Eight cell phones hit the pile. As I unholstered mine, I tried to push the emergency button that would reach Rodán, but my finger slipped and Johnson was staring at me.

Goddess.

My phone made phone number nine. "Let the pups go, Johnson." I tried to keep my voice even as my phone landed with a thud. "They're just children."

Johnson's expression kept changing from rational to irrational so fast it had to have screwed with his mind. He snarled and spittle flew from his mouth. "How dare you call these monstrosities *children*?"

"Shut. Up." I couldn't help myself. I said it with enough venom that I felt the words alone could have killed Johnson. More and more I thought my head would explode from hearing those words—to put it as Olivia would—*so many fucking times.*

Johnson's gaze was narrowed at me. "Under the microscope, this serum attacked and destroyed the weak gene of samples of both your and the blood of the 'Doppler,' as you call *it*." He nodded to Angel. She kept her expression neutral.

His next gesture was meant to include the Were children as he tipped his head slightly toward the other scientists who held pups. "The blood from these three beasts reacted in the same way."

We said nothing as he continued. "In each case, the blood turns the entire slides black, within twenty-four to forty-eight hours, proving the virus will destroy you all once I inject these beasts."

Muscles in each adult Were twitched or flexed but they kept their faces expressionless. Adam's jaw had tightened. Olivia was the only one who couldn't seem to control the emotions on her face. Her glare was deadly as she stared at Johnson. I knew her mind was working through every scenario she could think of.

The dryness in my throat made me want to swallow and I was almost afraid to make even that small movement. Yet I wanted to keep him talking to give us time . . . time to figure out what we would do. And what Joshua might be doing and have planned.

"What about humans?" I glanced at the poor norm children caged to the side.

"Their blood has no reaction." Johnson looked pleased.

"Unfortunately I did not have time to test this virus on the human children themselves or these abominations." A slow smile spread across his face. "But with the blood-test results I have no doubt I have found *the one*."

That burst of hope I'd felt earlier with Joshua nowhere in sight broke like a soap bubble as Johnson moved his gaze from one of us to the next and said, "Where is the beast who managed to gain entrance to this laboratory?"

When no one answered, Johnson's face took on that mad expression again. "We will inject one of the pups now if you do not cooperate."

Damn.

Joshua rose from a shadow in a corner not far from the scientists, and the expression on Johnson's face was between horror and hate. "Child of Satan. Abomination of Hell." He almost screamed at Joshua as he said, "Get with the others. Now!"

Damn, damn, damn.

Joshua moved toward us and stood in line next to Angel.

A thought occurred to me. Johnson hadn't injected the pups yet. Why? If the contagion would spread from the pups through the air, it would get to us. That eliminated us as a threat. So it was probably not an airborne virus.

There had to be a reason, or more than one. Johnson wasn't confident that the virus he'd developed wouldn't spread to humans; the virus wouldn't carry from paranorm to paranorm fast enough to stop us from killing him; the virus wasn't contagious and wouldn't carry at all from the paranorm he injected it with; or the serum didn't work at all and he was bluffing.

We couldn't take any chances on any of the possibilities. All we could do was assume that Johnson had what he needed and was buying time. He wanted to disperse the virus as well as get safely away from us before we could tear him to shreds. He might even be concerned about being exposed to the toxins.

Tension rippled from the Weres and my team and I could taste it in the air along with something foul and bitter. My sense of smell had almost fully returned and I could smell fear from the pups, children, even the junior scientists. The others didn't look afraid at all.

They should have.

I blinked as something caught my eye, but I didn't turn my gaze to look at it. A white mouse crouched in shadows cast by the cages. The mouse began to edge silently alongside the cages, working his way past Johnson, the other scientists, and Sanderson.

Ice.

Had to be. He was alive. I hadn't realized he could shift into such a tiny form. But I knew it was him. No doubt in my mind.

Ice moved, keeping to the shadows until there were no more for him to hide in. He had to scamper into the lighted areas. He passed under tables and other equipment when he could. I mentally crossed my fingers in the human gesture I'd have used if I dared to really move.

"What now?" I said to Johnson. Had to keep him talking. Had to keep him talking. "Every one of us will make sure you suffer in the same way you tortured the Werewolves. You will be mutilated and flayed like the Weres you captured and murdered."

No fear in Johnson's gaze, only confidence. "You will be dead before you reach me."

Then why hadn't he injected the pups already? I didn't want to ask.

A roar, the loud, terrible scream of a furious jaguar filled the laboratory, the sound coming from behind the scientists and techs.

The screaming roar startled the scientists and techs so much that they didn't know how to react. Didn't have time to react.

A huge white jaguar bounded onto the laboratory table, plowing into empty glass beakers and sending them flying across the laminate floor. The crash of shattered glass meshed with the big cat's roar.

The moment Ice appeared, Johnson and the four other scientists jerked their attention to him. Stark, immediate terror was on each of their faces.

At the same time Ice bounded onto the table, Beketov and his three remaining Weres shifted. In nothing more than an instant they were leaping, then attacked.

Ice grabbed one junior scientist by the neck, sinking his fangs into the man's jugular and shaking him like he was as light as a flag snapping in the wind.

One of the techs behind Johnson started to point his gun at Beketov. I ripped Storm from my belt and flung it before the man leveled his gun on the alpha Were.

The buckler sliced through the man's neck, beheading him. The tech's body collapsed to the floor. His head rolled away. My buckler made a small arc and returned to my grasp.

A Were had his jaws clamped on a junior scientist's neck.

Syringes toppled to the floor, still filled with green liquid. Two pups bolted away from the scientists as Ice and the Were released the dead men. The pups hid in a corner.

Shots zinged through the air from the living techs.

Olivia and Adam dove for the pile of weapons and grabbed a handgun. Each shot a tech, dropping him. Blood spotted Olivia's arm through her bandage, but she acted like nothing had happened to her.

Angel's whip cracked in the air, encircling another scientist's neck. She dragged the man toward her in a fast motion, then gutted him with a dagger she must have had hidden.

I didn't know how Joshua could have gotten to his flail so quickly, but he wielded it with ease and the spiked iron ball collided with one tech's head and smashed it in. The power in Joshua's swing sent the tech flying across the room.

Ice took care of the remaining junior scientist with another clamp of his jaws.

During all of the fighting, I grabbed one of my daggers and went after Sanderson.

I felt the dangerous white flash in my eyes. I jumped and forward-flipped twice, landing two feet from the huge man. His furious gaze met mine as he pointed the barrel of his gun at my chest.

Too fast for him to see, I swung my dragon-claw dagger—

And sliced off his gun hand.

Sanderson shrieked. In shock he held up his stump. I drove my dagger straight into the huge man's heart.

Surprise was still in his wide, glassy eyes as I jerked

my dagger out of his chest. His body toppled onto a broken glass beaker and I whirled to fight the next opponent.

Through the blood rushing in my ears I realized the room had gone completely silent.

Everyone on my team and Beketov's was staring in the same direction.

Horror grabbed my chest.

Beketov had shifted—

Into his full-moon Were form.

He was facing a terrified Johnson, who had plastered himself against a wall. Beketov's son and the syringe were no longer in the scientist's hands.

The misshapen and horrifying creature that had been Beketov stared at Johnson. The eight-foot-tall creature's ribcage expanded and retracted like bellows pumping within him. Its breaths were heavy, frightening.

Its body was pale, its veins showing through the opaque skin. Tufts of bronze hair crowned its head and patches had sprouted along its spine to its almost hairless tail that whipped back and forth. A ball of hair crowned the end of its tail.

The creature's face was misshapen—part wolf, part human. It bared its yellow teeth that glistened with saliva. Spittle dripped onto the floor near its huge, clawed feet. The creature raised its arms, long, clawed fingers near Johnson's throat.

A wet spot appeared at Johnson's crotch and pee trickled from the cuff of his slacks.

Johnson shrank away from what had been Beketov and now was something else entirely. Johnson's stutter was not much above a whisper. "A-abom-abomina-tion."

The creature's claws whipped out and shredded Johnson's face. Blood flew and splattered the floor. I caught my breath and watched as the huge creature flayed the scientist from his chest to his legs.

Johnson screamed the entire time. No coherent words came from his mouth, only cries filled with what must have been excruciating pain.

When Johnson had been flayed completely, like the Weres the scientist had mutilated, the creature stopped and stared at Johnson.

The creature drove its clawed hand into the left side of Johnson's chest. When it jerked its hand out, the scientist's heart pulsed once, twice, before the creature ate it.

A brief expression of shock crossed Johnson's face. It remained in his eyes as his body slid to the floor and lay there silent. Unmoving.

We were all still and it felt like we held our breaths as one.

That shouldn't have been possible. Beketov shifting to his complete full-moon Were form during the day.

Beketov wouldn't know who he was. He would turn on us and try to tear us all apart. We would have to stop him some way. Somehow.

The creature turned and its large, tawny eyes took in all of us in one sweep. Surprising intelligence was in those eyes.

"No!" I shouted as the bronze-haired pup bounded toward the creature. It might not recognize its own son.

The creature bent down, swept the pup into his arms as terror ripped through me.

I stepped forward, then stopped.

The creature was shifting.

Loud pops and crackles sounded in the room. The creature shuddered as it transformed and it held the pup tight.

In moments Beketov was in the creature's place. Naked and exhausted, the alpha Were crouched on the floor.

Holding his son like he would never let go.

TWENTY-TWO

After I racked the balls, I chalked my cue stick. I took an easy stance, sighted the eight ball, and broke the balls. Like I'd planned, I sank the solid red three and solid orange five. The balls spread across the table in a perfect set-up for my next shot.

Adam stood nearby, intent on looking over the paranorms in the Pit. It was the first time he'd been allowed to come to the Pit and by the expression on his face, the way he studied the room, I knew he was in cop mode, getting a handle on what was a completely alien experience to him.

I moved along the side of the table and angled my cue to drop the solid two.

My sense of smell had fully returned over the past couple of days. Even over all of the other smells in the nightclub, I breathed in Adam's scent of leather, coffee, and man, and I let it fill me.

No one ever beat me at pool, but if I continued to let Adam's presence distract me, my record would be broken.

I took my shot. The ball banked off the side, crossed

the felt-covered table at an angle and sank the two. I smiled.

A hand touched my arm. I glanced up to see Olivia and Nadia. "Rodán is ready for you." Nadia's red hair swung around her face when she glanced at Adam, then looked back at me. "He said you'll need to leave your human detective."

I opened my mouth to protest. I couldn't leave Adam alone with all of these paranorms.

Olivia gave a devilish grin. "I'll keep an eye on lover boy."

Her white bandages showed on her arm beneath the sleeve of her T-shirt. I read her shirt and I grinned, too. Her shirt reminded me that my Persian cat had shredded every bra and panty I hadn't taken with me. Would serve Kali right if she could read.

I love cats, but I can't eat a whole one.

Adam turned to me and I tipped my face up and kissed him. "I'll be back in a few."

Before Adam could ask any questions, I handed him my cue stick and left. Rodán was a little bit of a sore spot with him.

I made my way through the club to the mist-shrouded entryway to Rodán's "dungeon." Only those welcome could pass through the mist. Someone not welcome might break his nose on what would feel like solid concrete. It smelled almost like the forest we'd just spent time in. The mist had the clean scent of rain and the rich smell of loam.

When I got to the dungeon door, I placed my hand on the pad by the door and the colors swirled until they matched my eyes—with the addition of a white flash just for me. The door swung open and Rodán was waiting for me.

"Nyx." He gave me a soft kiss, just a friend's kiss. "Come."

He led me through the warm candlelit room that smelled of firethorn and had the largest bed I'd ever seen where he frequently "entertained." It was empty now, and I found myself glad, although I really didn't know why.

We went down stone steps to his den, entering the coolness of the smooth earthen walls, and I breathed in the scent of wisteria.

He sat at the opposite side of his large Dryad-wood desk that was clean of any papers, unlike mine and Olivia's. I took one of the chairs in front of his desk.

Rodán leaned back in his chair. "Fill me in on everything."

I explained all that had happened from the time we arrived in the Werewolf camp, to our experience in the NORAD facility, and to the death of the scientist and the clean up by the Paranormal Task Force.

Rodán studied me with his intent green eyes as I spoke. He said nothing, just listened as I explained it all. I told him of the amazing parts Joshua, Angel, and Ice had played as well as the other members of my team.

When I was finished telling him about the rescue, I said, "Jeanie was the Soothsayer who froze the scene." I brushed my blue hair over my shoulder. "Between her and the PTF, everything was under control."

"The Weres returned to and moved their camp in time," Rodán said more as a statement.

"The pack was safely away from civilization before the full moon." I rubbed my palms on my leather pants. "My whole team, as well as Adam, made sure of that." I frowned. "I have a question."

He nodded for me to continue.

"How did Beketov change during the day and control that change?" I shook my head. "That should have been impossible."

"Dmitri Beketov is a very old alpha," Rodán said. "And he has special talents. That is one of them."

"Thank the Goddess he had the control." I furrowed my brows as I thought of the danger we all could have been in. "We would have had to contain him in some way otherwise." *Or kill him*, I added silently to myself.

Rodán simply nodded, but not really in agreement, more in acknowledgment of what I was telling him.

"That's pretty much all there is to tell." I shifted in my chair as I realized there was something in his eyes I hadn't noticed before.

I leaned forward, a bad, bad feeling in my gut. "What is it, Rodán?"

"The Great Guardian intimated a storm is brewing," Rodán said. "Her words . . . 'Blood stains the paranorm world if those who care for it no longer care.'"

Despite the fact that chills prickled my spine, I wanted to roll my eyes. "I hate the GG's riddles."

"Nyx," Rodán said in a warning tone.

I settled back in my chair. "Bring it on."

FOR CHEYENNE'S READERS

Be sure to go to http://cheyennemccray.com to sign up for her PRIVATE book announcement list and get FREE EXCLUSIVE Cheyenne McCray goodies. Please feel free to e-mail her at chey@cheyennemccray.com. She would love to hear from you.

Turn the page for a sneak peek at Cheyenne
McCray's next Night Tracker novel

VAMPIRES NOT
INVITED

Coming soon from St. Martin's Paperbacks!

A Master Vampire living in the penthouse of the elite Hudson Hotel by Central Park.

Could things get any stranger?

Of course they could. This was New York City.

Arriving in the Vampire's personal elevator wasn't an option. Olivia, Angel, and Joshua were with me in the stairwell, taking the long way to get to Volod's lair.

Earlier today Joshua and I had continued "talking" with other Sprites. Even using bits of the information from Negel, we hadn't been able to get any Sprite to talk.

A couple of the creepy beings had looked shocked, if not scared, when they heard the Vampire's name, but still no one said anything. We'd been lucky with Negel.

Joshua's flail rocked at his side as we jogged the twenty-four flights of stairs to the penthouse of the Hudson. Shadow Shifters are as silent as Elves and Fae when they move, even when they're in human form.

I pushed long strands of my blue hair over my shoulder as I glanced behind me at Angel. She was incredibly quiet for a Doppler as she followed. Like me, she wore a form-fitting black leather fighting suit—only hers showed even more skin than mine did, which meant hers showed a lot of flesh.

The barbs on the whip at Angel's side had a dull look to them that didn't begin to betray their deadly knife-edged sharpness. Her beautiful features were set, a determined spark to her diamond-bright blue eyes, her blond corkscrew curls spilling over her shoulders like pale serpents.

Angel was a squirrel in Doppler form and as a human looked like a cover girl for a cheerleader magazine. A former Harvard graduate and NASA intern, Angel was one of the toughest Trackers I knew. She'd saved my butt more than once during the Werewolf op. Just goes to show you can't judge a Doppler by her human appearance or her animal form.

Olivia took up the rear. I winced every time I heard one of her shoes make a whisper of a sound. A former NYPD cop, she was pretty quiet for a human. But some beings have super-incredible hearing, and I just hoped the Vampire's hearing wasn't *that* good that they'd hear the slight sounds of Olivia's running shoes.

"Fourteenth floor and ten to go." I looked at the number on the door as we made it from twelve to the next landing. "The fact that some hotels don't have a thirteenth floor has got to be one of the silliest superstitions humans have."

"Humans have lots of silly superstitions." Angel's voice was deceptively innocent and sweet and I glanced at her again. "And Brownies looooove to play up to them."

I grinned as we hit another landing. "If they knew that Brownies are behind just about every superstition or haunting, then humans would really flip."

Brownies are Fae, and some of the most devious creatures known to paranorm kind. I dislike them as much as I dislike Sprites. But they can be amusing at times—when they aren't being malicious.

"Not all humans believe in that crap." Olivia might not be what anyone would consider slender, but she was in such great shape she wasn't breathing hard. "Don't even go there."

"Keep your traps shut," Joshua grumbled. Angel flipped him off. I grinned. "The bastards may have lookouts."

Joshua stopped on landing twenty and I came just short of running into him. I took his flail automatically as he handed it to me. The full weight of it caught me by surprise and I almost dropped it. Thank goodness I'm Drow and not simply human, because the thing was so heavy that I wouldn't have had the strength to hold it otherwise.

"Going ahead to scout." Joshua shifted—sort of melted away—and then I watched as a large shadow drifted up the stairs. Sometimes he blended with the stairwell shadows, sometimes not. And then he was gone.

Angel reached my side and gave me her whip. "Ouch," I said as one of its barbs dug into my palm, and blood formed where the small cut was.

"Sorry, Nyx," she said just before she transformed into a blond squirrel, jumped onto the railing and darted along it to cover the last few flights.

"What am I?" I muttered as I hurried up the stairs. "A coat rack?" As I moved, I hooked Angel's whip on my weapons belt next to my right dragon-clawed dagger and gripped Joshua's flail in my left hand. The blackness of the metal was dark against my pale amethyst skin.

Within seconds I was up the last four flights and at the penthouse, Olivia right behind me. A strange yet familiar odor that I couldn't identify cloyed the air. I frowned. Why couldn't I place the odor? So familiar . . .

Joshua and Angel were nowhere to be seen. As a Shadow Shifter, it was a given that Joshua had slipped beneath the door and into the Vampire's lair. But squirrels . . . I looked up at the low ceiling. Dust was slightly disturbed on an air vent. That explained Angel's disappearance.

"Like we talked about, wait here," I said to Olivia. "I know you don't think Vampires are dangerous because of the pukes at the Pit, but I think we have more to worry about than anyone realizes."

She scowled and I cut her off before she could say a word. "Don't come in, no matter what." I grasped the handle. "Your job is to shoot anything that comes through this door. And make sure it's through the heart."

"Just get your purple ass in there," she muttered as she positioned herself to the side of the stairwell door, her Sig held in a two-fisted grip and pointed upward.

I called to my air element and felt its reassuring embrace as it cloaked me and my weapons so that I was invisible. Most paranorms can still see me when I use a glamour, but Vampires are different.

Vampires aren't born paranorms, they were once human and in some ways they have human weaknesses. So to them I'm invisible when I draw a glamour. Thank goodness for that favor.

With my free hand I tested the doorknob to the penthouse's emergency exit. Locked. Joshua must not have been able to unlock it for me. I needed to be cautious because someone could be on the other side and see the door. I might be invisible to them, but they'd know something was up. A door being opened invisibly was bound to draw attention.

First I reached out with my senses, using my air element to search the area close to the door. To my satisfaction it was clear.

I focused on the lock and used a small amount of my air element to unlock it and cushioned the mechanism so that the sound wouldn't be heard. I used the same element to buffer any squeak the hinges might make.

Olivia couldn't see me anymore, but I looked at her over my shoulder before I slipped inside. Her features were set and grim.

The smell of Vampire—like old dirt and musty leaves—was strong as I eased through the doorway. Modern classic design greeted me. But, more than that, startled me.

Stark white walls with black accents towered to the vaulted ceiling. Muted city lights came through opaque drapes on the floor-to-ceiling windows.

Touches of red, like splashes of blood, were scattered on dead-white furniture. Crimson pillows were arranged on white sofa cushions, and I noticed hints of red in every one of the black-and-white paintings arranged on the walls. An enormous flat-screen TV was built into one wall. And I mean *enormous*. Go-to-the-movies enormous.

It shouldn't have surprised me, but apparently I'd

fallen for the old vampire stereotypes like everyone else. Like where would he keep a dusty old coffin in a place like this?

Voices echoed in the large room, words bouncing from one wall to another like the hollowness of a ping pong ball. I caught my breath as I settled the flail and barbed whip against the wall, keeping them cloaked in an air-glamour. Joshua and Angel should be able to see them—wherever they were.

I eased behind a potted black tree. The white pot was as high as my waist and the tree itself about six feet high. The tree was naked of any leaves and would have been worthless cover if I hadn't shrouded myself in a glamour.

My gaze narrowed at Volod and another Vampire as they strolled into the room. Volod's black shoes sank into the rich white carpet as he walked with his casual yet arrogant movements.

Dressed in a black button-down shirt and tailored black slacks, Volod looked like any one of New York's elite aristocrats—just a lot paler. He was outfitted from head to toe in Gucci, Ferragamo, and Versace. Obviously I have a well-trained eye for the finer things.

The other Vampire's white turtleneck sweater against the deadly white of his skin did nothing for his complexion. Except make him look more dead. Is that possible? The fact he wore Levis and Nikes as opposed to Volod's designer clothing might have indicated he was some kind of underling if it wasn't for the arrogant way he carried himself.

I peered at them both through the branches of the naked tree. It seemed bright in the room compared to the night sky barely visible through a slim part in the sheer drapes.

Despite my glamour, a tingling sense of danger rippled up my spine as I studied the two Vampires.

Volod picked up a black, smooth statue of a nude female and trailed his white hand down the statue's curves. I swept my gaze around the room. Joshua might be one of the many shadows, and as a squirrel, Angel could be just about anywhere.

I reached out with my senses, using my air power to guide me. I found, but still couldn't distinguish, Joshua on the other side of the room. In another second I felt Angel's presence beneath one of the sofas.

Vampires have extraordinary senses, but I didn't think they were able to sense Joshua and Angel like I could.

"Do you truly think that bunch of garbage can do it?" the second Vampire said as he tossed a crimson pillow on the floor and settled back in an oversized white chair. His skin was nearly as pale as his seat. "Can we put faith in the stupid creatures?"

Volod set the black statue on a glass table, and the thumping sound it made caused me to flinch. The irritation on Volod's angular features sent that creepy sensation up my spine again. "Questioning me, Danut?"

Danut didn't seem bothered by Volod's glare. Danut shook out his long black hair, which gleamed in the light. "If they complete their mission, is it wise to give them the *permanent* ability, brother?" It shouldn't have surprised me that he and Volod were brothers. The resemblance was clear to me now.

Volod didn't bother to answer Danut's question. "As

long as the Night Trackers remain ignorant, nothing will stop the Sprites from getting the information."

I caught my breath as thoughts spun through my mind. What was so important that he would be afraid of the Trackers finding out? I had a feeling that it had to be dangerous, whatever it was.

The Master Vampire turned to one of the windows, pushed aside the flowing sheer curtain. He studied the glittering Manhattan skyline through crystal-clear windows it bared. The view made the city's skyline seem almost close enough to grasp each light in my hand.

"I have given the creatures what they need to accomplish this task and this task only," Volod said.

Danut said, "It was brilliant that you gave the Sprites the ability to escape the elemental magic containment as only Vampires can."

So many questions ran through my mind that I had to set them aside to concentrate on what was being said.

Danut grinned, baring his fangs. "The Trackers have no idea what will happen tonight at the Paranorm Center or what we have planned for the future."

Tonight. Something is going down tonight. I gritted my teeth, torn between listening to the two Vampires and rushing to the Paranorm Center to stop whatever they had planned. If only there was a way to contact Rodán without the chance of being overheard on my cellphone.

"All will most certainly change with what you have planned for the Trackers later." Danut's grin vanished. "But for tonight the Sprites will gain the archives."

Disbelief at what the Vampires had said caused me

to shift my body backward. The Sprites in the detention center. How could we have not thought of that? I'd have bet my last Drow-mined diamond that the Vampires had intended to have the Sprites caught, so that the creeps could go after something in the archives.

I clenched my hand around the hilt of my sheathed dagger. Just like we'd thought, the Sprite mischief hadn't been random. But the realization that Vampires were behind it all made my skin feel tight.

"We have played the part far too long." Volod slammed his palms on the windowsill. He bent at his waist as he braced his hands.

My heart beat faster, my breathing grew heavier, my palms becoming sticky as I digested what I was hearing. What ability had the Vampires given to Sprites to break free of their cells and to get past the guards?

The Master Vampire straightened, then went still.

At once I knew he was searching for me with his mind, his senses.

Bless it. Volod had felt the strong shift in my emotions.

"You think you can enter a Master Vampire's domain and not be found out?" He looked in my direction.

My heart thundered harder but I maintained my glamour. In a rush I sought out my elements with my mind and senses. I could use water from the pipes behind the walls, fire from the stove in the kitchen, and of course I had air.

In the flash of a moment it took me to reach for my elements, his hand shot up.

Invisible power slammed into me. I bit my lip to

keep from crying out as the force of his power sent me skidding on my side on the carpet. The blast burned through my chest. Was my suit melting? It felt like the leather was sinking through my skin.

I rolled with the momentum of the power as it shoved me toward one of the floor-to-ceiling windows. My concentration on my glamour failed and I could be seen again.

With a shout and cry, I flipped my body into a crouch, drew one of my dragon-clawed daggers, and faced Volod. Shards of pain raked my lungs as I dragged in harsh breaths of air.

"Tracker." Volod tilted his head and studied me, his hand still outstretched. He looked at me as if not concerned at all. "The strange one. The Drow female."

"This creature is a Tracker?" Danut laughed, obviously not feeling threatened by me, either. "A purple woman?"

Give me a moment and I'll show you purple when I shove your—

"What are you going to do with her?" Danut asked, looking at his brother in a lazy, bored way. "Fun and games?"

Volod's black gaze held mine. "What do we do with all trash?" Volod splayed the fingers of his outstretched hand. "We dispose of it."

I surrounded myself with my air element, a thick cushion that would have protected me if I hadn't been so stupid and unprepared.

If I tried I couldn't have held back the dangerous white flash in my eyes. "Vampire scum."

I grasped the double-edged buckler from the front of

my weapons belt and flung it at Volod's neck. My air element shoved the buckler faster than a human eye could see.

Volod wasn't human. Not for a very long time.

He caught the buckler right before the razor edge would have sliced into his throat.

In a blur he threw the buckler at me. I dodged it. The buckler sailed through the floor-to-ceiling window behind me. Glass shattered with a loud *crack*. Icy wind whipped inside the penthouse.

Danut shouted something. From the corner of my eye I saw Angel's barbed whip wrap around Danut's neck. Multiple lacerations. Blood streamed down his body. Blood splattered the white sofas. Angel would rip the Vampire's head from his body.

I didn't have time to take pleasure in the sight.

My target was too powerful to allow myself to be distracted.

Faster than any Olympic sprinter, I bolted for Volod with my dagger. Blood rushed in my ears. My skin tingled. I'd carve his heart out.

Air cushioned me. Knowledge that I was protected gave me more strength.

My gaze was focused on the Vampire's grim expression. His bared fangs. A red glint in his black eyes. His pale raised hand as he faced his palm out to me.

I gripped my dagger. I was protected. Volod wouldn't be able to hurt me this time.

Five feet. Three feet—

An even more powerful invisible blast slammed into me.

It was as if I had no protection at all buffering me.

Breath rushed from my chest. Did my lungs collapse?

Fire. My body was on fire. Burning more, even more than the last time.

My concentration on my air element shattered. All elements.

The power flung my body backward.

No control. I had no control.

My back and head hit one of the massive windows.

Glass shattered as I was slammed against it, hard enough to break the thickness of it.

Shards sliced my skin and dug into my flesh as I sailed through the window.

I screamed as my body started to drop.

Twenty-four stories.